Daphne du maurier

Daphne du maurier

Daphne du maurier

Daphne du maurier

Daphne du maurier

maurier

du maurier

Daphne du Maurier
Maurier
Daphne du Maurier
Daphne du Maurier
Maurier
Daphne du Maurier
Daphne du Maurier
Maurier
Daphne du Maurier

VIRAGO
MODERN CLASSICS
509

Daphne du Maurier

DAPHNE DU MAURIER (1907–89) was born in London, the daughter of the famous actor-manager Sir Gerald du Maurier and granddaughter of George du Maurier, the author and artist. A voracious reader, she was from an early age fascinated by imaginary worlds and even created a male alter ego for herself. Educated at home with her sisters and later in Paris, she began writing short stories and articles in 1928, and in 1931 her first novel, *The Loving Spirit*, was published. A biography of her father and three other novels followed, but it was the novel *Rebecca* that launched her into the literary stratosphere and made her one of the most popular authors of her day. In 1932, du Maurier married Major Frederick Browning, with whom she had three children.

Besides novels, du Maurier published short stories, plays and biographies. Many of her bestselling novels became award-winning films, and in 1969 du Maurier was herself awarded a DBE. She lived most of her life in Cornwall, the setting for many of her books, and when she died in 1989, Margaret Forster wrote in tribute: 'No other popular writer has so triumphantly defied classification . . . She satisfied all the questionable criteria of popular fiction, and yet satisfied too the exacting requirements of "real literature", something very few novelists ever do'.

CASTLE DOR

Sir Arthur Quiller-Couch
and
Daphne du Maurier

with an Introduction
by Nina Bawden

Virago

A *Virago* Book

Published by Virago Press 2004

First published in Great Britain in 1962 by
J. M. Dent & Sons Ltd

Copyright © The Estate of Daphne du Maurier 1961
Introduction copyright © Nina Bawden 2004

Nina Bawden asserts her right to be identified as the author
of the Introduction to this Work in accordance with the
Copyright, Designs and Patents Act 1988.

A CIP catalogue record for this book
is available from the British Library.

ISBN 1 84408 067 6

Typeset by Palimpsest Book Production Limited,
Polmont, Stirlingshire
Printed and bound in Great Britain by Clays Ltd, St. Ives

Virago Press
An imprint of
Time Warner Book Group UK
Brettenham House
Lancaster Place
London WC2E 7EN

www.virago.co.uk

Introduction to this Edition

Castle Dor is a double find for me. Not only is it a novel written – or partly written – by Daphne du Maurier that I had not read before, but it is one that had been begun and half completed, before she took it over, by a hero of my youth, the writer and critic Sir Arthur Quiller-Couch. When I was at school in the forties, 'Q', as the great man was more generally known, inspired me to read – and I hope to recognise – the best in English literature. I still possess three of his excellent Studies in Literature, old and with yellowing pages but still serving as the best guide to literary judgement that I know. In his foreword to the earliest volume, first published in 1918 and reprinted many times since, he states his own position with beautiful clarity: '. . . before starting to lay down principles of literature or aesthetic a man should offer some evidence of his capacity to enjoy the better and eschew the worst.' And, as an example – he always gives examples: 'By "poetry", in these pages, I mean what has been written by Homer, Dante, Shakespeare and some others.'

That this exceptionally scholarly man whose judgements, always rich and sensitive, though sometimes austere, should have embarked on an intensely romantic retelling of the old Cornish legend of that famous pair of tragic lovers, Tristan and Queen Iseult, is intriguing in itself. But what makes it even more fascinating is that Daphne du Maurier, asked by 'Q''s daughter long after her father's death to finish this novel that he had set aside 'near the end of a chapter, halfway through', did so in such a skilful fashion that it is impossible to guess with any certainty the exact point at which she began to write. She says, in a modest foreword, that she 'could not imitate "Q"'s style . . . that would have been robbing the dead', but she had known him when she was a child, remembered him as a genial host at many a Sunday supper, and 'by thinking back to conversations long forgotten' she could recapture something of the man himself and trust herself to 'fall into his mood'.

She has succeeded superbly. 'Q' had set his retelling of the ancient legend in the early 1840s, in the Cornish countryside around the Fowey river that he loved and knew so well. The Tristan of the legend has become Amyot Trestane, a young Breton onion-seller from the *Jolie Bris*, a small schooner that plies the Breton coast and sails to Cornwall regularly with seasonal cargoes of strawberries, apricots, onions and lime – the last in great demand by the Cornish potteries, since the kilns which had once burned at the head of every creek had by this time been abandoned. The Captain of the *Jolie Bris* is a monster, a vicious drunk, and Amyot jumps ship to escape from his sadistic cruelty. After rescuing her when her horse runs away with her carriage, he falls in love with Linnet Lewarne, the beautiful new bride of Mark Lewarne, the landlord of the Rose and Anchor inn at Troy. Mark dotes on his young wife but he is a cantankerous old man and wildly jealous. And so the stage is set.

Each of the doomed lovers has moments when he or she is seized by confusing sensations of being part of something older and stronger than themselves, some force that links them with the past, and sets them on the same tragic path as the legendary pair who lived and died so many centuries before. Central to their story is a certain Doctor Carfax, who seems to have been intended by 'Q' as the main mover and shaker, controlling events, Daphne du Maurier suggests, a little like Shakespeare's Prospero. He is, for her, the most sympathetic and rounded character in the novel, which opens with him in his role as the local doctor, waiting one night upon the earthwork of Castle Dor for the blacksmith's wife to give birth, and being seized by wonder at the earth that holds so many universal secrets that might 'never flower again, yet be unable to forget or desist from the effort to throw up secondary shoots'. Doctor Carfax is present throughout the story, explaining, holding it together, and at the end he is still there, an old man pondering the mysteries of love, and dreaming about one of the 'saddest love stories in the world'.

There are a number of different versions of the Tristan and Iseult legend and Daphne du Maurier tells us that she read all she could discover before she took on the task of completing the novel, and found inconsistencies and confusions that she had to resolve in order to satisfy her own 'sense of order'. In 'Q''s unfinished half of the novel, the earthwork of Castle Dor where King Mark, Queen Iseult's husband, had his palace in the legend, has become the site of Lantyan, a farmhouse that belongs to Bosanko, a local farmer with whom Amyot finds refuge and a job. Although Bosanko and his wife and two children play no part in the original story, there are many deliberate connections between the old tale and the new. In 'Q''s version, Linnet contrives to fall from a hay wain into Amyot's arms, and when her jealous husband accuses her of infidelity, she laughs at him, saying that she can hardly claim no other man has touched her, since the lowly farm hand, Amyot, has just saved her life. Centuries before, Queen Iseult had made the same mocking answer to King Mark after she had been helped ashore from the Fal by Tristan, disguised as a leper, and had tumbled with him, wrapped in his arms, on landing. A somewhat more laboured connection is made between Tristan's unintended death by a friend's poisoned spear, and Amyot's death, after he has misunderstood Doctor Carfax's attempts to rescue him from a disused mine shaft and inadvertently cut himself with the doctor's clasp knife that had just been used to remove a stone from a horse's hoof. There were no antibiotics in 1840, as Carfax's musing over the results of the terrible accident reminds us.

Daphne du Maurier is often – and automatically – dismissed as a 'romantic novelist'. Sir Arthur Quiller-Couch is, above all, a scholar. In the first of his Studies in Literature he includes an essay, or discourse, on the terms 'Classical' and 'Romantic'. He considers these labels, as they are often applied to great poets, novelists, playwrights, to be meaningless, and is against considering literature as if it were something that could be studied in compartments under abstract headings: 'influences', 'tendencies', 'isms'. Books, plays, poems, he insists, I think rightly, are written using the rare skills their authors were born with and have honed over the years. 'Shakespeare, Milton, Shelley did not write "classicism" or "romanticism". They wrote *Hamlet*, *Lycidas*, *The Cenci*.'

This immensely complex but extremely readable novel is a splendid story of love and loss with fascinating links to two widely separated centuries by two very different, but very skilful writers.

Nina Bawden
2003

It was my father's intention
to dedicate this book to
Mr and Mrs Santo of Lantyan
F. F. Q.-C.

Contents

Book Three

BOOK ONE

You and I and Amyas,
Amyas and you and I
To the green wood must we go, alas!
You and I, my lyf, and Amyas.

William Cornish

Prologue

Many years ago, in the early 1840s, on an October night very clear and lustrous, a certain Doctor Carfax stood sentry with a field-telescope upon the earthwork of Castle Dor in Cornwall. He had arrived on a summons to the blacksmith's at the crossroads near by, the blacksmith's wife being in labour. He had arrived to find the travail going well and naturally: and being a one who believed in nature being left to herself, put his bag on the kitchen chair, and strolled off across a dewy meadow, having told the competent midwife to hail him when necessary. After a while on the earthwork, which lay but a field away from the forge, the doctor, accustomed to such vigils, found himself passing familiarly enough through three stages of sensation, to arrive upon a fourth at once novel and most magical.

First came that feeling of aloofness which, while it seems to be regal enough, belongs to any man of ordinary imagination who stands on a high ridge under stars. They are a crown we can all fit upon us, to cheat us into derisory thoughts of this planet and a mood in which all man's fret upon it becomes as a weaving of midges beneath a summer bough. This mood contains its own rebuke. Being men, we belong to earth: belonging to earth, like Archimedes, we must stand somewhere: and wherever we stand to play at astronomers, it is a condition that we cannot be aware of what hovers at our feet.

Ignoring these considerations, and still intent on the firmament — where over the plain of the sea Sirius sparkled as a flint under the heel of the Hunter, Aldebaran was a ruby and the Pleiads aloft on its right hung like a cobweb in the cross-moonshine — Doctor Carfax passed to a second apprehension again familiar — of the vast dome inexorably, almost visibly turning, and of our earth (himself with it) spinning 'widdershins' or back-somersaulting beneath it, at incredible speed.

This (for he was a commonsensical man, albeit imaginative) hitched him back to his feet — to be aware of the dark brambles around him covering grass-blades innumerable and minute leaflets of the thyme by the million; these in turn covering asleep the insect life to be released in its myriads next summer and fill the air and all the field with humming. Of a sudden our world grew enormous again — a rounded world with curved uplands that dipped to the sea's more gradual curve. The sea itself . . .

> the great sea
> Lay, a strong vessel at his master's gate,
> And, like a drunken giant, sobbed in sleep.

No — Sea and Land were giant and giantess, rather, locked in exhaustion after tremendous embraces: and it seemed to him — now turned from watcher to listener — that while the giant audibly snored, his mate could not sleep: that her bosom heaved with an inarticulate trouble, a word that could not be told; and somehow that the secret was meant for *him*, and concerned men and women just here where he stood. Yet it could not concern — it was too important to concern — any of the folk who slept in the valley cottages beneath him or the immediate trouble at the forge-house nearby on the high road, or anyone in the vale below him there who perchance lay awake remembering a sorrow locked away in this or that folded churchyard among the hills . . . He knew — as who but a medical practitioner can know — these folk.

No, again. This most ancient cirque of Castle Dor, deserted, bramble-grown, was the very nipple of a huge breast in pain, aching for discharge.

Day broke slowly – closing a shutter on space to open another on time. For the rampart overlooks on the one hand a bay of the sea, on the other a river ford deep-set in a vale: From a nook of the bay, centuries ago, a *soi-disant* Caesar pushed out with his ships to win Rome. In a field sloping northward from the ramp, the guns and foot of a Parliament Army capitulated to King Charles on his last campaign of the West. The king had his coach anchored under the lee of a hedge yonder, and slept in it on the night before the surrender. Across the ford below regiments have stormed and shouted.

But these memories lifted themselves with the valley mists, to dissolve and trail away over woodland, arable, pasture; and he knew that it was not for any secret of theirs he had been listening, nor yet for any lowly tale decipherable of quarrel, ancient feud, litigation, which had parcelled the fields at his feet or twisted the parish roads. All England is a palimpsest of such, scored over with writ of hate and love, begettings of children beneath the hazels, betrayals, appeals, curses, concealed travails. But this was different somehow. It had no dimensions, small or great. In a way it had escaped dimensions, to be universal; and yet just here – here, waiting . . . An owl hooted up from the woods. A titlark on a stone announced the day. A moment later in the daylight the blacksmith, coming across the meadow, panted that all was well but he was wanted. Doctor Carfax closed his telescope, musing, and retraced his steps to the forge. The word, for a moment so close upon utterance, had escaped him.

1

The onion-seller

'Amyot!'

The unintelligible word was spoken in a liquid foreign voice; not, however, as the French would pronounce it, but closing with a sharp 't' – sharp as if plucked on a lute string. A sigh lingered after it. Word and sigh seemed to melt together off the old mirror in which Mrs Lewarne had been admiring herself.

She turned about. Someone had spoken within the room, close, at her shoulder. Her maid, Deborah?

But no Deborah stood in the doorway. Indeed on a quick second thought she knew that the old mirror, for all the tarnish of its quicksilver, would have reflected anyone standing there. Into the panelled triangular bedroom, frowsy with disuse, the sunshine, reflected from a whitewashed house-front across the narrow street, filtered as if stealing its way. Linnet Lewarne, half an hour ago, had pulled up the blind and lifted the window before falling to study her image in the glass; an excusable dalliance, she being a bride of twelve months. Also she was mistress of this house – the Rose and Anchor, Troy – an old well-reputed house, owned by an old husband who idolized her in his way. She had, as folks said, 'done very well for herself'. Her maiden name had been Linnet Constantine; her father a one-time blacksmith, having owned, some nineteen years ago, a forge and cottage, high on the hill, by Castle Dor.

If the smallest shadow of demur or of discontent had clouded her brow as she lifted the blind, set it down to her pure youthfulness upon which the waft of age through the old bedchamber acted repulsively. And now all trace of demur – if such it had ever worn – was gone from her face as she stepped half a pace back, then a little more than half a tiptoe forward, turning a little this way and that before her image that the old quicksilver clutched like a miser.

For her husband had given her a new gown of her choosing, to drive with him to Castle Dor races. It was of a very pale green muslin sprigged with rosebuds; and her hat matched it – a broad hat with pale green ribbons meeting under the chin. And her sunshade matched. She had half opened it, to try its effect; but desisted, remembering that it was unlucky to open any sort of umbrella indoors.

'*Amyot!*'

The voice had not been Deborah's quite, and yet was mixed up with hers, as well as with some preoccupation over a foreign gentleman. It was annoying of course that he should have chosen Castle Dor race day of all others for moving in. All yesterday had been spent by her and Deborah in cleaning, dusting, airing bed linen, polishing the old uneven floor with soft brooms and beeswax. Stepping to the window, she heard Deborah's irritable voice, now from the doorway close around the angle of the house.

'Two shillings! Highway robbery!'

'*Plaît-il?*'

Linnet divined. This was the time of year when the Breton schooners arrive, and their cabin-boys are sent ashore to chaffer strings of onions, asking a price which can be cheapened by a fifth at the shop next door. It had happened so last September, her first month of housekeeping.

Linnet could never afterwards tell why she turned so quickly from the mirror and slipped out past the door of the large

8

Wagon Room, within which glasses jingled, and her old husband, from the chair of the Ordinary, led a 'tally-ho' to the company over some sporting story. She paused by the door for an instant, just to listen like a good wife and make sure he was not drunk, then passed down the stair.

She foreknew more or less the scene in the doorway: the town square, empty as usual in the dinner hour – today even emptier than usual, the populace having tramped up the hill to the race field. The farmers and sporting men, now finishing their brandies and cigars in the Wagon Room, would presently push themselves into two-horse brakes and be borne away to the field, puffing bad tobacco between the hedgerows. She would follow after an interval, seated in a barouche beside her husband, who had a craze for exhibiting her. Her name appeared on the placards of the race-meeting as donor of a twenty-guinea steeple-chase cup, which she was to hand to the winning jockey. She had practised her gesture in giving it twice or thrice before the old looking-glass.

Down the stair to the porch she came. On the step Deborah, hand on hip, stood denouncing a young man in patched blue jumper and worse patched trousers that, being all too short, showed naked ankle and three or four inches of naked leg above his wooden sabots, a beret on his head and, across his back, a pole with five or six ropes of onions slung on it.

'Heathen boy! Go and ask two shillings off the Pope – no, but hi, you! Come back!'

The onion-seller had turned to go as Mrs Lewarne reached the porch. At Deborah's sudden outcry he wheeled slowly about in the roadway: a singularly handsome fellow with a sullen set of the jaw and fine brown eyes, his skin deeply tanned by wind and weather.

Deborah darted at him and spun him roundabout.

'See here, mistress!'

'Oh, it's cruel!'

A broad smear crossed the young man's back, over the

shoulder blades and just beneath the onion pole: a smear that at one point ran down to five or six inches, purpling and still damping his blouse with blood.

'Who did it to you?'

'What is your ship?'

'Your name, anyway?' demanded Deborah.

'Amyot.'

'Foolish woman!' said Mrs Lewarne. 'When he told it to you not five minutes ago!'

'Told it to me? I never . . .' protested Deborah.

Mrs Lewarne stood all confused, putting out a hand to a pillar of the porch. She had a strange sensation of something breaking out of the past to connect itself with something immediately to come. The square all seemed to be hushed as an empty space . . .

'Amyot,' repeated the onion-seller. 'Amyot Trestane.' For a second or two he searched back among their questions; then added in his broken speech: 'Of the *Jolie Brise*, schooner, from Brest. *Mais tenez, mesdames – le patron!*'

A giant of a man had lurched out of the bar, where he had been dozing off his liquor, and stood in the porchway, pausing for the moment to wipe his mouth. Over Mrs Lewarne's shoulder his gaze fell on the onion-seller.

'*Petit cochon!*' he roared. '*Pas un chapelet vendu! Attends seulement!*' and with that passed into a torrent of mixed French and Breton curses.

Linnet understood a little French, but nothing of his Breton. She faced around on him.

'All his onions are sold: I have bought them. But did you do *that*?' She pointed as Deborah spun the young man about again. 'If so you are a beast!'

The giant grinned tolerantly, as one who understands women.

'These fellows, madame, are all lazy swine. They will learn nothing but at the rope's end.'

With a sharp cough Linnet's husband, Mark Lewarne, peered

10

out from behind – a man of some sixty years, proprietor of the Rose and Anchor.

'What's all this?' he demanded in a high voice, half dictatorial, half querulous. Then, his eyes falling on his wife, he became of a sudden insensible to the rest of the scene. 'What's all this?' he repeated, more shrilly. 'Didn't I expressly ask you, my dear, to come in and hand around the cigars?'

'Didn't Deborah hand the cigars?'

'It's not the same. It's not the same thing at all. And afterwards to sit and take a sip out of my glass. There was a chair set by my side. That gown of yours – I shall pay a pretty penny for it, this side of quarter-day. A man's own is his own, eh?' He appealed to the Breton skipper.

'Above all, when he owns an armful of so much charm,' agreed that ogre, turning from him to leer knowingly at the two women.

Mrs Lewarne avoided Deborah's eye; yet her next words were addressed to Deborah.

'I have bought those onions. Take them off his back.'

The skipper stepped forward, possibly to help in a half-drunken way, while she felt for placket-hole and purse.

'At two shillings the string?' he demanded, looking back at the landlord to make sure.

But he spoke too soon. The onion-seller, as Deborah released the pole of its weight, caught it off his shoulders, swung it high and made for the giant as if to brain him. Deborah screamed. Linnet caught her breath. The giant stepped back half a pace. He had arms like a gorilla's. But just then the scene came to a ridiculous pause. Feet of the revellers came tumbling downstairs from the upper room, and almost simultaneously a voice commanded:

'Stop that! What the devil! . . .' followed, in the instant, by '*Halte la!*'

11

2

The Notary Ledru

The occupant of the barouche opened his eyes and lifted his shoulders from the cushion against which they reclined – this with a slight start, as of one suddenly awakened from a doze. Yet it was incredible that he could have dozed through that precipitous descent into Troy, which has been known to terrify strangers half out of their wits.

He wore a black travelling-cape. A black hat of velvet, extremely wide of brim, covered his white locks. It had fallen forward a little over his eyes; and as he pushed it back with a black-gloved hand Linnet had a sensation that he was the oldest man she had ever seen in her life – old past belief, so many were the lines on his shaven face; and yet (as she put it to herself a moment later) most wonderfully young for his age. For his complexion was as of ivory, almost transparent, and seemed to hold an inner light of its own.

As a rule old things made Linnet shiver – or had made her shiver of late. But the aspect of this old man did not repel her. It mastered her, rather. It mastered at any rate, and at once, her curiosity.

She had a quick eye. 'A gentleman,' she said to herself, as Deborah stepped to open the carriage door.

The visitor too had a quick eye. It flickered for an instant

13

on Linnet and then selected her husband from the group on the step.

'Monsieur my host, if I am not mistaken? But pardon me, I seem to have dropped, at your doorway, back into my own country.'

He spoke in excellent English, with scarcely a trace of foreign accent, looking meanwhile from the onion-seller to the skipper, whom he next addressed, gently enough.

'My friend, our meetings would seem to be providential. The last, if I remember, was at Landerneau, when the bishop was forced to interrupt a pardon because you were beating an ass unmercifully at the back of the fair.'

'As I am an honest man, Monsieur le Notaire—'

'Which, in fact, you are not,' returned the stranger, dusting his hat. 'It was not, if I remember, precisely for that virtue that you, Fouguereau, left Quimper two years ago and opened a cabaret at Pont l'Abbé. A theft of fowls, was it not? And I had the pleasure of prosecuting. You afterwards purchased a ship at Loctudy. You remember me also, I dare say?'

'I do, Monsieur Ledru. Why, of course—'

'You see, he already introduces me.' The stranger turned to address the landlord. 'Yes, my name is Ledru, Notary of Quimper: and my room will be ready for me, doubtless, as your carriage was waiting at Lostwithiel railway station, even though', he added, lifting his face to a sudden roar of laughter from some belated drinkers in the Wagon Room upstairs, 'You entertain more company than I had expected.'

'The races—' began Mark Lewarne.

'Yes, but your room is ready for you, sir,' Linnet interrupted, stepping close up behind Deborah, who still held open the carriage door. 'The oldest in our house; but a pleasanter one, freshly papered, if you prefer it.'

Monsieur Ledru's eyebrows went up a little. '*Tenez*, and are *you* the charming mistress of this house?'

'Your hot water shall be ready at once; and after that a grilled plaice, and an omelette to follow.'

'With onions, if you please.' He nodded at the ropes still encumbering Deborah's left arm.

'Shredded and fried: and Deborah here can make an omelette,' Linnet promised valiantly.

'Then I am more and more at home.'

Monsieur Ledru bowed, distributed a benign smile on everybody and turned slowly about. He had by some power of command held the whole violent scene arrested. There stood the onion-seller in the roadway, with yoke-pole lowered; there the giant skipper, a bully; Deborah's hand still hung at the carriage door. The driver stood as he had climbed down off the box-seat: Linnet stood with lips half parted; her husband stood on the step behind her like a man who has received a message of which, for the moment, he can make nothing. And always in the upstairs room the noise of silly laughter continued.

'Then all is providential and I feel more and more at home.' Monsieur Ledru, standing erect, unwound the travelling rug from his legs. 'And this fellow? It seemed to me, as we drove around the corner – turn right about, my son! . . . Ah! But this is abominable, you Fouguereau! May I put it to you that it discredits our country? No; for such as you do not understand. But let me at least assure you that this young man does not voyage back in your ship.'

Then followed a swift exchange of words in Breton, at the end of which the skipper picked up the stick which the onion-seller had dropped in the roadway, and slouched away with hunched shoulders.

Monsieur Ledru, still standing upright in the barouche, turned on the other.

'From where do you hail, my son?'

The answer came after a pause and as if with an effort.

'From L'Ile Tudy.'

'So look up at me and answer. What is your name?'

'Amyot.'

15

'Amyot, eh? And will that be Christian name or surname? What other, if you have one?'

The onion-seller was still staring after the retreating figure of his employer.

'My mother, sir, was called Trestane. She belonged to Douarnenez, so she once told me, and that we came to L'Ile Tudy, I think she said, soon after I was born . . .'

He shrugged, as though indifferent to past history, the light in his eye suggesting he had but one thought in mind: to renew the struggle – despite disparity of height – with the brutal skipper.

'A trouble-maker, if you ask *me*,' pronounced the landlord, asserting himself from the upper step of the porch. 'But I never pretended to understand foreigners – if you'll excuse me, mister.'

Monsieur Ledru, in the act of stepping from the carriage, politely ignored this remark.

'The first thing to do,' said he, composedly addressing Deborah and signing that he wished to descend, 'is to take this fellow indoors and bathe his back. Afterwards, if he be recovered, he shall row me some way up your river – that is, if you have a boat for hire, sir?'

'There's a boat, of course—'

'Yes, I know; you would not be bothered about that just now. You are going to the races and on the point to depart for them, you and madame.' He bowed to Linnet as he climbed agilely down the carriage step. Then, after feeing the driver: 'I saw the advertisement of your races on the blacksmith's shutter at the crossroads. Madame is giving a cup, I understand.'

'Well, you may put it so,' the landlord conceded. 'Of course, as a fact—'

'To be sure, and as a gallant husband . . . I think I hear your equipages coming downhill. Before they arrive and, rather than incommode these sportsmen' – with a bow to the general company in the porchway – 'shall we pass in?'

3

May and November

Mark Lewarne, his wife and their guest entered and went up the stairs in single file, Deborah following with the valise. At her command the onion-seller waited in the passage below. On the landing Lewarne, with an apology, turned aside to open the door of the Wagon Room and announce to the remnant of the diners that the wagonettes were approaching: Linnet and Monsieur Ledru went on to the best bedchamber.

'We have done our best with it, sir, but, as I said just now, we have a brighter one, newly papered, should you prefer it. Deborah, you may set down the gentleman's portmanteau: then run, get some hot water and attend to that poor young man. Afterwards you can unpack for the gentleman in whichever room he decides upon.'

'But what is the matter with *this* room, madame?' asked Monsieur Ledru, looking about him.

'For my part I hate everything old,' Linnet confessed.

'Ah?' Monsieur Ledru turned, and with his back to the window looked at her quickly. The light, such as his opposing figure admitted, fell full on her face. 'Now for my part I can understand your view, madame, though you can see with your own eyes that I must not share it.'

Linnet's face had flushed, almost as soon as the words were

past her lips. The manner of this fine old gentleman at once invited speech and rebuked it.

'I did not mean, sir—'

'Why, of course you did not. And if you had I should have no resentment. The old, madame, as they draw nearer to God, grow to share a little in one attribute of His – or if you prefer in a vacuity of His. He has no silly touchiness.'

'I only meant,' Linnet stammered, 'that I dislike the smell of all this old oak. You see that Deborah has laid a fire, sir. We have been burning a fire for two days past, to air the room: but we agreed that, in this weather, it might be too hot for you. Still, if you are taking a boat, you may find the sight of one cheerful, later – and after travelling so far.'

'Thank you: yes, I should like a fire. At my time of life, madame, what used to be luxuries tend to become necessities. And unlike you I love old oak. There is nothing like it, madame, to last. We sleep in it, some endlessly; in our old age we like to dream by it and watch, waking, the fire in its core. But we dream of the birds that one built in the high branches, rocked by the wind.'

At this moment Deborah opened the door, carrying a can of hot water; and almost as though her opening of the door had admitted the noise through the open window opposite, the train of wagonettes rumbled below, rounded into the square and deployed, their drivers calling one to another for room with many facetious objurgations. Deborah announced first that the gentleman's luncheon would be ready within ten minutes; next that the onion-seller was below, sponging himself, and she wished the mistress could see his wounds. She added, with a glance at Monsieur Ledru, that time was getting on.

'With your permission, madame, I also should wish to examine the young man's hurts,' said the Notary, holding open the door.

So, Deborah, having deposited her jug, all three went their way out into the narrow corridor and were intercepted by the last-leaving diners at the door of the Wagon Room.

Mark Lewarne led them and, heading off his wife, faced about on her so that there was at once a block on the corridor and in the doorway behind him. He was clearly in an evil humour.

'I thought I told you – I thought I told you—'

Linnet's face went white for an instant before hoisting a red flag of defiance. Monsieur Ledru could not perceive this, for he stood immediately behind her: but, noting the quick back-tilt of her pretty head, he surmised.

'I forget just what it was you told me,' answered Linnet, picking her words very deliberately. 'But I think it amounted to this: that you wished to show me off in this new gown you have bought for me. Very well; if you will stand a little aside from the doorway, please, I will walk past very slowly with this gentleman, and your other guests can tell you very freely, as no doubt they will, what they think of your wife.'

'A man is master in his own house,' 'tis agreed.' Mark, some-what quelled, was conscious of a strong masculine backing in the doorway behind him. In face of a woman at once young and beautiful and in the devil of a temper such a backing is not always to be relied upon. A Scots skipper in the rear of the group, tall enough to look over the heads of those in front, half hummed, half chanted:

> 'What shall a young lassie—
> What shall a young lassie
> Do with an auld man?'

Mark overheard it and a titter that followed.

'A man is master in his own house,' he swore.

'And his wife its mistress,' Linnet answered. 'Attend to your guests, and I will attend to mine'.

Her husband at once stepped aside and made way for her. Like a queen she passed the doorway. But she alone knew that he gave way chiefly through hopeless adoration. She passed the doorway in triumph, however, followed by Monsieur Ledru and Deborah.

The trio descended the stairs, and on the ground floor, at the end of a passage permeated with the smell of onions frying and sizzling, entered an ample stone-paved back kitchen, within which over a tub of hot water young Amyot bent, sponging himself. He stood up at their entry, naked to the waist; smiled on all gratefully and bent over the tub again. His back was cruelly scored, from the shoulderblades down to the line where the tucked trousertop covered hip and loin. But his shoulders were firm and muscular, very delicate of skin; and down the back, half embedding the backbone, ran two high muscular ridges such as only come of long and powerful rowing.

'I can prescribe for this,' announced Monsieur Ledru, after some close peering into the young fellow's wounds. 'If you have a chemist near by—'

'But,' said Linnet, 'I have ointments here in the house. I was brought up, sir' – she turned to the Notary – 'on a farm, across the water, where it is hard to fetch a doctor, and help had to be handy for men who cut themselves at hedging or shearing.'

As she spoke she had put out her hand to Amyot's shoulder. Unwittingly, for she was facing the Notary, her fingers touched it; and at the same moment, as unwittingly, Amyot lifted his sponge backwards and squeezed a rush of warm water over her hand.

'These local specifics,' the Notary was answering, 'are usually the best – especially in the manner of ointments—'

'Linnet!' called her husband's voice from above-stairs. 'Where the devil are you delaying?'

Linnet snatched her hand away suddenly from the young man's shoulder. The Notary caught, this time, the look of her eyes as she faced to the doorway through which her husband's voice sounded, sharp and querulous. At first it was the look of a wild thing trapped. But in a moment the eyes contracted under a frown: their pupils narrowed and the iris, violet, lovely, seemed to narrow and sharpen with them.

'Linnet!' her husband's voice called down to her.

She dropped the hand to her side, wetting her gown, paused and went upstairs.

'She has turned obedient of a sudden,' commented Deborah, after a pause filled with the sound of sponging and laving.

'I am not of that opinion, though to be sure you should know her better than I,' the Notary answered gravely. 'I think rather that she has locked her door and is at this moment beginning to cast off her finery.'

Deborah stared at him, picked up a towel and began gently to dab the onion-seller's back.

'If that's so,' she asked as she dabbed, 'what's to be done, sir?'

'In your place I should follow her, knock at the door and remind her that we are ready for the ointment.'

Deborah went up.

She found that Linnet had indeed locked the bedroom door. But she came also on a sight that the Notary had not prophesied – on Mark Lewarne crouching outside, almost kneeling, at the keyhole, imploring.

'Leave her to me, master,' said Deborah.

She tapped on the door.

'Go away, I tell you!' commanded the voice within. 'I tell you I am not coming!'

Deborah tapped again.

'It's *me*, mistress – Deborah only. I have come to fetch the ointment.'

After a second or two the key was heard turning back the lock. With a sign to Mark that he was on no account to follow, Deborah tried the handle, opened the door just sufficiently, entered and closed it after her.

Linnet Lewarne went to the races after all.

4

Troy River and Castle Dor

ater that afternoon, Deborah, having led the way down
Mark Lewarne's private quay stair to the boat, and having
heftily drawn it alongside by its *frape*, launched the Notary
and the onion-seller Amyot. For a minute or so she stood
watching them – long enough to assure herself that the young
man understood a boat and could pull, bandaged as he was, a
pair of paddles deftly.

Monsieur Ledru, however, was inclined to doubt the lad's
capabilities when he found himself being pulled dangerously
close (as he thought) to the stem of a black schooner anchored
in the tideway.

'Take care!'

'It is all right,' Amyot assured him tranquilly. 'This is the *Jolie
Brise*.' He hailed the vessel with a queer sharp cry which
Monsieur Ledru remembered later, and quite skilfully brought
the boat alongside, close under the fore-chains.

A seaman came forward and leaned over the bulwarks.

'Yann, will you fetch and hand me down my kit – or shall
I come? It is all in a bundle, in my bunk, with my fiddle beside
it.'

'So I saw, just now, cleaning up the fo'c's'le,' returned the
seaman; 'and I allowed to myself you were meaning to break
ship. Not that I wonder.' He glanced over his shoulder, and

again looked down with a good-natured grin. 'Well, I will fetch the gear for you. But keep very quiet. The *patron* is below and, I do believe, in a worse humour than ever.'

The skipper was indeed below, and was moreover very wide awake. He had heard and recognised the cabin-boy's hail; and now from the after-companion he emerged and drew himself forth to his full height just as the seaman tumbled himself down through the fore-hatch. He lurched forward and looked overside.

'Eh?' said he, addressing Amyot. 'So you've thought twice and are coming back, little fool?'

'To fetch his belongings,' answered Monsieur Ledru.

'His belongings? His belongings?' Fouguereau thundered. He took a step back to the open fore-hatch, bent over it and bellowed down: 'Hi, below! What are you about, down there?'

The culprit, though frightened – for the power of a master, aboard his own ship, is wellnigh absolute – was a courageous fellow and a truthful one.

'I am fetching Amyot Trestane's gear,' he answered, and came clambering up with the bundle in one hand and under his armpit a rude box-shaped fiddle.

'Without my permission, *hein*? You wait awhile, my friend, and I'll teach *you* too what is discipline. For a beginning, there!'

He snatched the fiddle away from under the seaman's arm, broke it across his knee and flung the two pieces overboard, to float upward on the tide.

'There!' he repeated, having snatched the bundle in its turn, and holding it aloft over the bulwarks. 'As for this trash, I keep it – or do you prefer that I throw it too into the harbour?'

'My friend,' said Monsieur Ledru, speaking almost as in a sleep, his old eyes half closed; yet he said it distinctly, 'if you insist on the one or dare to attempt the other, I take this young man straight to the custom-house, and from that to the police inspector, whom I shall instruct to take out a summons against you. We shall next find a magistrate to certify it, and – well, I

24

do not envy you your interview with your owners when you return to them with a conviction for brutality and a long bill of claim against them for the ship's demurrage. I am not for punishment myself,' the old man continued placidly. 'I am a Notary, not a judge. But I know the law in these matters rather better than you.' He unclosed his eyes, and looked up as if recalling himself from slumber. 'So you had best hand down that bundle at once.'

Fouguereau considered for a moment, then thrust the bundle back upon the seaman.

'Here, toss it down to them – and good riddance, after all!'

'Excuse me,' Monsieur Ledru corrected him, this time sternly; 'but you shall lower it with your own hands, and quite gently – yes, gently all the way.'

The bundle was handed down.

As it was received with a 'Thank you', the skipper swung about to curse the seaman. But again the old precise voice spoke up with authority, inflexible.

'We are going some way up the river. But I return towards evening, and shall be lodging at the Rose and Anchor for some while. If I hear of any more complaints about you I shall examine them, and they may find themselves reported in and about Loctudy and around the coast. Good day.'

About a hundred yards upstream they recovered the floating sound-box and neckpiece of Amyot's fiddle; also the bow. But this, snapped in two, was unmendable.

'I will buy you a better one,' Monsieur Ledru said, seeing tears in the lad's eyes.

'But I made this myself, monsieur.'

'And maybe out of your own head, as the saying is,' Monsieur Ledru answered sarcastically. 'It looks as if it could be mended. I am no musician for my part, and anyway you cannot play on it just now: for to begin with it is broken, and moreover you could not row me and play on your fiddle at the same time.'

It was at all events evident that Amyot could row. The muscles of his back, stiff at first and sore with their wounds, warmed to the work and gradually became pliant. His lengthened strokes grew easier.

With a strong tide under them they swept up the harbour and past the lading ships; threaded their way between these and the vessels moored amid-stream, waiting to be stemmed; turned the bend of a pool under a wooded cliff; turned again by a low isolated rock on the starboard hand, and, all noise and business of commerce fading away behind them, found themselves opening entrance upon a sheet of water, some three miles long, silent and still as a lake of dreams.

Hanging woods embowered it on the one hand: on the other, rough untilled land ran down, sheeted with bracken, to a fringe of coppice, thick bushes, wild vines and woodbines – all mirrored in this Sabbath sheet of water, all seeming to bend lower and lower as the tide rose to them. There was no sound on it. A cart track, tufted above highwater mark with wild valerian, ran down along the right bank of this loch under the woodlands, out of which (the one sign of life) a heron ahead flapped slowly across, flying not so high but that the smooth water accurately glassed every movement of his wings. Far ahead a wooded promontory, bluish-green in the haze, appeared as closing the flood.

'Ah, it is beautiful,' said Monsieur Ledru. 'Rest on your oars for a moment, son: turn about and look . . .' But he added quaintly, almost with a sigh: 'I was hoping against hope. There is no island. The map is right. Now if only there were an island!'

He pulled forth a map from his breast pocket and spread it on his knees.

'That rock we have just passed is the Wiseman's Stone. There is a pool within the base of it frequented, they say, by otters. But there is no island, eh? Use your eyes, my boy.'

'It reminds me—' began Amyot, gazing.

'Eh? – of what?'

26

'I do not know, monsieur.' The confession came slowly, after a pause. 'Of no place that I remember – and yet it reminds me.' Thereupon he too made a queer remark. 'If the *patron* had not broken my fiddle, maybe it would tell me.'

'You suffer from fancies, my son,' said the Notary. But it seemed that he too suffered from fancies, for he went on: 'You shall have a new fiddle tomorrow, if it will only conjure up an island hereabouts.'

'But mine – but this one – was of my own making,' Amyot objected passionately, staring down forelornly upon his wrecked instrument. 'Perhaps that would make a difference – and the old one could conjure up, as monsieur puts it, but fancies: not an island – not a *real* island. It may have been that I never asked it, however. *A propos*, what sort of island would Monsieur require?'

'I know nothing of its shape or size,' Monsieur Ledru confessed. 'But it ought to be here somewhere . . . It was an island where two knights fought centuries ago – the one for his master's gain, the other for a lady. This was as it should be, according to the old saying that a knight should undertake no quarrel save for the truth's sake or for a woman.'

Amyot considered this.

'Then I am afraid, monsieur, I can never hope to be a real knight. For if ever again I come across this – this Fouguereau who has smashed my poor fiddle . . . But about this island – it seems to me that knights in armour would not fight on a rock but on some sort of sandbank; and of such there may be a dozen left when the tide ebbs.'

'You think so?' said the Notary aloud, and under his voice, 'Then perhaps you are not the dreamer I have been taking you for.' Aloud again he said, after Amyot had been rowing in silence for another half-mile or more: 'The map shows a track somewhere near, leading up through the woods to a spot I particularly wish to visit. Can we leave the boat and explore? Or will the tide desert us, I wonder?'

'The tide will make for four hours yet,' Amyot answered him. 'And I tried the depth under us with a paddle while you were talking. There is plenty of water: and in the pool we passed just now I found no bottom. As for mooring her, I can find a stone on the cart track yonder and use it for anchor.'

But by and by, upon the left hand side, they came to a tiny creek, with a ruinated quay close inside, and at the upper end a deserted saw-mill whose water-wheel had ceased to work. Amyot jumped ashore, hooped the boat's painter with one turn of the hand in a clove hitch over an old bollard and helped Monsieur Ledru to step ashore.

They followed up the bank of the creek until it shallowed under the blank windows of the saw-mill: found a line of step-ping-stones, crossed by them, and struck a steep foot track up which they thrust their way between hazels. It led them out upon a high moor, short-turfed, dotted with furze. At their feet lay the river, broad in expanse.

Beyond the round of the hill they covered a couple of stiles, struck towards an orchard lane darkened by overhanging boughs, crossed the village street at its head, under garden walls over-hung by drooping fuchsias, and mounted again by a cart-way between hedges draped with fern over the roots, and here and there over the fronds of which water poured in runnels.

The Notary pressed his pace up this hill, at a speed aston-ishing in one of his years. Once he halted for a moment, as if listening to the laps of water in the roadway gutters, and his hand twitched towards his pocket. 'But no, we will wait,' he said. 'The map, it is true, marks no island. If it marks no castle we have come in vain.'

Amyot's face expressed nothing but puzzlement. He did not in the least understand what quest he was following. It might be for a flower. He had heard of men of science – botanists – who would travel over countries in search of some little plant – a moss maybe. It was all one to him.

Monsieur Ledru pushed on with an unrelaxed stride; and

now, as the road at the top of the acclivity made a traverse out of the confined lane upon a broader road which disclosed a more gently sloping country of parcelled arable and pasture, he began to trace and retrace his steps from right to left, from gate to gate; for the hedgerows, though diminished in height, were still above a man's stature and allowed no prospect save through these gaps. Three or four times his fingers twitched towards his pocket; but always, as upon a quick afterthought, refrained. He zig-zagged across the road, as a hound works to pick up a line of scent.

At length, climbing two bars of a gate on their right, he gave tongue:

'*Voyons!* The castle!'

Clutching the upper bar with his left hand to balance himself, he cried again:

'The castle! See, boy – there on the very ridge!'

'I see no castle, sir. I see only a round clump of bushes.'

'But that is the castle, I tell you, Castle Dor! Let us make a short cut for it – I daresay now,' added Monsieur Ledru, as Amyot unhasped the gate upon a wheatfield, 'I dare say you think me mad. An old man – and in such a hurry not to be late, *hein?*'

The late-left wheat in the field grew tall, with its millions of ears all full-ripe. It grew almost to the hedge, with just a swathe left for them to pass along in single file. From the gate they had overlooked the whole surface of the field, undulating with shine and shade, but here in the pathway the wheat out-topped them. They could see nothing to their right but its stalks; nothing save here and there a scarlet poppy, a shoot of blue flax, a butterfly drifting in a quiver of heat.

After fifty paces or so Monsieur Ledru turned about, lifted his hat and wiped his forehead.

'One gets the like of this,' said he, 'at times, sailing between Ushant and the Main. Near the close of day, when the wind turns offshore and comes out over the water in a sudden warm breath of hayfields and strawberry-fields, straight down Brest harbour – I suppose,' he added, 'when I promised you a castle just now, you expected some sort of a tower – a tall massive building, with fortifications, was it not?'

But Amyot had turned indifferent. 'I had indeed expected – I cannot tell what, monsieur.'

The Notary clapped on his hat, and they resumed their way. It led them around an angle to a second gate, which admitted to a field of stubble. Amyot's heels by this time gored him worse than the stripes on his back and loins.

A third gate opened upon a broad field of close-cropped pasture, the sides of which converged to a mound, now discernible as a cirque – and by and by as a double earthwork, each vallum overgrown with brambles, topping thorns and the elder that sprawls and kills all its neighbours. Straight ahead of them a wide gap opened in the rampart: and through it they passed into an amphitheatre of close turf, screened from all winds: in diameter some two hundred-odd feet across, level and smooth as a table.

Monsieur Ledru, in an ecstasy which forbade speech, started pacing and counting. The inner side of the enclosure was almost bare of bushes. He found a seat on a cushion of wild thyme, and at length drew the map from his pocket.

'This is better than I thought – I said just now that we should be yet in time – I meant only that I should be here in time, to pay homage to the kings and their knights and ladies that once kept court within this very circle. It has been my long race against time and opportunity.'

He climbed through a gap in the encircling thorns, plunged down and across a tangled ditch, and clambering, led the way to the top of the outer vallum, which just here abutted on the high road. From their feet the country descended to a bay of the channel, blue beneath the summer haze. Turning about, they could descry at the foot of the ascent they had mounted, the river ford deep down in a wedge-shaped funnel of the woodlands.

'Castle Dor – you see it commands all approaches,' cried the Notary, pointing, 'bay, river, road along the ridge – but hallo!'

His gaze, travelling along the ridge, fell on an enclosure dotted with tents, vehicles and human beings in clusters – a field full of folk. There were white-topped booths too outside the enclosure, lining a rise of the highway. On distant banks tiny flags flickered.

'Ah, to be sure – the races!'

On their way they had neither met nor passed a living soul, with the single exception of an aged woman filling her pitcher from a chute at the head of the village street. Here of course lay the explanation. The entire countryside had gathered itself yonder. Afar there a bell tinkled – a saddling-bell for the next race. Listening, the Notary and Amyot could almost articulate the cries of the bookmakers, shouting one against the others.

'It might be an ancient religious festival at this distance,' said Monsieur Ledru drily; 'only it isn't. At this distance,' he went on meditatively, 'what an ant-hill it looks! The divine Homer, my son, likens the generations of men to the leaves of the forest. To me they resemble rather the spring's renewal of grass, covering the world's mistakes. You see where we stand at this moment: you see where the hucksters have planted their sweet-stalls yonder, beside that exposed patch of the road? Well, many centuries ago, here, where we stand, to this same rampart – yes, to this very yard of it, since it gives the best view along the road – a queen came, making excuse to her husband, but in truth for the first glimpse of her lover, as his horse rounded that same corner. It is a tragic story – one of the saddest. They trysted among the woods a little beyond and below the race field – there, where, without a wind a dark cloud is gathering and a darker cloud wheeling, foreboding a thunderstorm.'

'*Lantyan!*'

'Eh? But how, name of thunder—?'

Amyot dropped the hand with which he had been shielding his eyes. 'Nay, monsieur, but the word came to me . . .'

At that moment an outcry, shriller than any they had heard heretofore, came borne to them from the race field. Groups of folk were seen breaking up of a sudden and detached dots of figures running towards the entrance gate.

'The ant-hill for some reason is in commotion,' observed Monsieur Ledru.

Gazing, they saw a booth by the gate collapse like a diminutive house of cards: then a scurry of figures to right and left of the road.

'It is a runaway carriage,' announced Amyot, using his young eyes.

He knelt and slipped off his sabots.

5

The runaways

Linnet Lewarne, after re-tying her hat ribbons very leisurely under her chin, which was none the less beautiful just then for being petulant, and after a prolonged look at herself in the mirror to make sure that disdain did not ill become her, unlocked the door and paused on the threshold.

'I will go with you to the races – on one condition: that you don't ask me to speak one word to you.'

'Eh?'

'You have insulted me. Of course I can't prevent *your* talking: you may chatter as much as you like. But my terms I can keep: and if you don't agree to them I go back and take off this finery. I shall not speak to you before we get back to this door, and only then after you have begged my pardon—'

'But I beg it *now*, Linnet.'

She shook her head. 'Not properly. You are doing it just to coax me to come and be shown off. Well, here I am. If you still think me worth it, show me off to your friends as much as you like.'

'And you won't even speak to *them*?'

'Of course I shall speak to them. *They* haven't put any affront on me – or none that wasn't of your getting – oh!' She struck the point of her parasol sharply on the floor, and checked herself. 'Well, those are the terms.'

Mark bent his head. She passed him, descended the stairs and stepped into the barouche, her husband following. 'Like a queen she done it, and like any queen she looked,' said Tim Udy, the coachman, afterwards,

Tim Udy, somewhat tipsy and in a sweat to be at the races, put the two horses, Merman and Merlin, furiously at the breast of the hill. They were young horses, spirited animals both, sons of one sire, in colour bright bay and beautifully matched: unusually matched too, for each carried one white 'sock' on the foreleg, Merlin on the near one, Merman on the off, and these left and right birthmarks tallied to within an inch. Mark Lewarne, penurious by habit until marriage converted him to ostentation, had paid a pretty penny for the pair. No owner could see his valuable horseflesh treated in this fashion. Mark moreover had just been humiliated and had to take his wrath out on somebody. He staggered up from his seat, was jolted back against the padded cushions, and again staggered up, imprecating.

'Can't help it now, master,' called Tim Udy over his shoulder. 'Thought you was in a hurry – ought to be anyhow. Whir-roo! You sit down and they'll do it!'

A timorous woman would have cried out, or at least have clutched at the rail of the carriage: for at the first bend the off hind wheel had grated and almost locked itself against a lean-to block of granite that protected the inn corner. That shock past, a good, dutiful, nagging wife should have told her husband that Tom Udy was drunk and anybody but a fool could have seen it before starting. Linnet did not stir a hand, but sat composedly, with set lips.

At the top of the hill Tim Udy called a breather to his beauties, before sending them along the safe level. 'That's the way to do it!'

Mark Lewarne exploded again. 'The way to break any horse's wind!' he shouted. 'Damn you – don't you know what money's worth you're driving?'

'They're fresh, master,' Tim Udy explained lucidly. 'Nothing like a hill to take it out of 'em. I didn't ask 'ee to keep 'em frothing and waiting. They'll go like lambs now, tell the missus.'

Mark Lewarne cursed again – but to what use? 'There's no danger now,' he assured Linnet, bending over her uxoriously as the horses broke into a trot and almost at once settled to a free stride. 'Not badly frightened, were you, dear? Not feeling faint?'

She was certainly not feeling faint. But her half-closed eyes and a pallor on her face excused the question.

She opened her eyes. They were languorous, as though drowsed by the smooth motion of the carriage wheels. She opened them upon her husband as though upon a stranger leaning over her. Then they sharpened, hardened and closed again at once. Her lips tightened.

Many centuries ago there came into the west of England a certain Theodore Palaeologus, whose tomb or monument may today be inspected within a little tide-washed church beside Tamar. He had been in fact the last stout man of imperial race to hold the Turk out of Byzantium. Why, beaten, he chose this shore, to end his days upon it, is now a question past solving. But he did: and, being a vigorous man, he married in these parts and had legitimate heirs who, with their branches, have quite faded out. But also (tradition has it) being a vigorous man, he begat other children, who accepted the name of Constantine which he bequeathed to them with what wealth he could spare. Certain it is that today, 'across the water', as they to the west of Troy harbour say of folk on its east, Constantines abound; and whatever he or she has lost of estate, a Constantine seldom fails to inherit a nobility of feature shared by themselves, somehow alien to their neighbours; especially the womenkind, however subdued by necessity to farm tasks.

Now of these women Constantines, the most are dark, handsome, low-browed; but sometimes a child will be born with strict type of feature but light-coloured or auburn of hair, and with a complexion of crystalline fairness. Such a girl was Linnet Constantine, whose mother (a Constantine wedded to a black-smith cousin) had died when her child was two years old.

Linnet Constantine – her father dandering, with all spring of ambition broken in him having exchanged his smithy for a farm – had grown up three miles from anywhere, and almost two from the elementary school, where, however, she found an outlet of ambition in beating her fellows, and a mistress who dressed fashionably (for those parts), spoke with a refined accent and lent the child books. From the age of fourteen, 'three years she grew in sun and shower', sheltered by a poor roof over-grown with house-leek down to the very eaves under which in early summer the martlets built.

She had no money to purchase fine clothes, but she carried beneath her growing breasts an inner command never to show herself in mean array. Looking back on these years, it is hard to imagine that even in cheap finery she could ever have demeaned herself to attract rustic lovers. At any rate, she hid herself; and she hid herself so carefully that even her father found her avoidance of company a strange freak – when he happened to think about it at all.

Then one autumn day in the 1860s Mark Lewarne came across the water to have a look at Prosper Constantine's yield of apples. His look wandered more than once in pauses of chaf-fering to Prosper Constantine's daughter, as she balanced herself on the orchard ladder, reached to pick the fruit, and climbed down with an apronful to bestow it delicately on the pile beneath the tree, no apple bruised. She appeared to pay no attention to the visitor.

Mark Lewarne bought the whole cider crop at a generous bid. Early next spring he brought Linnet to be his wife. She was just eighteen.

She did not know love, or what it was. She had read books. She craved for the world over the hills. She would stand, that spring, by the gate, watching with eyes half closed the martlets and swallows as they skimmed and wove circles over the farm pools. They came all the way from Egypt to her door.

One day – about a week after she had accepted Mark Lewarne, and as she watched these birds circleting and swooping for midges, she heard the gate at the head of the rutted farm lane unhasped and reclosed: then footsteps. The oncomer and she caught sight of one another almost simultaneously: and the oncomer was a woman, a girl almost or but a year or two older than Linnet. She was tall, dark, handsome in a way, and she surveyed Linnet, halting in the dusk.

'Are you wanting to be told the footpath down to the creek?' asked Linnet a little nervously.

'No,' was the answer, with a backward jerk of the head. 'I came by the ferry and must cross back by it. But seeing as you're to be my mistress, it seems—'

'You came to have a look at me? Well, look!' Linnet spread out her arms against the darkening sky.

'Well, you're a beauty – an armful – I must say,' responded the other, with a half-curtsy: and her wrists went over her breasts as if they gathered the edges of her shawl closer against a sudden chill in the air.

'Do I understand that you are to be my servant – one of my servants?'

'Yes, mistress, and the faithfullest, I hope. My name is Deborah, Deborah Brangwyn.'

She was gone in the dusk. By and by Linnet heard the latch of the gate click twice.

'What you don't see,' said Mark Lewarne, leaning over the barouche towards his wife, 'is that I've planned all this for your pleasure. Men are longer-sighted than women: but it's the women that help. You're mistress of all, this afternoon – that's one step up: and if you play the cards, one of these days we'll sell out and be gentry with the best. Eh, dear? Don't you see what I'm planning for you?'

Silence.

'See these fields to the left,' he began again presently, 'I've one—two—three – mortgages on the bunch of 'em. And I showed you my will, didn't I?'

Still silence.

On the race field Linnet behaved with composure and graciousness to everyone who approached the barouche. When the time came for her to hand the cup to the winner of her own steeple-chase, she did it with a pretty regal grace; and even turned to her husband, as she handed it, with a charming small bow of acknowledgement that seemed to say she transmitted the gift from its actual donor. But she did not speak to him.

Now before this ceremony, and in an interval of the races, Tim Udy had unharnessed Merman and Merlin, and taken them around to the back of the refreshment tent, between it and the hedge, to tether them there and water and feed them: after which he had dived into the tent and consumed whisky.

The ceremony over, his master, in the very devil of a rage, dragged him out and commanded him to harness up for the return journey. There was only a Consolation Stake remaining to be run for. Tim Udy fetched around Merman and Merlin and harnessed them up obediently. His own movements during the operation were deliberate and painfully thoughtful. No horses even for the king's opening of Parliament were ever harnessed with a minuter care. Tim Udy was in fact as drunk as a lord.

The Consolation chase had been started and had already proceeded some way before he climbed the box and steered his pair out into the high road. Then someone by the gate called out sharply:

'Morning Star's down!'

Morning Star was not only down by a nearby fence, but had broken a leg. Tim Udy pulled up drunkenly to listen. There was a long pause, then a revolver shot rang out over the hedge, in the Lewarnes' ears.

38

It rang in the ears also of Merman and Merlin, who forthwith plunged through the gateway at an angle, shedding their driver off his seat and stunning him against a post. Scattering the sweet-sellers' booth, left and right, they were off on the road towards Castle Dor at a mad gallop, hampered only by a loose trace that, now trailing and now flicked up like a whip, lashed Merlin's belly. The reins too would be dangling somewhere among the hind hoofs – the occupants of the barouche could not see. They were helpless.

Mark Lewarne was on his feet, clutching a hold somehow and screaming. Linnet heard his screams above the pounding of hoofs. Once, with a sway and a jolt, he was flung right across her lap.

She did not help him to recover. She leaned back in the rush of the air, her lips tight for that something which must inevitably happen.

6

First fate becomes second

It came heralded by a wild screech, that began as it were with the ripping of a calico screen between life and death, and was hideously prolonged in her ears to a yell utterly maniacal. For half an instant it had sounded human – had a child been run over and killed?

She thrust off Mark's weight from across her lap, and he fell in a limp heap. She staggered up and forward: clutched for the rail of the driver's seat: caught and held it; and stood swaying, her feet treading her husband's body amid the rugs. She managed to slew her right shoulder for a glance over it along the road behind.

No body lay there. Back for a long stretch it was void: beyond this a couple of horsemen pounded, following at a gallop – a short interval divided them: behind them her glance took in but a cluster of dots or specks.

But the scream continued. It was somewhere ahead – and now close. She clutched the rail harder and, swinging about again still treading Mark's body for foothold, had a vision over heaving loins and plunging shoulders of a dazzling road and a dark figure against the dazzle with arms stretched wildly . . .

And with that – as to the last moment the screech kept piercing her ears – Merman and Merlin went suddenly back on their haunches, and the scream as suddenly ended with a

41

snap and rending smash of the carriage-pole. But Linnet scarcely heard this. The jerk of it flung her forward, her brow striking the rail, and then as violently backward among the cushions.

She scrambled to her feet, and recognised the Notary Ledru, gallantly holding Merlin short of the bridle and working around in front of the pair, who reared and plunged, entangling their legs in the broken pole: confused by it perhaps; cowed, at any rate.

'Steady, madame! and descend with speed,' he panted. 'You are saved, thank God! Now if they go again, they go – there is nothing to hold them.'

'Did *you* stop them? Can I help?' – the two questions almost in a breath.

'In God's name, no! *Eh, eh, calmez-vous donc – soyez tran-quilles, assassins!*' (A struggle.) Run around, madame – quick – at the back there!' he called. 'See if the lad lives – you went right over him . . .'

Linnet fled around. A body lay huddled sideways in the roadway, some twenty yards back. She ran, reached it and knelt in the dust. She was lifting the inert head as the two pursuing horsemen rode up and jumped from their saddles. The leader ran to the Notary's help. The second, after a glance, turned about and stooped over Linnet and the lad.

'Dead, ma'am?'

'Oh, I hope not! No. I am sure not! Listen – listen again!'

She bent her ear to the lad's lips, tore open his shirt and listened against his heart. The only visible hurt was a wound welling through the hair above the forehead where the splin-tered bar had gashed him as he went down.

'No bones broken here, seemin'ly,' said the stout newcomer, kneeling and feeling up and down the patient's legs. 'You know me, missus? – if so be as we can get him alive to Lantyan –'

'Oh, Mr Bosanko!' cried Linnet. 'See! his eyes opened – now they've shut again! – A-A-ah! . . .' she cried it out upon two things happening swiftly, as everything was happening swiftly.

A blinding flash lit up road and hedges: many folk – faces even – crowding in from everywhere out of nowhere: this and a sense of blood everywhere: drops of blood oozing from the lad's skull wound and simultaneously splashed on his naked chin and throat, whence, how could she guess? She heard Farmer Bosanko calling to the crowd to hold back and give air.

'But he is bleeding – bleeding everywhere!' she called. Her voice lifted but to be smashed by a peal of thunder. As it died down she heard Mr Bosanko saying, repeating:

''Tis your own blood, mistress – your own blood dripping, ma'am, if you'll excuse me. Your face is a mask of it.'

He found and tendered a huge red handkerchief. But already her hands had gone up to her face. They came away covered with blood. The jerk against the rail had cut her sharply across her eyebrow.

From a child she had secretly despised herself for a tendency to faint at the sight of blood. She spread out her hands now, and the rain-burst of the storm fell on them as if invoked. It fell as from buckets. It drenched down in a white veil cutting off the ring of the crowd: it mastered the five or six men at the heads of the already mastered horses – within ten seconds it had drenched Linnet to the skin. Her hands were washed white as she raised them again instinctively, foolishly, to ward off a second flash that jagged down and smote earth somewhere close to the left. The glare of it revealed Amyot's face; and that too was clean, pallid, wet as a drowned man's. The rain beat up from the roadway, hissing, almost to her hips . . .

Then – and all as suddenly, it seemed – the rain ceased; the clouds parted into two dark battalions rolling seaward; and through the partition shone the sun. An arm was about her – Farmer Bosanko's.

'Your pardon, missus, but I reck'ned you was goin' to faint. When you cast up your hands that way –'

She raised herself on her knees, a runnel from the farmer's hat brim pouring over her breast as he bent.

'No – attend to *him*!'

But already the Notary, relieved from charge of the horses, was stooping over Amyot, feeling the lad's body. He looked up side-ways and commanded Farmer Bosanko sharply:

'Take my handkerchief too, and bind her forehead.'

While the farmer fumbled, up hurried Linnet's husband. He had crawled out of the barouche unhurt. Like most timorous men, danger past, he was viciously angered; and at the sight of his wife's expensive gown bedraggled, bedaubed and besmeared with half-washed-out bloodstains, he started to vent his anger in the face of the crowd which a newly arrived police constable was brandishing out into a semicircle.

'What made you so mad as to jump?' he demanded furiously. 'You might have killed yourself! – and look at the cautch of your dress, damn it all!'

Linnet heard him and turned about slowly, under the bandage which Farmer Bosanko had clumsily begun to adjust. Words were on her lips: but she spoke not one.

'You are hurt! You are hurt!' At sight of her face, down which the blood had begun anew to trickle and spread, his wrath emptied itself back into terror, solicitude. Almost his knees knocked together. And Linnet, regarding, despised him in her heart more than ever.

But as they stood confronted someone raised a cry: 'The doctor!' The crowd took it up in a loud murmur, 'The doctor! the doctor!' and edged back to give way.

Down against the sunburst now gilding the road and the wet hedges there came at a canter a cobbish grey mare; and on her, and sitting her easily, a middle-aged man in the act of closing an immense umbrella; in this performance negligent of his one snaffle rein save to hitch it loosely over a crook of his left little finger. The umbrella closed itself high above a rusty silk hat. Doctor Carfax rode into the arena. He lifted a leg over the butt end of a butterfly net under his off saddle-flap, and dismounted – clean-shaven, of middle height, very plain of feature, but with a carriage of easy dignity and, beneath bushy grey eyebrows, the assured gaze of a country gentleman accustomed to command respect. As if by instinct he singled out the Notary – a stranger to him as to the crowd – and addressed him sharply.

'Sorry if I am late, sir! Sent to fetch a wagonette for Udy: bad concussion: nothing worse. The Lord looks after such. I sent police for second vehicle. It is needed seemingly. Lucky thing I chanced to be passing by.'

He stooped and made his examination, the first act of which was to draw up the lad's shirt gently and expose the bare chest. This done, he paused and looked up at the Notary into whose charge he had yielded his umbrella.

'Pass it over to friend Bosanko, sir, and take this' – he produced a roll of lint from an ample tail pocket – 'and attend to Mrs Lewarne if you will. By the look of your hands you'll make a better job of it than he.'

'I never could manage a knot,' confessed Mr Bosanko modestly; 'not even in my own neckcloth. As I've said times and again, the Lord send I don't outlive my missus!'

The cut on Linnet's forehead was not deep, and the blood had almost ceased welling. Someone fetched a cupful of water from the near ditch, and with this and the lint and the Notary's clean handkerchief Linnet was soon put to rights.

'Let's see, let's see!' muttered Doctor Carfax, pursuing his task with rapid, delicate hands. 'Collar-bone, of course: two – three ribs, and a scalp wound that doesn't amount to much. Now help me lift him a little, somebody – carefully – very gently, I tell you.'

He slid a hand under the back of the shirt and was passing it up towards the shoulder-blade when of a sudden he paused and looked up, puzzled interrogation in his eye.

'What the devil!'

The Notary nodded. 'You saw?'

'No, I did not. But I can feel.'

'I will tell you about it later – it is another story. It has nothing to do with this business.'

'Well, I was wondering – but here comes the wagonette –'

'They can take him down to Lantyan,' offered Farmer Bosanko; 'and welcome. My wife's a motherly woman, as you know, doctor: and a lad that has the nerve – I saw it, and never the like . . . He'll recover all right?'

'Of course he will! The pole must have struck him slant-ways, and slantways he went down. How the wheel missed him is a miracle and a closer miracle how the hoofs missed. See the shoe mark stamped on his cap here – printed so that even the rain hasn't washed it out – in a fortnight he'll be hale and about again.'

'That's good hearing. And when he's fit to be moved – well, I'll speak to my wife about it,' said the farmer.

'Don't speak to her now. Just take the lad in; lay him on the floor of your hall, and say I'll be round within twenty minutes.'

Doctor Carfax turned to the two wagonettes approaching, the one empty, the other laden with the unconscious bulk of Tim Udy. After a brief secondary inspection of this sufferer, he commanded one of the brakes now returning from the races to bear Udy in to Troy to the small hospital in Fore Street. Its occupants cheerfully tumbled out and packed themselves into other vehicles. Amyot was placed in the wagonette.

Already Merman and Merlin, sobered of their madness, were being led homeward to stable. A cart-horse had been enlisted from a near field to tow the barouche to the wheelwright's shop at the crossroads. The invalids bestowed, room was found in the second wagonette for Linnet, her husband and the Notary. And so all rolled back towards Troy, Doctor Carfax, after a word or two with Mr Bosanko, mounting and jogging in the rear of the first wagonette.

7

Doctor Carfax and a discussion over lunch

'Lantyan was the word,' said the Notary, 'and the lad said it distinctly, pronouncing it English-wise, with the strong accent on the "y", so that it slurs over the "a" following, and the word becomes *Lantyne* with just the shade of difference I noted when you spoke it just now, and when the farmer spoke it – Bosanko, I think he calls himself.'

'Well, and that is how we call it in these parts,' answered the doctor, delicately peeling the rind of a lemon. 'You are something of a philologer, I take it, and maybe something of an historian as well. So we needn't bother about the old ecclesiastical fight between the *lans* and the *sows*. The point is that in any place name *lan* or *stow*, as with *cester*, is very naturally the unaccented part – Morwenstow, Brid-estow, Landulph, Lankelly, Exeter, Dorchester, Leicester.'

'Excuse me, that is not quite the point: or, to put it more politely, it is not what puzzles me – I am not thinking of philology just now. Of course I know my Breton, and some Cornish: enough to distribute the stress rightly on any place name I see in print.'

'You are putting it modestly.' The doctor dropped the whole rind of his lemon, perfectly circumvoluted, into the punch-bowl.

'Well, suppose that I am – I break down, then, at two points; the first is, that this Amyot anticipated a word, almost certainly unknown to him, that was on the tip of my tongue; the second, which is more wonderful, that he anticipated my pronunciation, to correct it. I should have called it Lantaien – something like that.'

Doctor Carfax stooped over the fire to push the kettle back on its trivet. He had invited Monsieur Ledru to drop in and have a smoke with him after dinner, and the Notary had accepted gratefully, with some prospect of being amused, in this corner of the world, by an 'original'; and his quick readjustment, on being received by a courteous and fastidiously dressed gentleman in a well-furnished library, before a log fire burning in a basket of polished steel, did his manners all credit. The room was low-raftered but ample: its far end abutted a wide bow window over the harbour tide, the surge and lap of which murmured through a lifted sash. Over the chimney-shelf hung a portrait, in watercolour of a young woman. It was his one picture in the room, dimly lit by four wax candles on the table. These shone in candlesticks of old silver, beautifully polished. Monsieur Ledru noted also that the room smelt fragrantly of lavender: two large bowls of which he had presently perceived – one on the polished oak table, the other on a tallboy just within the penumbra of the candles. For the rest, the walls were brown to the ceiling with books, with here and there a glint of old gilt, answering a jet of flame from the logs.

'Let us take your two puzzles in order,' said Doctor Carfax, stepping back to the table and filling his pipe from the tobacco jar. 'For the first I may tell you that I am no sceptic at all. Why, man, thought transference is a fact. Who hasn't, once or twice or many times in his life, anticipated the exact words the other fellow was going to say? I get a good many confessions in my trade: and I am convinced on accumulated evidence that between any given man and wife, sleeping side by side, this happens quite frequently.

'Once upon a time' – here he chose a spill from a jar on the chimney-shelf to relight his pipe – 'once upon a time,' he resumed, 'I quite often leapt to what – to what *somebody* was going to say . . . But I never possessed second sight, I'm glad to say.'

'I was thinking,' said the Notary, 'about that boy.'

He had told Doctor Carfax the story of the stripes on Amyot's back and shoulders. He bent forward. 'We'll allow for the moment that one human being can anticipate another's thought, to put it into a word or words. But that doesn't satisfy me. It doesn't wholly explain – I have omitted to tell you that already, on our way up the river, he had confided to me that the scene – the sheet of water and the wooded hills – reminded him of some spot he had once known, he couldn't say where. When I questioned him he could recall nothing definite – might have seen some such place in a forgotten infancy, as we'll say, or maybe but in a dream. You detect any possible connection between that and his taking the word *Lantyan* out of my mouth later on? *Voyez vous*, I mean only some *possible* connection?'

'Certainly I do. I also see that a youngster, friendless till rescued by you from that abominable ship, with every nerve tortured up and quivering, must have found himself in that dinghy unexpectedly floated into heaven.'

'But with a broken fiddle.'

'To be sure – but with the breaking of the fiddle a real heaven found, eh?'

'You said just now,' objected Monsieur Ledru politely, 'that at one period of your life you anticipated what a certain person was going to say.'

Doctor Carfax removed the pipe from his mouth. '*Touché* . . . I was young at that time and undergoing the pangs of first love.' he answered.

'Ah!' Monsieur Ledru breathed his thanks softly. 'Then you think—'

'No, I don't,' the doctor snapped, as if double-locking a shutter

49

incautiously opened. 'No, I don't,' he repeated. 'Perhaps I ought to tell you that, of a sort and in my obscure way, I am a man of science. Oh, not a man of science with any letters to my name! You may call me a naturalist, if you choose to be polite and so reward the impoliteness of my asking you to come around by the surgery door. The truth is, my front porch is occupied by a lady – rather an unpleasant lady. She killed her husband yesterday and ate him. In short she's a garden spider whose ways I have been observing for the last week or two. Why did she choose my front porch? Why did Leto choose Delos for her parturition of Apollo? Anyhow, I had the front door locked, rather than disturb her, and put up a card asking visitors to come around to the surgery entrance.'

Doctor Carfax rose, lifted the hissing kettle and concentrated himself upon the mixing of the punch-bowl. Speech was clearly forbidden during this operation. When it was finished he took up a pair of tall-stemmed glasses, held them swiftly to the candle-light, and almost as dexterously brimmed them.

'Pronounce,' he challenged, handing one steaming glassful to the Notary.

'Delicious,' pronounced Monsieur Ledru after a sip; and after a second: 'Oh, but absolutely delicious; you are an artist, Doctor Carfax.'

'I am a naturalist, I tell you. My grandfather was a naturalist too, greater than I, because he stuck to observed facts without any theorizing whatever.'

'Was he a doctor too?'

'Oh yes – we've been doctors these three generations and now myself a childless man and the last of us all. But we've all had, I suspect, an inkling that our practice is mere empiricism – that the best we could do, each in his parish, was to alleviate suffering and win that confidence which does in fact alleviate it. I'm not speaking of exceptional cases, or any refinements of surgery, but of that mysterious confidence a doctor can inspire by the simple act of entering a house and laying down hat and gloves.

'As I say, we Carfaxes have all been doctors, yet all intrigued by something outside the empiricism which is about the summary of what we know, and at the back of our minds, always seeking for some sixth sense in nature – be it in man's brain or a spider's. You perceive what I am working around to?'

'I begin to,' said Monsieur Ledru, lazily amused. Old men when not themselves garrulous make the best listeners.

Doctor Carfax went to a corner-cupboard, produced from it a kind of cup of silver with a cover, and, filling it with hot wood-ash from the hearth, dropped it tenderly into the punch-bowl to reheat the liquor.

'It's curious,' said he reflectively, 'that spirit likes silver. So does cider. Whereas to any kind of wine metal is poison. Let the best wine run over metal and it's ruined – on the instant.' He swung around upon Monsieur Ledru and proffered another steaming glassful.

'Well, as I was saying, or was about to say, you were the one who had the word *Lantyan* in your head. All the way up the river you were preoccupied with Lantyan. Further, you were half hoping, or hoping against hope, to find an island. May I ask whether you were looking for the island where one, Tristan, fought the Irishman Morholt?'

As though the question had been an actual shot and had struck him, the Notary jerked himself erect, staring. 'What! You know the connection then?'

'Why not?' Doctor Carfax, with a dry smile, sought a book-shelf, pointed to several slim volumes packed tight together, half withdrew one, then replaced it, and turned again to his guest.

'Who', he asked, 'can ever tell how information travels, when men are curious for it? Before I became a naturalist I collected books, and the Antiquarian Society of which I was a member has affiliations with a similar body your side of the channel. Treatises passed between us, the similarity of place names in Brittany and Cornwall, and their legends too, being a favourite subject. To begin with I was an ignoramus. Like most

Cornishmen and all Englishmen, I believed Lyonesse lay between Land's End and the Lizard, that King Mark held court at Tintagel, that Iseult landed there from Ireland – an impossibility if you look at the coast – and it was not until I read Béroul—'

'Ah!' sighed the Notary, 'then you have read Béroul.'

'Manuscript 217,' quoted his host, '*du fonds français de la Bibliotheque Nationale, le commencement et le fin du poeme sont perdus*: twelfth century – and the earliest extant manuscript of the whole Tristan series. Yes, I have read Béroul's *Roman de Tristan*; or as much of it as the professor of the learned society I have just mentioned cared to quote.

> Oiezpue dit la tricheresse!
> Mout fist que bonne lecherresse.

The tale originated here in the sixth century, or before that even, and was handed down from father to son, or more likely mother to daughter, until your wandering troubadours got hold of it and turned it into poetry.'

'Romanticizing lust and licence into deathless love,' murmured the Notary.

'You can put it that way,' said Carfax, 'but my experience as a doctor suggests the result has been beneficial on the whole. Man cannot live by bread alone, or, to be blunt, by copulation. The dreaming self must be satisfied too. Let me tell you something. Some nineteen years ago I was waiting up at Castle Dor for a child to make its appearance in the world – the same young woman, as it happens, who so nearly came to grief in a runaway carriage this very day – and as I vigiled under the stars it seemed to me that I was near to stumbling upon something; what it was I could not say, the secret was beyond me. And then, many months later, reading your poet Béroul, I found the word *Lancien*, the ancient rendering of our *Lantyan*, and realized, if his words held truth, that all my boyhood – bird's-nesting,

52

blackberrying, nutting, or merely loafing and dreaming – I had been treading the very tracks of one of the greatest love stories in the world.'

'And so?'

Doctor Carfax considered a moment, as though endeavouring to recapture an experience blunted by time, whose fragrance now lay stored in memory's labyrinth like a flower pressed between the pages of a book.

'The revelation overpowered me,' he answered finally. 'I took Béroul's *Roman de Tristan* – or to be more accurate the extracts from it reprinted in the journal of our society – to read the poem through once more under Castle Dor and in the woods of Lantyan, where, according to your poet, Tristan once trysted with Queen Iseult. I recollect they had been felling oaks there to serve the commercial purpose of some firm beyond Bodmin, and the trunks were sledged down to a creek to be rafted away – God knows where. But where they had fallen, what sheets of foxgloves clothed the hill bringing first aid to its shorn beauty!'

He rose from his chair, and stood looking out of the window across the harbour. Memory was not so blunted after all. He could remember the drowsy bumble-bees sipping the nectar from within the flowers, the brilliance of a dragon-fly on the wing, the sudden startled flight of pigeons.

'One of Nature's happier tricks,' he commented, 'is how, after devastation, the wild flower grows. Demolish a house, lay waste a city, and the following year you'll find a field of ragged robin. Gazing at that wealth of foxgloves amid the forest penury I wondered if a soil having once brought to birth such a story as that of Tristan and Iseult would never so flower again, yet be unable to forget or desist from the effort to throw up secondary shoots—'

He broke off abruptly, and shooting a quick glance at his guest from under bushy eyebrows, returned to his chair.

'Forgive me,' he said. 'You will observe that I am not so

53

entirely a man of science that I cannot sometimes have – romantic theories. Or had them once. *Revenons a nos moutons*.'

The Notary brushed an imaginary fly from his cravat.

'I was not aware,' he said mildly, 'that we had strayed from them. And your romantic theories, as you term them, hold far more interest for an old man like myself than your field work with the common spider. Tell me though: having read Béroul, what do you make of his geography?'

'Why, that he was accurate,' Carfax replied, 'and he can be proved so by research into old manor histories and by the study of place names. This Lantyan you seek is indubitably the Lancien of the original story. I believe, as Béroul knew, that King Mark held his court just there below Castle Dor and ruled all this part of the coast of Cornwall from it; that Tintagel, in the north, never came into the story at all; that Iseult and Tristan loved and suffered on the very spot and under the parent boughs of those I will show you in leaf tomorrow. Be prepared though for a mere farmhouse – no palace. On the way I shall introduce you to another patient of mine, who, at my behest, studies rooks for his health's sake instead of taking physic.'

The Notary smiled. It was not often he came across anyone so immediately sympathetic to his own notions of how life should be conducted as this general practitioner of a small Cornish seaport.

'A moment ago,' he said, 'it was on the point of my tongue to ask you a seemingly absurd question. You are a precisian for scientific method?'

'Without it all conjecture is the child of conceit.'

'Then tell me, as man to man: how do you hold it conceivable that a certain spot – a place, say, of waters, woodlands, old buildings – can hold a memory, a thought almost, and even utter it, once in a while, through human lips?'

Doctor Carfax stood up, added a log to the fire, stirred it and faced about.

'How, sir?' he said; 'because nobody but a philosopher with

a system would deny the possibility. You see this poker? Your systematic fellows pour scorn on the poor woman who, having lit her fire, sets a poker upright against the bars. How can he know anyhow – how prove his negative? Against him he has the practical experience of generations of women who have kindled fires. They don't know *why* they do it, but they do it. All he can know is that he can't explain why an upright poker should help a fire – which, as a fact, it often does.'

Doctor Carfax leaned his poker against the hearth by way of illustration.

'The word impossible should be in no scientific man's dictionary,' he continued, 'any more than it was in Napoleon's. How do we know that a spray doesn't blossom with pleasure because a bird clings to it? A blade of grass has intelligence: a convolvulus – and climbing pea – has intelligence enough to do business for itself and actively realize its Maker's idea. Do you suppose they take no pleasure in it, or fade back and revive without memories?'

'A plant is a plant,' Monsieur Ledru objected. 'A whole scene of forestry and river is a different question. It's a congeries – a composition – of a thousand, a million separate things, even allowing them to be sentient.'

'Tush man! So are you: so am I, or any cabbage. There *may* happen something – say once in a thousand years – to draw all this patch of elements together upon the moment for which, on our fantastic but not unscientific hypothesis, this patch – this infinitesimal patch, after all – of creation is in travail – but you have journeyed far and are weary. Let me light a lantern and see you along the street to your inn. Tomorrow, if you have nothing better to do, you shall mount my trap and let me drive you on my round to Lantyan.'

8

Doctor Carfax prescribes

Doctor Carfax sent around to the Rose and Anchor early next morning a messenger to say that he would be starting on his country round at eleven o'clock; that it would include a visit to Lantyan; that the day was fine; and that he would be honoured by Monsieur Ledru's company in the dogcart. The Notary accepted with eagerness.

'Cassandra,' said the doctor as they set forth, 'was first broken to the saddle, and her stride – eh, old lady? – is a trifle rugged when she steps out at any speed between shafts. She knows it too, and she knows that I know it; wherefore on a delicate understanding between us she usually sets her own pace and adapts it to my habit of reading a book as we go. She quarters intelligently for any vehicle or indeed any object on the road save a pig. If we should happen to encounter a pig, or a clergyman . . .'

The doctor here plunged into a discourse on the aversions of certain animals for certain others, particularly among the quadrupeds, appositing a number of human superstitions. From these depths he rose to surface with an exclamation on the beauty of the weather and of the drive ahead.

Monsieur Ledru praised the smooth running of the dogcart, and at this point as they were passing a farm gate a sheep-dog flew out raving, recognized the doctor's uplifted whip, and on the instant turned tail.

'I had once,' said the doctor equably, as Cassandra resumed her trot, 'to give that dog a lesson. He is known to us as the Reverend Doctor Vulgar.'

He divagated to the Odyssey, to the best way of encountering an attack by a dog or by dogs. 'Of course if you happen to carry a stout stick, a sweep with it at the forelegs is infallible. It cripples at once. But my father has left it in manuscript, as a recorded experiment, that to sit down abruptly and laugh will defeat the most violent dog, and instantly. For my part I have never had the nerve.'

'*Chemin faisant*, my friend,' said Monsieur Ledru, as they bowled along between tall hedges, 'what do you make of that extraordinary yell produced by our young friend yesterday?'

'Tell me. I did not happen to hear it.'

'It seemed to me, standing on the rampart over the road, that one must have heard it across three fields.'

'Well, I did not. There was a brass band playing, as I remember – our local champions. I seem to remember also that on the first bar a covey of partridges broke shelter and way-to-go across the vale. I don't blame 'em, capable as I am of shutting my ears against brass.'

'That screech,' said Monsieur Ledru reflectively, 'was like nothing on earth. It stopped the runaways almost as if a shot had been fired across them.'

'Has the lad any acquaintance with horses?'

'Not to my knowledge. I should guess from what I know of his birthplace that his acquaintance with the larger quadrupeds did not reach above pack-donkeys.'

They had now by passed the head of a green lane, and almost at once came upon the entrance gates of a neat gravelled drive, with a thatched lodge close inside to the left. A cheerful middle-aged woman, whose ears must have caught and recognized the sound of the dogcart's wheels, came bustling forth at once and opened to them with a bob and curtsy, at the same time calling over her shoulder:

'William Henry! William Henry!'

A rosy-faced urchin aged about eight came running out.

'William Henry, run along and open gates for the doctor.'

'Oh, Mrs Carne, Mrs Carne! Why isn't this lad at school?'

'He's my youngest, doctor, and he's delicate.'

'I know he's your youngest, missus, not being a fool; and by the same grace of God I know he's not delicate.'

'He had a hacking cough early this morning. You should have heard it.'

'Lucky for you, sir, I did not.' The doctor shook his whip at the boy. 'This can hurt worse than schoolmaster's cane – here, run along with you.'

The urchin scampered ahead. The drive for a short way ran midway through a narrowish belt of trees, and then, just as Monsieur Ledru was expecting this plantation to thicken, turned aside to a gate admitting upon a wide open field of noble prospect. Steeply to their left the pasture descended to a rim that hid the waters of a tiny creek. On the farther bank a pastoral landscape dotted with a farmstead or two, swept down from the high ridge on which Castle Dor humped itself to break the skyline. Ahead of them, far below, guessed rather than visible, lay the gorge of the main river, and beyond its hanging woodlands; and away beyond their uplands, fold upon fold of inland Cornwall shone up to the moors, striated with shadows.

The doctor drew rein as the boy opened the next gate.

'You heard me say just now,' he remarked to his companion, 'that I'd reason to know this child to be the woman's youngest? She's the mother of seven, and has punctually paid me for each childbirth on my attending the next. "And the last", she has boasted to her neighbours, "I'll never pay for, please God." Nor has she, by George! William Henry must be well outside the Statute of Limitations. Oh yes, they're queer folk in these parts: but wonderful the more you know 'em.'

'They strike me as very frank and polite: much like, strangely like the folk of my own Brittany.'

'Polite – yes. But frank? Well, yes again, when you get to it: but you have to go deep for that stratum, devilish deep – down to "old, unhappy far-off things", as Wordsworth puts it. We are an ancient race, sir: frank and joyous among ourselves, and especially joyous and childish with our own children, but bred in-and-in and secretive.'

'"Old, unhappy far-off things",' echoes Monsieur Ledru, almost under his breath. But the doctor was not listening.

'I doubt', said he, 'if a general practitioner could pick up a livelihood in these parts unless by following my example, economizing in medicines, and letting the most of his patients die a natural death – hear those rooks, down in the next field?'

'I hear them – a few only.'

'T'wards nightfall you could hear a couple of hundred – and cawing. They're another of my prescriptions, supplied by Nature – to a rich patient too; and I am going to use him presently as a prescription for another case. You are to make his acquaintance. His name is Tregentil, and the name of this place Penquite.'

Doctor Carfax shot a quizzical glance at his companion. 'Well,' he resumed, 'I have saved up my *bonne bouche*. Yonder woods, on the promontory' – he pointed his whip to the left – 'are the veritable woods of Lantyan, or a fringe of them. They stretch over the hill to Lantyan itself in the father vale. By the by we will explore them.'

'We shall not go down to the house,' Doctor Carfax instructed the boy William Henry, 'that is, if Mr Tregentil be busy in his summer-house, as I expect. Shut the gate after us, my son, while we alight, and see to it that Cassandra gets into no mischief.'

The child grinned shamefacedly. The doctor hitched the slack of his reins loosely round the whip socket, motioned Monsieur Ledru to alight, and alighted himself. Cassandra, left at ease, drew to the bank and started to crop at the grass.

The drive here in this third meadow wound in a pretty steep curve down and around a slope protected on the summit of its high right-hand bank by a double belt of trees, towards which the doctor struck obliquely across the short turf, Monsieur Ledru at his heels.

The inner and nearer belt of trees consisted of beech, sturdy and of no very considerable height, planted in a rough semi-circle on the round of the slope: the farthest belt was of elms, taller and crowded with the nests of a rookery.

At the head of the farthest and sharpest bit of their ascent a tall man emerged from the beech boles and stood awaiting them.

'Ah, I reckoned so,' said the doctor; and, drawing close: 'I have brought a visitor – from Brittany. Let me introduce him: his name is Monsieur Ledru.'

Mr Tregentil bowed. They were not close enough as yet to shake hands. 'Let me spare Monsieur Ledru the rest of the climb, and lead him down to the house,' he called.

He was a gaunt man, extremely thin-legged as seen from below, past middle age, of withered yellow complexion and emaciated features.

'No, certainly not,' announced the doctor. 'You will be no sooner indoors than out will come the brown sherry: which for you, who will insist upon keeping us company with it, is the most pestilent drink you can imbibe.' He turned to the Notary. 'I should explain that Mr Tregentil has all but ruined his liver by a thirty year's residence in India. But I am patching it up, please the Lord!' Then, to Mr Tregentil: 'Any report of the rooks this morning?'

'Very little. They went off at seven-fifteen this morning, for Lantyan or beyond. I wrote my notes out in fair copy, and was just completing my daily map when I heard your wheels.'

'Take us up to the summer-house. I want a look at the papers.'

'You disturbed me, doctor, as I was tidying them up.'

'Never mind that. You are looking a healthier man already, and I have a commission for you that will make you a healthier man yet.'

Mr Tregentil stared suspiciously. 'If you only knew how I suffer at night—' he protested.

'I know perfectly well. And I'm engaged to cure you, but *progressively*, you understand. Take us to the summer-house and show me today's map and jottings.'

Mr Tregentil led them between the beech boles to a small thatched summer-house, a clearing which gave a clearer prospect of the rookery. It had, to Monsieur Ledru's eye, been placed there with that purpose since other prospect it had none: and it contained for furniture a bench, a rustic chair and a rude oak table, on which, very neatly arranged, lay a telescope, a pair of binoculars, writing materials, a pile of small notebooks, a box of cheroots and some sheets of manuscript held down by a bronze paper-weight. Mr Tregentil invited the Notary to a seat on the bench, with an apology for its lack of cushions, while the doctor, without leave asked, dropped into the chair, affixed his spectacles, took up the papers and with a 'H'm!' began to peruse them, at first silently. At the second page, however, he turned back and started to read aloud.

'Day fine and warm almost as midsummer. Rooks away early. Many returned from their breakfasts as early as six a.m. From six to seven a.m. and later they were exceedingly noisy and sportive. The jackdaws flying about in flocks chattered even louder than the rooks.

'The autumn note of the birds – the change perceptible to my ear as beginning (*v.* note *supra*) on 16th or 17th August – is now beyond mistake. It indicates the recurrence to their winter habits after the business of rearing their young . . .'

Doctor Carfax paused and pushed up his spectacles. 'You are learning, Tregentil,' he commented. 'But you should not say "it indicates". Very likely it does; and your observation is sound so far as it goes; but it merely correlates two facts. When you say boldly that one is cause and t'other effect you go beyond your strict knowledge and talk like a lawyer.' He sorted the papers back carefully, and laid them under the bronze weight. Then he leisurely filled and lit his pipe. 'Now just you listen to me, Tregentil,' he said slowly between the puffs. 'You have immensely improved as an observer during the past eighteen months; and what is more, though you'll not admit it at once, you are practically a hale man. Go on keeping your diary; but from today I prescribe walking exercise – or we'll say from next Monday. Every day from next Monday you are to walk to Lantyan and back.'

'What, doctor!' protested Mr Tregentil. 'Why, that would be about four miles, around the head of the creek.'

'And I'm not advising you to shorten the distance by swimming. A hale man you are, I say, save for your nerves and your liver, the seat of 'em. You are fit enough now to work it back to normal by gentle exercise: and now you must complete the cure by walking over to Lantyan daily.'

'I couldn't possibly—'

'You can, and you shall. You will take the first volume of *Robinson Crusoe* under your arm, and Mrs Bosanko will give you a drink of milk when you arrive.'

'But why *Robinson Crusoe*?'

'Because I have a patient there, a Breton lad, to teach English to whom will be a part of your final cure. He knows something of the sea and it occurs to me that to a man of your intelligence *Robinson Crusoe* is a textbook made to your hand. As soon as you have taught him to speak English and perhaps write a little, you will have a lad competent to make notes for you; and thus you may gather what the rooks are doing when they absent themselves daily for the woods of Lantyan.'

'I doubt if I shall be equal to it, doctor.'

Doctor Carfax smoothed his nose between forefinger and thumb. 'The ways of science,' said he gravely, 'are seldom easy. At the beginning a small anti-phlogistic in the shape of brandy and soda. On no account rum. A pint of light wine – Graves for choice – on your return, and a well-earned nap till teatime.'

'If it will oblige you, doctor—'

'Tut!'

He and Monsieur Ledru, refusing a second proffer of hospitality, sought back to the dogcart. William Henry opened the gates for them along the return journey, and at the lodge accepted shamefacedly a penny and a promise of the bad end little boys came to who minched from school.

9

Lantyan

A few yards beyond the lodge Doctor Carfax swung the
dogcart off the high road into a lane that at first sight
appeared to run back and almost parallel with the drive
from which they had just emerged. For a little way it skirted
the entrance plantation, but presently swerved and dived, making
down and across the vale on a perilous rutted slope. Cassandra,
sure-footed though she was, slithered twice or thrice in the
descent, and at each jolt or slither Monsieur Ledru clutched at
the cart's rail. Between shock and shock he was aware of the
ridge on his left hand lifting itself higher and higher, and ever
on the mountain in skyline, commanding it, the thorn-set crown
of Castle Dor.

At the foot of the declivity they came to a rushing brook
which swept noisily across the lane, issuing from a thicket of
elders, and plunging down to the right through ferns and under
a side-bridge of two granite blocks, iron-clamped, set for pedes-
trians. Cassandra waded half way through the water and lowered
her head to drink: a right which Doctor Carfax allowed her,
as by custom. 'This stream, sir,' he observed while the mare
drank, 'has no name on the maps: but the old people hereabouts know it as Deraine Lake. It rises at the foot of the camp,
Castle Dor, and has but a short run before plunging to the
creek, Woodget Pyll, below on our right, where of course it

joins the river. A queer name Deraine Lake – and no known history or etymology for it. I record to you only that the very old man who first acquainted me with it affirmed that there had once upon a time been a real lake here. On the far side of those elders – a lake with swans – and that a king had made it. Hey? Deraine Lake – *lac de reine*? What's the use of guessing? But the same old fellow told me something even more curious. Come up, Cassandra. You've had more than a bellyful!'

Beyond the stream the precarious roadway climbed, fading now almost to a grass track that followed the windings of the shore, though the shore was now hidden by woodland. To the left, thick hazel overhung them. 'A good year for nuts,' said Doctor Carfax, indicating some clusters with his whip. 'There's a saying in these parts that a good year for nuts is a good year for bastards. I have never used my opportunity to trace the connection.' Meanwhile Doctor Carfax stuck his whip into its socket, motioned Monsieur Ledru to alight and, hitching up the reins, allowed Cassandra to grass at will and do as she would with the cart. He led the way to the right, to a gate that opened upon a rounded meadow and a view that fairly took Monsieur Ledru's breath away.

Below him lay the placid river, and across it and glassed in it on the brim of the farther shore, a grey church set among elms overlooking a tiny quay. The woodland above and to left and right shone over the water exquisitely mirrored. To the right even the breasts of many herons were mirrored with the foliage into which they had retreated, driven by the early flood-tides from their fishing on the flats and in the low-water channels.

But the meadow in which Monsieur Ledru found himself with his guide on this hither side of the flood took the imagination at least equally. Between the rounded curves of the greenwood where this narrowed up to a waist, it rolled itself in two ample symmetrical curves of bright grass, globing with a deep dip between. The dip went down, down, to a thicket; in which, faintly, a well could be heard gushing.

'About this meadow,' said Doctor Carfax with a wave of the hand. 'Its name is – and I know no reason for it – Thunder Park. But the same old fellow who told me about Deraine Lake told me also that a king in old times – he could not say whether the same king or no – had shaped this lovely field by art to resemble the breasts of his bride. That is all he could tell me, and that is all I can tell you.'

'Great monarchs have had such fancies,' Monsieur Ledru murmured. 'Was it—'

'Yes, Montaigne quotes it. I know the reference too.'

'I know not what it is,' the Notary confessed, 'but ever since we crossed that brook which you called Deraine Lake a very strange heaviness has settled on me.'

'Meaning by that, a depression of spirits?'

'No.' Monsieur Ledru mused, as though he had but half heard. Then with a start: 'Oh, but most certainly not. No, it is rather a heaviness upon the mind – a weight as of lead upon brain and thoughts, while my legs are like paper under me.' Lifting his hat he passed a thin hand over his forehead. 'It is such as when one cannot recall a name and goes under a burden until memory releases it.'

'Let us go back to Cassandra,' said Doctor Carfax. 'It is downhill all the way now to Lantyan.'

Now while they were talking, a young woman had been riding up the farm lane returning to Troy: and as they stood preparing to re-climb the dogcart she came along, the sun through the hazels dappling her and her tall chestnut horse. She reined up, smiling happily, albeit with a guarded compression of her beautiful mouth.

'Good morning, Mrs Lewarne!' Doctor Carfax, reins gathered, withdrew his foot from the step of the dogcart and lifted his hat. Monsieur Ledru had already climbed up and seated himself.

'Good morning, doctor: and good morning again to you, sir.'

'You return, of course, from visiting our patient?'

'From visiting Lantyan, to inquire for him,' Linnet corrected. 'I did not see him – that is, to speak to him. He was in some pain early in the night; but fell asleep towards two in the morning, and is asleep yet.'

'Good.'

'Mrs Bosanko is nursing him like an angel – as anyone can see. I felt it only right to ride over early.'

'Right. But I must say that you had some nerve to ride over on Merlin after his behaviour of yesterday. He is not properly a saddle-horse either.'

'He is not: and to tell the truth, doctor, I had some trouble with him on the way over. But when a horse picks up a trick of bolting, the sooner you start teaching him out of it the better. I learned that when I was ever so young.'

'I wonder your husband allowed it though.'

'My husband doesn't even know! Why *should* he?'

She laughed, lifted her whip and rode on.

The farmstead of Lantyan lay under Lantyan woods, secluded at the base of converging hills. A lately constructed line of railway on an embankment crossed the view from its side-windows, and trains rattled past within fairly close earshot, to plunge into a tunnel.

The farmhouse, itself of fair age, stood a furlong or two from the site of the old manor and its surviving kennels, where the quality kept their hounds. And this manor house had been built centuries later than the dead-and-gone palace for vestiges of which Monsieur Ledru had travelled to seek.

'But what a site, my friend!' he exclaimed, as the cart swayed slowly downhill, Cassandra skidding continuously slantwise in places, like the wise mare she was. 'What a site for those times! The palace sequestered somewhere hereabouts: the camp on Castle Dor to watch over sea and river ford and send down timely notice of a foray: and withal, thus sheltered, a demesne royal and most delectable!'

It amused Doctor Carfax to introduce his friend to their hostess, Mrs Bosanko, and to watch him from the first moment as he gracefully adjusted his hearing to someone who did not in the least resemble an ordinary Breton farm-wife. Mrs Bosanko in fact was a cultivated woman, and one of those rare ones, though not so very rare in this country, who, marrying 'on the land', accept its traditions faithfully, throw down roots in remote houses and yet bring with their presence a subtle and compelling refinement. Her garden blazed with late autumn flowers, trimly ranked. Her porch and doorstep were spotless, admitting to a wide low-bowered hall, ancient, with a small bright fire in the basket grate and a bowl of home-grown chrysanthemums on the mid-table. To the left by the fireplace a flight of stairs, rose-carpeted, led up to an old audit chamber, transformed into a drawing-room.

Doctor Carfax smiled to himself as he left Monsieur Ledru to make what he best could of this and went up the broad polished staircase to his patient's bedroom.

He found Amyot in bed and slumbrous, as Mrs Lewarne had reported; and awakened him very gently.

'You'll need to move but a very little. I just want to make sure that my bandages are firm, and dress a cut or two. Ah, here is water – hot, by George! – and a sponge, and lint set beside me. She must have heard Cassandra sprawling down the hill.'

The lad muttered something in Breton.

'*Ne m'eveillez donc pour l'amour de Dieu! . . .*' The words rambled off. '*Ah non, patron! Je viens de Paradis . . .*'

Again the voice trailed off and the boy nestled to his pillow drowsily.

'Now I wonder,' mused Doctor Carfax to himself as he unrolled the lint, 'if that young woman really contented herself with looking in at the door.'

Down in the farm-hall he found Mrs Bosanko by the mid-table spreading out a map under Monsieur Ledru's nose.

'It came with the property,' she was explaining, 'when my

husband bought it. He is away today, at the cattle market. He could explain better than I, because he has known all these old fields from a boy. Will you study the map, gentlemen, while I lay the table? For you must certainly give me that pleasure! And you must stay, doctor, please, to have a look at the children when they come home from school.'

Of her hospitable kindness to the strange lad upstairs she made no mention. It would be time enough to talk about him and his plight in private conference at the door. Moreover she had guessed from the doctor's face that there was no ground for anxiety.

She was moving away, when Doctor Carfax, leaning across the shoulder of Monsieur Ledru, bent and, poring over the map, suddenly dashed a forefinger down upon it:

'My God, man – look at that!'

'Hein?'

'Cannot you see? A field in the very place entered as "Mark's Gate" – "Mark's Gate"! King Mark's Gate! Oh! it's a clincher! And Woodgate would be t'other approach from the river, up through the plantation – hey? And look here!' He jabbed a thumb upon another purcelled field on the large map. '"Pilfer Door" – and, if we're right, just where a postern door would be. *Plus ça change* – yes, "Pilfer Door" leading to an angle of "Prior's Meadow"! Oh, this is glorious!'

'You go too fast, my friend,' protested Monsieur Ledru, but his bent shoulders trembled. 'But, madame, what is this brown oblong marked just in the bed of the river?'

'That means a sort of island, sir. I never heard that it has a name. It lies there, a short way off the viaduct—'

'A sort of eyot, as we call it,' supplemented Doctor Carfax.

'An island – a sort of eyot!' Monsieur Ledru sprang upright. There was no trace of heaviness in him now. 'We have it, doctor!' he cried, hurrying Doctor Carfax to the door. '*Mon Dieu!* we have it! lead me – show it!'

'But your pasties, sirs, are just crisp in the oven, and the children will be home in a few minues,' protested Mrs Bosanko.

'Ah! but pardon me, madame! This island has been waiting a thousand years longer than your excellent pasties!'

Doctor Carfax, laughing, led his companion out of the house, and so downhill towards the viaduct and beyond.

It was an island indeed, though cut off from the shore by a narrow channel across which one could toss a stone: a long, narrow eyot of two furlongs or less with undercut banks of mud, and for vegetation a mat of salt meadow-grass, grey from frequent flooding by the high spring-tides. A heron, surprised in his fishery, arose with a cry from the muddy channel, balanced himself in the air and flapped clumsily away to the farther woodland.

'A veritable island!' repeated Monsieur Ledru slowly, sinking voice to a kind of inward ecstasy. Then aloud: '*Voyons*, let us reconstruct! Those old romancers exaggerated by custom, but they built on fact.'

Hitherto and throughout the morning he had played a mild second fiddle to Doctor Carfax's talk. But now his voice quavered no longer, his aged treble deepened to strong baritone, and as it deepened he seemed to grow a full two inches in stature.

'*Voyons!*' he commanded. 'You know the story – how Morholt came to King Mark's court here to collect tribute for the King of Ireland; and how, while Mark faltered, the young Tristan stood up and defied the Irish messenger, challenging him to single combat to decide the issue: how the challenge was accepted and how an island was chosen for the encounter; and how the two knights pushed across in separate boats for it. Mark and his court gathered on the shore as spectators. Where – granted his palace to have stood in the high woods yonder – where, I ask you, can you conceive a scene to fit more exquisitely with the tale than this island with that slope there overlooking it?'

'You make out a case for it to be sure,' answered the doctor, 'but to my way of thinking the island was more likely one of the sandbanks, uncovered at low water, that lie in the main river yonder; but no matter. Béroul, if you remember, never mentions the fight, but Gottfried von Strassburg, rewriting the poet Thomas, gives us the incident in detail. Oh yes, it could all have happened on the sandbanks between St Sampson's and the opposite shore, or on the mudflat by St Winnow, or on this eyot here, if you prefer it. Come, you have had enough excitement for one morning. Let us return to the farm house and see what good Mrs Bosanko can produce for us. I recollect she spoke of pasties.'

Monsieur Ledru stared at the doctor in reproof. 'We have between us,' he said solemnly, 'made a discovery of historical importance, yet you preoccupy yourself with the claims of the inner man.'

'If I do so,' replied Doctor Carfax, 'you must blame my professional eye. You stumbled twice as we descended the hill to the viaduct, and I suspect that like all Frenchmen you breakfasted on coffee.'

He turned his back firmly upon the island, the Notary following with some reluctance; and as the two men retraced their steps towards Lantyan, the Notary endeavoured to reconstruct a scene of centuries past, when the narrow rivulet beside them had been a flowing stream, a tributary to the main river beyond, and the ancient palace of Lancien, sited below the present farmhouse and by the water's edge, would have had – even as Béroul described it – a stream running past the queen's chamber window. The Queen Iseult – here, beneath his eyes, at the base of the wooded hill, where the great railway viaduct stood today, Iseult had waited in the moonlight, while the shadow of her lover Tristan, his finger to his lips warned her to be silent, for the king her husband was hiding near at hand.

'They trysted in an orchard,' murmured Monsieur Ledru, 'and lo and behold, here is an orchard, even to this day but the olive tree, beneath which the dwarf Melot and the king lay concealed – the olive tree is absent.'

His eye lingered on the neglected apple trees, misshapen by

72

time, hoary with age, their lichened branches growing athwart the stream, while his companion, whose quick eye had caught the *sotto voce* monologue, followed the glance, and smiled.

'No, your eyes have not deceived you,' said the doctor, 'apples there are, but not within our immediate reach, nor ripe enough yet for plucking. I've tasted them myself before now. Cassandra appreciated them, but I find them sour. Bosanko, who has a fine orchard close to the farm, and knows more about apples than anyone living, cannot pronounce upon the species. He declares them to be a hybrid. Yes, I know what you are thinking, and agree with you. These trees may be eighty years old, certainly not a thousand. But men are conservative hereabouts. We tend to plant and till where our forefathers did before us.' He stepped down onto the grass verge beneath the viaduct, and, reaching out across the narrow stream, broke off a twig from an over-hanging branch and cast it in the water. Slowly the twig revolved, bobbing towards the current, then, gathering momentum, drifted off downstream and out of sight.

'Thus the twig passed the women's quarters,' said the doctor, 'with the initials T and I carved upon it. And Queen Iseult and her servant Brangwyn knew that the coast was clear.'

'Brangwyn, her accomplice and kinswoman,' capped the Notary, 'through whose neglect the love potion, intended orig-inally for King Mark and his bride, was swallowed instead by the bride and Tristan.'

'H'm,' the doctor grunted. 'If I muddled my prescriptions in the same fashion' – he flicked his wet shoe with a fine cambric handkerchief – 'the attendance in my surgery would be doubled. Or perhaps not,' he added in afterthought. 'The experiment might be worth trying. A dose of the baby's gripe-water for Tim Udy should prove efficacious, who can say? With Tim's ale in the baby's bottle – but see, here come the young Bosankos to welcome us. They have very good manners; the girl is not yet of an age to be self-conscious about her pretty face, and the boy is still young enough to believe in fairies and to appreciate cough lozenges.'

He waved a hand to the two children racing down the hill towards them, and his companion sighed. The reconstruction of the ancient palace of Lantyan must be exchanged for childish prattle.

The childish prattle, aforesaid, had the Notary but known it, ran as follows.

'Wonder who he is?'

'Who?'

'Why that old sport with the doctor.'

'I wonder where you pick up those vulgar words. "Old sport", indeed. I'll trouble you not to go on being low. Especially at this moment when nobody knows what's happening at home to that young man in the spare bedroom. Mother told me he was a young man – and I've got an idea.'

'Tell me.'

'If you ask *me*,' said Mary, 'I think they're hushing it up, Father and Mother; and that young man is going to die. If you ask *me*, that old gentleman had come with the doctor as a second opinion.'

'Think there'll be a funeral?' Johnny speculated. 'I hope they won't make it Saturday – whole holiday.'

'Don't get excited. It's Thursday now, and Mother wouldn't allow it because I've nothing to wear. Besides, there has to be an operation first.'

'Sure?'

'There usually is. And then the patient is going on well, and there's a relapse. That ought to carry us on to Tuesday at earliest.'

'Tell you what,' Johnny suggested, aglow, 'we might practise it tonight upon Araminta, with my new knife.'

'Practise what?'

'The operation. She's old, and you can't lift her without the sawdust trickling. We could pretent to operate for that: and you've kissed all the colours off her years ago. She'd look a lovely patient.'

'I don't like the notion at all.'

'And afterwards we could practise a funeral,' went on the tempter.

'I've outgrown dolls, to be sure,' hesitated Mary, her eyes glistening under the larches. 'I'll have to consider it. What no boy understands is that there's such a thing as sentiment.'

So the babes ran down the hill.

Monsieur Ledru sought his bed that night soon after dinner. A lingering drift of daylight floated in through the window of his room: but a lighted candle stood on the table at his bedside and, propped high on pillows, the old Notary, without the aid of spectacles, was studying a map. The candlelight flickered on the foot bedposts and was lost in a dark angle of the room beyond. It faintly illuminated the pomegranates scrolled on the beam above him.

A light tap on the door startled him out of his musings. After a moment or two it was repeated somewhat more sharply.

'Entrez!'

The door handle turned and the maid, Deborah, slid into the room bearing a small tray which she set down on a table at the bed's foot.

'The mistress sends her compliments, sir. She took note that you were weary when you came back this afternoon, and begs your acceptance of a cordial.'

'She served me an admirable wine at dinner,' answered Monsieur Ledru. 'Nevertheless I am a foreigner, and if this be a custom of the country—'

'You must not undervalue it, please, as a usual thing. Our house has good wines to be sure, and some very old spirits, they tell me. But this is something quite special – the secret of it kept in the mistress's family. I have never seen the recipe, for she has it locked in her jewel box. And I have never even sipped the cordial. No maid may except on her bridal night,' added Deborah in an easy matter-of-fact tone. 'May I borrow your candle, sir? For it has to be taken with hot water – as hot as you can bear it. I have a small saucepan here, and a spirit lamp and matches. But I want more light or I may over-fill the glass.'

Taking permission for granted, she slipped to the side-table and carried Monsieur Ledru's candle back to the other at the bed's end. She stepped noiselessly – it seemed in list-shod slippers. Monsieur Ledru stuck an elbow into his pillow and lifted himself to watch. She made an uncanny figure there as she struck a match and held the saucepan over the bluish flame of the spirit lamp – her dark-browed, pallid face bluish also. Her gown or dressing-robe was all but indistinguishable from the shadow into which that end of the room deepened as the walls tapered away.

'It will not take long,' she assured him, watching the flames not looking up. 'The saucepan is of silver and soon heated. That also goes with the drink and is necessary to it – or so the mistress says.'

'What was her maiden name?'

'She was a Constantine, and they tell that the Constantines come from the East, where they were royalty once upon a time.'

'A Constantine?'

'Yes, but you need not fear it. The most of it is neat brandy, she says – I saw her offer a glass of it on her wedding night to Mr Lewarne, but he would have none. He said he had drunk enough champagne already – here you are sir; and it's an honour the mistress would do you, believe me.'

She returned to the bedside noiselessly, the candle in her one hand and a long-stemmed steaming glass in the other.

'I thank you, mademoiselle – a-ah!' said Monsieur Ledru, sipping and recalling Doctor Carfax's punch. 'But you brew the most delectable drinks in this duchy. Put your lips to it, my dear – if your lips only.'

'It is forbidden,' said Deborah, standing over him as he drank.

'But it is a marvel!' said he as he handed her the empty glass. 'It is an *eau-de-vie* indeed. And I was tired, I confess to you. What is your name, my daughter?'

'Deborah, sir.' She was collecting the contents of her tray with a faint tinkle.

'But your surname?'

'Brangwyn'.

'Say it again.'

'Brangwyn – you are half asleep already. Shall I spell it for you? B-R-A-N-G-W-Y-N.'

She was gone, as softly as she had come. Monsieur Ledru lying back on his pillow continued for some time to stare at the oaken beam. The cup, though not at all fiery, was certainly very potent. It embalmed him rather, and yet he was young and the dead carved rafter was young, throwing out buds, tendrils, vivid green shoots. He retained just enough of consciousness to blow out his candle before sinking to a sleep in which the window curtains, stirred by the faint night wind, waved and whispered and turned to the boughs of an infinitely deep forest.

10

The potion without the apple pips

Just a week later Doctor Carfax dined and slept at the Rose and Anchor as Monsieur Ledru's guest. They had paid two more visits to Lantyan, where the patient was making good progress: but the Notary had snatched a flying visit to Plymouth, whence he returned with a parcel of light weight but considerable bulk.

'It is a parting gift,' he explained to the doctor, 'and I beg you to hand it to him tomorrow, with my regards. It is in fact a moderately good violin – with some elementary instructions and exercises; also some spare twists of gut. The instrument and the extra string to it will no doubt puzzle him at first: but the effort to get some mastery of it may while away his convalescence.'

'I don't see them whiling away Mrs Bosanko's spare hours; or why you should reward her with this probable torture,' replied the doctor. 'However, I understand that, having to depart tomorrow, you leave me to hand on this *damnosa hereditas?*'

Monsieur Ledru smiled. 'From what I know of you, my friend, you will execute this little commission gladly – and one other.'

'H'm – I think I can guess. You wish me to search at my leisure the manor rolls, tithe maps and what not hereabouts and report to you if I can hitch any name back (through *Domesday*

79

or not) to Béroul's story or to Gottfried von Strassburg's or to any other *conte* or *lai* of Tristan, Eh?'

'May I rely on that service of friendship?'

'And you might add, on my curiosity, which I confess you have excited. Yes, you may. But I warn you of two things; the first that I am busy but desultory, painstaking but indolent; a slave (I trust always) to my poor patients, but for the rest – slave or master – I care not to determine which – of my own whims.'

'At all events I can count upon you?' asked the Notary.

'You can,' returned the doctor, shooting a quizzical glance at his companion, 'unless, like Béroul, like Gottfried von Strassburg and the rest, you and I find ourselves cut short in the quest of the original Tristan. It is a curious coincidence that no poet, or shall we call him investigator, has ever lived to conclude this particular story. His work has always been finished by another.'

Monsieur Ledru smiled. 'As to that,' he observed, 'I am content to leave my part of the investigation in your capable hands. And remember, the only poet who did complete his poem, and that one lost, was Chrétien de Troyes – so possibly Carfax of Troy—' He paused, and, passing the decanter, added: 'Troyes and Troy. You must admit there is some similarity.'

The doctor was not to be won so easily. 'I will have nothing to do with you philologers and your *peut-êtres*,' he said firmly. 'Hand me, if you will, that book on Celtic names which has so intrigued you.'

They had reached their dessert; and Doctor Carfax, after helping himself to a third glass of port, cleared a space before him for the thin volume which Monsieur Ledru passed over.

'I suppose,' pursued Doctor Carfax, sipping delicately in the intervals of turning the pages, 'that our host Lewarne bought the cellars of the Rose and Anchor, stock and barrel. It is ungrateful, perhaps, but it irritates me that he cannot tell the vintage, and that I am not connoisseur enough to date it by taste. One likes to know what one is drinking, as the saying is

– let me see – yes, here is the reference. It's on the name *Tristan*, supposedly carved upon a monument near here, not a mile from Troy. "*La forme* Drustagnos *n'est pas une simple reconstitution*: *elle existe dans une inscription de Cornwall*: DRUSTAGNI *hic jacet* Cunomori filius"'.

'Why, man, I pass that Long Stone (as we call it) at the Four Turnings, almost every day of my life: have examined it many times with the aid of a ladder – for it has been planted upright since its removal from its original site, a rood or two distant, and was a funeral slab carved to lie horizontally – in which position it was found. You have seen it. I helped your fingers to trace the *Cunomori* or *Cunowori filius*. The *jacet* can be deciphered by aid of faith. It is anyhow clearly a funeral slab; for on the nether side – much less weathered, of course, because bedded in earth originally – is the *Thanatos Tau*, which even a casual passer-by cannot miss. But as for your *DRU*, why, good Lord – Le Dru! it might just as easily have been an inscription over *you*.'

'Yes . . . I wonder,' the Notary murmured.

Doctor Carfax ran on unheeding. He could ride several of his many hobbies at once, jumping from one back to another:

'So I won't have any truck with your Celtic derivations – your Destanes and Drustagnis and the rest. Our hero of a hundred legends may have lain beneath that tombstone once – I rather doubt it, I say that those lays of Tristan, written in French if derived from Cornwall, called Tristan by his name for the simple reason they give – that his mother, overtaken by birth pangs as she followed an adored husband, and dying, named the child so – *partus tristis* – and that's all. All your philological guesses, sir, are pure rubbish, but Béroul's topography is exact. He has King Mark appeal to St Evol, St Stephen and St Tresmer of Cahares almost in one breath, parishes I can show you any time. *Par St Estienne le martyre*: *par St Tresmer de Cahares* – and Carhayes the other side of Dodman, across the bay from Troy.

'Furthermore, when you get to names like *Lantyan*, for

instance, to Mark's Gate, to St Sampson's hard by where Iseult went to hear Mass, to Malpas on the Fal, or *le Mal Pas*, where she was helped ashore by Tristan disguised as a leper, and tumbled with him on landing, so that she could swear her audacious oath that no one save this leper had ever — save Mark her husband — why, then we begin to multiply coincidences which—'

The door opened and Mistress Lewarne entered followed by Deborah with a tray holding, beside the apparatus of coffee, two tall-stemmed glasses, a spirit lamp and a silver saucepan.

Monsieur Ledru and Doctor Carfax rose to their feet. Over the candleshades they beheld her, tall in a gown of pale blue, straightly cut from the shoulders down, naked arms exposed through low-falling sleeves with a glint of gold on their edges. Later that night it occurred to Doctor Carfax to wonder that the child he had ushered into the world some nineteen years ago, and now wife to the innkeeper, Mark Lewarne, should so attire herself: and together with his wonder, or swift upon it, occurred the thought that she was solitary, childless, unlikely to have children; with a second and meditative reflection on the eternal claim of women upon lineage and forfeited rank. But for the moment the two men stood, astonished at the beauty of this apparition. The blue flame of the spirit lamp made bluer her pale blue dress as she stepped forward and with a motion to Deborah, who deposited the tray at Monsieur Ledru's elbow and instantly withdrew into the shadow, bowed to her guests.

'You leave us tomorrow, monsieur: and I have brought you a stirrup cup, if you will pardon the fancy and my boldness.'

'If, madame, it is such a potion as you sent me the other night—'

'You were over-tired, and I knew it would do you good.'

'It was a draught, as the poet says, to renew old Aeson. I assure you, madame, it sent me off to sleep, and to such dreams that I awoke feeling twenty years younger.'

'No more than that?' Linnet's eyebrows arched themselves a

little maliciously as she lifted the saucepan, about to heat it over the blue flame.

'My word, Linnet,' exclaimed Doctor Carfax, 'what a piece of silver you have there! Can you tell us anything of its age?'

'Nothing, doctor; except that it has belonged to our family for generations – oh, for an unknown length of time. It is handed to the heir on his marriage day, with a recipe – Deborah, you may leave us.'

As the door closed behind her woman Linnet went on hardily: 'I think, doctor, it has something to do with marriage. For two recipes go with it, and at the end of the second is signed and written *Prosper Constantine. Prosper the race.* "Prosper" is a Christian name in our family, sir. It comes up again and again in an old Bible that my father keeps. And the queer thing is – or it would be queer if there weren't a story about it – that the two recipes are the same, word for word, except that in the second three apple-pips must be crushed and heated; and this is for a bridal cup only, or so it is headed.'

'You have these prescriptions?'

'Yes, for as you know I am the last of us, and a daughter. But I keep them locked away. All the same, I have them by heart, and the first – I brewed it once for my father when he had ridden home drenched and shivering from Liskeard market. I brewed it the other night for Monsieur Ledru—'

'And I can testify to its virtue, madame. I slept, and awoke invigorated.'

'But the story, Linnet!'

'It is an old, and I dare say a very silly, one, doctor. My father told it to me once. He said that when Adam grew old with tilling the wilderness, and felt his end near, he called his son Seth to him and said: "I am dying but cannot rest in the grave you shall dig for me unless you travel to the gate of the garden which is called Paradise and bring me an apple from the Tree of Knowledge, which grows in the very centre of the garden. And if you find me dead when you come home, then cut the apple in two and lay three pips under my tongue as you bury me." So Seth went to the garden of Paradise, chose an apple and travelled home: but Adam was dead. Seth cut the apple in two and found it had three pips, and these he put under his father's tongue and buried him. Then, my father said, from these pips grew three different trees. The first was an oak and bore oak-apples and had galls on it: and this one Noah cut down for the keelson of his Ark. Then after lying for hundreds of years it was fetched out and made into the Cross on which Our Lord was crucified—'

'*The beam which the builders rejected*—' murmured Doctor Carfax.

'The second tree,' continued Linnet, 'was a holly: and under this in a thicket Abraham found the ram when he was going to sacrifice his son. But its berries were pale then, and only turned red hundreds of years after, when plaited into a crown of thorns. But the third tree was an apple – the same sort as Eve's. This found its way to King Solomon's garden: and my father said that when the Shunammite woman ran away from the king with her lover, who was a shepherd, she took a basket of fruit with her, in her bosom, and a slip of this tree. Solomon chased the lovers through the hills and down to the coast; but there they escaped on board ship, and were landed out of his reach at the foot of a mountain – Ida, I think, was its name. I forget just how the tale goes hereabouts: I was very young when I heard it. But father will remember and tell it to you, doctor, any day you are passing.'

'I think,' said the Doctor, with a smile across at Monsieur Ledru, 'that I can continue the story without consulting your father. Years after these lovers were dead and gone, there came along another young shepherd who plucked an apple from the tree the Shunammite had planted: an apple so perfectly golden that three goddesses claimed it for a beauty prize. Their names were Royalty, Wisdom and Love; and the silly lad gave it to Love.'

'Yes, I remember now – though the names were different. Is it an old story then?'

'A very old story, my dear. As old as that Mount Ida itself.'

Linnet poured out the steaming potion and handed a glassful each to her guests.

'Well, the tale ends that one of my mother's family – you know, doctor, that we claim to have been great folk once on a time – came here to Cornwall and brought this apple with him. They call it still the Constantine Pippin or Gillyflower, and it fruits only on the tip of the spray. My mother planted a slip at Castle Dor the day after her wedding.'

'Linnet!' interrupted a querulous voice calling from below stairs.

Mrs Lewarne stepped to the door and opened it on an invisible Deborah, who apparently had been standing sentry outside.

'Deborah!' She blew out the spirit lamp and carried it, with saucepan and tray to the door. 'Take these downstairs, and tell your master that I am coming as soon as I have finished waiting on these gentlemen. Is the cordial to your liking, sirs?'

'Linnet!' – again.

'It is marvellous,' pronounced Doctor Carfax after a sip or two, cautious only for fear of scalding his mouth. 'But I detect no trace at all of apple-pip in it,' he added, holding his glass up by its stem so that the candlelight shone through the orange-ruby liquid.

She faced him and the steam above the glass floated thinly up between him and her challenging eyes. In the film of it their blue seemed to darken into violet, even to the red-violet of the lost imperial murex.

'Belike they would not have been good for either of you,' answered Linnet with a short laugh.

She was gone.

Doctor Carfax murmured to himself, but more than half aloud:

> That look was Heaven or Hell,
> As you shall please to take it—
> Enormity of love or lust so fell,
> The Devil could not slake it—

'What is that you are chanting to yourself, my friend?' asked the Notary.

'Nothing – or a tag of verse by an old poet who once honoured me with some poetic confidences. That was a queer story of the witch over this delicious brew. Talking of poets,' said Doctor Carfax with a sudden shine in his eyes, casting off their veil of thought for naked mirth, 'I have sought everywhere and without success to trace the author of the following – hark ye:

> 'King David and King Solomon
> Led very merry lives:
> They had very many concubines,
> And very many wives.
>
> But when old age crept over 'em
> They both of 'em had qualms—
> So Solomon wrote the Proverbs,
> And David wrote the Psalms!'

As Monsieur Ledru, that night, rolled himself up in the bedclothes with an old man's foreboding of a long journey to be taken on the morrow and almost a prayer for a sound night's sleep as a preparation for it, again a light tap sounded on the door, and again, as once before, Deborah entered bearing lamp and tray. 'The mistress's compliments, sir. She wishes you to drink this last little wineglassful for a stirrup cup.'

The fire still burned up cheerfully, throwing flickers of light all about the room, deepening the shadow of the old bed-curtains. It pencilled an occasional ray of light along the curved oaken rafter at the bed's foot.

Monsieur Ledru drained the glass, blew out his candle, lay back on his pillow. Still the firelight flickered around the oak of the room. As before, the wood started to shoot out a green arm across the ceiling. He was passing under them, a lover. He was hurrying to meet his first love. The flicker of the fire upon dead panels turned to a chequer of sunlight falling down through the boughs. Then, one small spasm of the heart took him, and he died – quite peacefully, his aged face composed slowly from the sharpness of death to a smile.

Doctor Carfax also had a wonderful dream that night. It began with a remembered waft of sweet brier, and while in some unremembered byway he halted to inhale it, a girl in a broad sunshady hat came riding up out of the past. She smiled and alighted: their lips touched: they were in one another's arms – when a knock awakened him and Mark Lewarne broke in with his news.

BOOK TWO

Full well I know many there be
Who have the tale of Tristan read.

11

The hay cart

On a warm evening in the following June – dusk so faintly gathering that a sickle moon, westering over Castle Dor, travelled as a ghost scarcely visible in the blue sky toward her setting in Ocean – Farmer Bosanko's hay harvesters sat in a wide semicircle under the hedge of the field (Mark's Gate), drinking tea which Mrs Bosanko dispensed among them along with plates of saffron cake and splitters piled with jam upon clotted cream. The hay crop had been well and truly saved; all but its last load stacked in the mowhay below. This last load remained to be carried home ceremoniously – the farmer believing in all old rites. After the coming corn harvest there would be supper in the barn with cider and songs to celebrate it. But the hay harvest concluded with a tea drink under the hedge. Doctor Carfax and Mr Tregentil, by invitation, completed the party.

Before the tea-urns came up some of the harvesters had been essaying a dance to the strains of Amyot's fiddle. But they had worked hard all day, and were parched; and were passing country jests and rude compliments now, while eating and drinking voraciously. They wiped their foreheads from time to time while Mrs Bosanko plied them with cake and tea – the men brushing the sweat off with a sweep of the naked forearm, the women more delicately pushing up handkerchiefs under the pent of their sun-bonnets.

The wagon laden with the 'last load home', piled and tedded with special care, waited a few yards to the right, its empty shafts resting on the ground, a pitchfork stuck in its summit. A little beyond it the two horses, Lion and Pleasant, moved in the deep gripe's shadow, cropping hazel, now and again shaking their head harness musically or swishing off flies and gnats with their long tails. They had no tethers, but they kept within a limit which Amyot had indicated, a little before, merely by drawing with his hand an imaginary line across the ditch.

He was Farmer Bosanko's wagoner now, and the pair adored him. So for that matter did the two children, Mary and Johnny. He told them stories, but in a queer way. He seemed to fetch them out of himself, out of fairyland, anywhere; not playing on his fiddle, but laying it across his knees and plucking at a string at times, as if to help his memory. And then, maybe at the most exciting moment, he would break off, protesting that he knew no more of it, and asking the children to continue.

Now, as he sat between Doctor Carfax and Mary, he glanced up at the sky as a company of rooks came flying in close phalanx, across the zenith, homing for Penquite.

'They are flying higher than yesterday,' said Mr Tregentil.

'The families are coming into flocks again,' replied Amyot, plucking on a string of his fiddle. 'All the spring they've been plying in pairs, each for his own.'

'What's that air, lad?' asked Doctor Carfax.

'I can't tell you, sir. It's a silly old song I heard as a boy, years and years ago.'

'Any words to it?'

'Oh yes; it goes on and on. But I remember only the last two lines; nothing, sir, of what the song was about.'

Amyot caressed his fiddle and half hummed, half sang, intoning:

'Iseut ma dru, Iseut m'amie,
En vus ma mort, en vus ma vie.'

Doctor Carfax, in the act of lighting his pipe, paused, and stared at the singer, allowing his match to go out

'Would you mind repeating that?' he demanded slowly.

Amyot obliged, phrasing his words more clearly, and then breaking off, with a shy glance at the company. 'It was a love song, they told me, sir,' he murmured, 'but who wrote it I cannot say. It's too sad perhaps for this occasion.' He launched forth into a lively jig:

> 'N'y pleurez plus, ma fille,
> Ran, tan, plan, Tireli!
>
> N'y pleurez-vous, ma fille,
> Nous vous marierons riche.
>
> Nous vous marierons riche
> Ran, tan, plan, Tireli!
>
> Avec un gros marchand d'oignons
> À six liards le quarteren.'

Doctor Carfax frowned, and proceeded with the lighting of his pipe. It was not the moment to pursue his line of inquiry, but he had been reminded, all too suddenly, of poor Ledru and his fatal seizure the previous autumn. The Breton lad had made progress with his English under Tregentil's tuition, but how had Tregentil himself progressed with the tracing of local place names, an additional prescription to that of rook-watching? He must remember to ask, but not now.

'Tell us a story, Amyot,' Johnny pleaded.

'Yes, tell us a story,' echoed Mrs Bosanko. 'Only let it be a cheerful one, or the children won't teen an eye tonight.'

Johnny nestled up against Amyot, who began, plucking softly at the strings:

'At the back of the land where I lived when I was Johnny's

age there was a forest – I think that behind everybody's thoughts while he is growing there must be a forest. But this was a real one, though the most wonderful things happened in it. At first you came to pine trees, a sort of fringe, but very deep, and the trees like pillars in a church. And beyond this you came to a lake, with an island in its middle, and swans that bred there – oh yes, this is all true enough: the old people used to tell about it. Well, beyond that was a spring with a stone basin, out of which the lake was fed. The lake, I remember, was called Louc'h Rouan – which means the Queen's Lake: and the fountain had red sand all about it, red as blood: but the water was clear and green, and so deep that though it lay in a trough no one could see to the bottom of it. The old people said that if anyone dipped a fork into it and then stuck his fork into the red sand, a thunderstorm would come up out of the woods, and a wind so roaring that it stripped all the leaves off the trees. Then it would pass and the birds all come together and sing on the bare branches. I never dared to try this – I was very young, but beyond the fountain a path went up zig-a-zag through the trees, with waterfalls . . . Now you take it on, Johnny.'

'It's all true,' said Johnny eagerly. 'I went that way yesterday – up past Milltown. Mother had covered me up with a shawl and told me to go to sleep like a good boy. But when she was gone I got up and out past Milltown—'

'He bolted anyway,' put in Mary, secretly jealous. 'I hate lies.'

'It *isn't* lies,' protested Johnny. 'It's a dream if you like . . . well, first of all I came to the viaduct, with the trains making their noise over me: and then there was Billy Tregenza, taking a grasshopper out of the rushes and eating it—'

'That's a tarnation lie anyway,' objected old Tregenza. 'I never done such a thing in my born days.'

'You were as real as real,' asserted Johnny. 'And behind you the path went up through the trees – what d'you call 'em – larches? Yes, Billy Tregenza told me they were larches—'

'I never did.'

'Hadn't you better put this – this urchin to bed?' Mary appealed to her mother.

'No, let's have it out,' said Doctor Carfax. 'Its quite a remarkable tale. And I'm interested.'

'By an' by,' purused Johnny, 'I came in sight of a naked boy at the top, the water pouring down all under him. I can't tell you how naked he was—'

'Mary is right,' said Mrs Bosanko. 'You'd better come off to bed, and at once.'

'He was so naked,' Johnny went on, hugging himself closer to Amyot's side, 'that I wanted to fight him. I called up, but he took no notice at all. I was out of breath, or pretty near, and wondered if I should have wind enough to hit him . . . And then, at the top, he turned out to be a stone boy, stuck in a fountain: with goldfish in it and a lady, t'other side, walking beside a dark hedge—'

'What sort of lady?' demanded his sister.

'Silly, a lady's a lady. You always know—'

'But what *like*?'

'What like . . . Azackly like Mrs Lewarne.'

For at that moment Linnet Lewarne came walking to them alongside the hedge. She wore her riding-habit, the long skirt of it looped across her arm.

'You be just in time, mistress,' said the farmer, jumping up and making her welcome. 'Will you condescend to a dish of tea?'

'No, I thank you,' answered Linnet. 'But I rode over to the forge by Castle Dor and left Merlin there to have a new shoe fitted. They told me you were carrying the last of the hay tonight, and I just wandered down to wish you well.'

'Yonder it is,' said Farmer Bosanko, jerking his finger towards the wagon. 'And it only wants a maid 'pon top of it. Harness up, boy!' – this to Amyot – 'and fetch the ladder, Mary child, what do 'ee say to riding Harvest Queen?'

But Mary, cut out by her brother in the late tale-telling, had turned sullen.

'Another time, Father,' she said. 'I've always been allowed to ride home with the heck at corn harvest.'

'Well-a-well! Then up you gets, Mrs Lewarne,' A pause and half a chuckle. 'But it ought to be a maiden by rights.'

'Never mind that,' snapped Mrs Bosanko, with a sharp glance at Linnet, who on the instant had turned rosy-pink. 'Let Mrs Lewarne climb up an' honour us if she will.'

Linnet bent her neck and climbed the short ladder which Amyot ran and fetched for her. He harnessed up Lion and Pleasant.

The wagon was swung out accurately through the gateway; thence down a narrow road to the right; so narrow that the bushes on either side held wisps of hay caught from the sides of previous wains; so steep that Amyot's hand had always to be on the touch with Pleasant's bridle. In the deep cutting between the hedges horses and guide moved in shadow. The harvesters followed them likewise in shadow, humming tunes and breaking out in choruses. At a turn of the road the sun's last rays illuminated Linnet aloft on the load, and the fork handle to which she held was a staff of gold.

Once Amyot looked up. She sat above him against the sky, radiant. She, looking down, marked his strong shoulders and the skilled movements with which he guided the two horses.

They swung again into the mowhay and were fetched up alongside the great rick. Tregenza and another labouring man (by name unknown to her) had gone ahead of the wain and clambered up by a ladder. Their figures, each with pitchfork in hand, stood silhouetted against the pale last of the day.

Amyot, leaving Pleasant's bridle, ran back to her. They had come to anchor, and she might descend.

Then, in a flurry of half a dozen seconds, the disaster happened and was over. Afterwards Linnet remembered only Amyot's looking up at her, his collar open, his naked throat all powdered with hayseed. A moment later, attempting the descent, she had caught her heel in her riding-skirt and clutched at the pitchfork handle to steady herself. It came away – Amyot caught it and with a twist of the hand flung it away as it was within an ace of piercing her side with its prongs. For the moment she had tumbled into Amyot's arms and was held. Then a pile of hay, dislodged by the pulling out of the fork, topped over and fell, smothering them both.

'Neatly manoeuvred,' murmured Doctor Carfax.

'Sweet hay, if ever there was!' cried the farmer jocularly. 'But you did that nibby–jibby, lad.'

He pulled the covering smother from the shoulders of the pair. Linnet's cheeks were hot and flushed; Amyot's white as a man's who has just seen a ghost. No wonder, either, so near a thing it had been. He stared around him blankly, towards the fork which, whirled from him, had bedded its deadly prongs into the midden-heap of the mowhay.

12

'Comfort me with apples'

The next day was a Sunday, and the cuckoo sang loudly through the June woods – albeit with a breaking note. Linnet, her maid Deborah rowing, had come up the river on a full spring tide, their excuse being that they were to attend evening service at St Winnow and after service, the tide just suiting, fall back quietly home on the first ebb. They had brought a tea basket with them, into which Deborah had quietly slipped a drinking flask.

They passed the church, a good hour before its bell would ring for service, and penetrating the screen of a retired weather way, then flooded up almost to the arches of the railway viaduct beneath Lantyan. Here amid the spongy odorous sedges they landed, and sought higher ground, where Linnet sat while Deborah foraged for dry sticks and leaves, to pile them for a fire at the foot of one of the viaduct's arches. A deal of coppice had been cut in the previous autumn, and its shrivelled leaves lay more than ankle-deep. She built the fire, lit it, and set the kettle to boil.

The kettle had scarcely begun to make its noise before Amyot came down to water his horses – as the women knew he would – he riding Lion with Pleasant on his right-hand rein.

He pulled up, astonished at their presence there. He had his fiddle slung at his back, and apologised for it.

'I come down in the evenings here to practise,' he explained, 'and the trickle of the water helps – you cannot tell how.'

'Well, put it aside and have tea with us.'

They drank, and Deborah, having piled a great armful of leaves on the fire, moved away towards the boat and was lost.

A train rattled over the viaduct above.

'That's the night express,' said Linnet. 'It stops at Plymouth: and after that one can fade off into another life and wake up in London.'

'It all depends,' said Amyot seriously, 'on if one wishes for another life. Do you?'

'Foolish lad! Of course I do!' Linnet leant back on the bank and lifted her face to the arch of the viaduct. 'I come here as often as the tides serve: but I was not born for this. These trains – think of them, all carrying numbers of folk to some kind of life.'

Linnet unscrewed the top of the drinking flask as Amyot, with a smack on Pleasant's rump, commanded the horses to go home and stall themselves.

He came back and stretched himself beside the fire with a 'By your leave, mistress'. In his innocence he had unstrapped his fiddle and laid it across his knees, thinking that some tune on it might please her.

She had filled a small glass and was holding it to him across the fire, the faint flame of which lit up its amber liquid.

'Last night,' said she. 'I came on purpose to explain – last night, on the wagon, I slipped on purpose. Do you understand?'

'It was a very dangerous trick,' he answered firmly, not yet comprehending. 'You don't know how nearly the prongs missed to pierce you. They were close on your side when I caught the handle.' He shivered. 'I didn't know where I flung it – a mercy, mistress, it pitched clear of everyone!'

'Oh, of course *that* wasn't intentional. I just caught at the thing to steady myself – I suppose, now, if it had pierced my side I might have bled to death, there, in your arms.'

'Ah, don't – don't!'

'But I am alive, you see, and come to thank you. Yes, it's good to be alive. Drink to me, Amyot.'

He faced her across the glow of the fire and took the glass, dazedly, looking into her elfish eyes. Having drunk he passed it back to her and she too drank.

He fell back on his elbow. There was a spurt of flame as she tossed the dregs of the glass upon the embers. She also leant back her shoulders pillowed upon a cushion of moss. The dying fire faded between them. Fair and alluring though she was, Amyot dared not cross the fire to touch her. A constriction of the heart held him; half faint, he only knew that this wonder of beauty wanted him, and that, wanting him, she must be his for ever and ever.

The late June cuckoo sang its last through the wood and was silent. As though its silence broke the spell, Amyot sat up, reached for his violin and began with finger and thumb to prick out an echo of the cuckoo's forlorn call.

'I hate that song,' said Linnet suddenly. 'It's sorrowful, like someone wailing for the dead.'

He stood up, snapped the violin across his knee and dropped it into the fire, which licked almost instantly its varnish and thin frame.

As their eyes encountered, as all trembling he made half a step to pass through the fire and lean over her, a twig crackled and Deborah came down through the dark wood.

The woman glanced at the two figures and at the fast-fading fire still between them.

'The tide has begun to fall, mistress. Even now you will find it hard to miss soiling your shoes in the dimpsey. But here is the boat – half in grass, half in water. You have come as you came, and we have missed church and the sermon. Let us pull home.'

13

Mrs Bosanko intervenes

'Gabriel,' confessed Mrs Bosanko, early one morning, 'my mind's in trouble. I've scarcely slept a wink this night – you awake?'

'Moderately,' the farmer responded heavily, then fetched himself around with the quick solicitude of a husband who had never from the hour of his betrothal forgotten to be a lover. 'Eh? Trouble?' he repeated. 'You don't say the children are sickening for anything?'

'No, I thank God.'

'And Patch calved the day before yesterday – of a heifer, too; and the others true to pail – though Slow-coach is running dry, o' course. But that's the Lord's ordinance upon cows. Balance in the bank all right – likewise deposit account?'

'Yes, of course. I told you.'

'Then I don't understand. Here, put your head in the crook of my arm, dear heart, and tell me about it. Trouble, says you?'

'It's about Amyot – and Mrs Lewarne.'

'I don't see the connection – you've been dreamin', and thoughts all get mixed up in dreams – putting two an' two together and making 'em five. Well, rouse out 'em, my dear, and tell me.'

'She's fond of him.'

'Well, so we all are, the children included.'

'She's too fond of him. And the mischief is, he's fond of her. That she was fain of him I saw from the first. But he being so simple—'

'Have you noticed any change in him lately?'

'Only, now you come to mention it, that I have to speak twice to him at whiles before he answers. On the whole, a quicker chap at his job you couldn't want.'

'That's my trouble, dear,' said Mrs Bosanko. 'We're here living in a fool's paradise. The horses love him and the children love him. But all the while there's wickedness brewing, and he'll have to go.'

'Wickedness?'

'Of course it's wickedness. She's a married woman.'

'Well, if it be as you say—'

'I'm certain of it.'

'Well, if it be as you say, what's to be done? If old Lewarne chooses to marry a girl half his age, that's his look-out. I reckon it's none of our business.'

'But it *is*. Listen – lean closer – don't you know by this time that any woman, early or not, or past a certain age, simply raves to be loved? Don't you know? – Ah, my dear, don't you?'

'We'll grant that. Still, I don't see—'

'Don't be foolish, but just listen. I've thought it over while you were snoring, manlike; and the upshot is, Amyot will have to go.'

'I never did fancy Mark Lewarne; never could stomach him somehow,' the farmer muttered sleepily. 'And anyway – supposin' you're right – why can't he look after his goods? I don't see what business 'tis of ours. I like the lad, and so do you; and if he's to be turned adrift what excuse will I give him, I'd like to know?'

'You leave that to me, I'll do the talking.'

'You always do, mainly – thank God!'

'But first of all, I'm going to Troy—'

'Here, hold on!' Mr Bosanko sat upright suddenly. 'You don't mean to say that you're going to tell Lewarne?'

'No, my poor witless one! Lie down again. I shall go to the custom-house and ask if any skipper happens to want a hand. I know the collector of customs down there, but very slightly. McPhail his name is, and he's well spoken of as a kindly man. I shall just go to him and state the facts: that Amyot was brought to us as a lad off a Breton ship; and took your employ; but that coming from the sea he now wants to go back to it.'

'But suppose he doesn't?'

'He will, when I've talked to him,' answered Mrs Bosanko firmly. 'But that, I allow, will be the hard part of it. As to Mrs Lewarne, I don't feel like bearing her any ill will at all. I pity her, poor soul. I understand her in a way. But then there's the principle of the thing – and on top of that there are the children. You wouldn't have our two innocents mixed up in any such ways.'

'No,' agreed Mr Bosanko; 'that's a clincher, my dear. Don't I hear 'em chitterin' in the next room?'

'Chittering and twittering like a pair of sparrows.'

'Why so early?'

'Because it's Mary's fourteenth birthday, and Johnny has awoken her with his present – such a pretty prayer book that I chose for him to give, all bound up in ivory boards, bound up with Wesley's hymns!'

Mrs Bosanko travelled down to Troy by the jingle and returned before three o'clock. This gave her plenty of time to pack the birthday tea-basket, to be carried down by Amyot and Zillah to the place the children had chosen – the foot of the viaduct, under the larch woods.

She sent Zillah to the gate of the mowhay and went upstairs to titivate herself. This operation took a very short while, and when Zillah returned Mrs Bosanko stood awaiting her on the back doorstep.

'He's coming straight away,' Zillah reported.

'Who was that woman talking to him? I saw it from my bedroom window?'

''Twas that maidservant of Mister Lewarne's, down to Troy. I never seen her but twice in my life at the most. But I reck-ernized her as she slipped away. "Courtin'," said I to myself, though not knowin' as they'd ever met. Well, summer's the season for it; and I've a-heard the cuckoo myself in my time. But he went away and was lost at sea next winter.'

''Tis late July. "In July he prepares to fly",' quoted her mistress.

The family held the birthday tea-drinking under an archway of the viaduct. The children, building a fire in contention, scooped together the ashes of an earlier fire.

'But what's this?' demanded Johnny, holding up a charred piece of wood.

'It's my fiddle neck,' Amyot confessed. 'I found I should never be able to play on it rightly, and I burned it here.'

'And aren't there going to be any more tunes?'

'Nor any more stories?'

'Oh yes – heaps and heaps, I hope.' Being pressed, he told them some rough Breton version of Rudolph and the Lady of Tripoli – one of those stories that float everywhere about the world. His voice was more animated than ordinarily, his colour higher, his gesture quicker. Mrs Bosanko watched him narrowly. Her husband's gaze rested on the shore across the river and the wheat thereon, beautifully whitening to harvest.

Then the rooks came across the creek, homing towards Pen-quite, and Amyot, counting the birds, told them which were the parents and which the younger birds learning to fly and range, day by day, higher and farther.

When they had packed up and finished, Mrs Bosanko touched the lad's arm.

'Stay behind, Amyot. I want a word with you.'

Amyot started, and stared at her.

'But why, madame? Have I by chance done anything wrong?' he asked.

'Oh, I hope not – I trust not; and, if not, I am in time.'

'If the master has any complaint of my work—'

106

'He has not. He was praising it only this morning.'

'Then if by chance I have given you some offence, for which you cannot give me pardon—'

'None, Amyot: you have given me none. You know that we all – that Mr Bosanko and I and the children have come to be very fond of you.' ('The Lord help me,' she thought to herself, 'that I should be sending him away on this evening of Mary's birthday. It will go near to break the child's heart.')

'Then I see how it is. You are not rich – you and the master – to the extent of your charity and kindness to me: I ought to have thought of this. But if that be all, the master can pay me no wage – it was he who surprised me by offering it; and it is all in a little knot in the corner of my handkerchief within the top drawer of my room. What should I want with money here? And as for eating, why, I find of late I can do with little or nothing in that way.'

In the midst of his distress Mrs Bosanko could almost have laughed aloud. Why of course she had noted it – shrewd house-wife that she was – and alas! she knew it part of the indictment.

'Lad,' she said, 'it has nothing to do with that: nothing at all. We love you, I say: and I have watched you of late as a mother might watch her own son: and I say to you, just as I would say to my own son, were he of your age: "You must go out of this!"'

'Yes, you have been the best friend of all to me. I don't ask to know why: for I know that. It just came to me, a stranger and unfriended, out of the goodness of your heart. But have I not paid back all that I had to pay?'

'You have, lad.'

'Then tell me at least the one little thing I ask. What is my sin?'

'You are in love.'

He dropped his eyes and then looked at her straight and long.

'I am. Is that a crime?'

'You are in love, Amyot, with a married woman – Linnet

107

Lewarne. She sends messages to you by her maid. She sent one this very evening. Isn't this true?'

'It is, madame. But *married*, you say?'

Mrs Bosanko winced. 'What has she told you?'

'She has in effect, madame, told me nothing. But I have my thoughts necessarily, as you have yours. Perhaps even more necessarily. But you are wiser than I. What are yours?'

'She and her husband are one in the sight of God,' said Mrs Bosanko.

'I know very little about the sight of God,' returned Amyot. 'As you know, I was thrown into the Iceland fishery early without any school-teaching to speak of. On board my first boat I heard a great deal of filthy talk. But this is all different – so different!'

'See here, Amyot. It is indeed as to my own boy that I would talk to you – you must go away this night, and out of this calf love you will grow into a man.'

Yet all the time Mrs Bosanko knew that, talking as to a boy, she was addressing a man – a man strangely grown, love having made him one.

'I went down to Troy today,' she went on: 'and you can ship aboard the steam-packet *Downshire* tomorrow morning on good pay. You can carry your belongings on board there tonight. She is laden and sails tomorrow for Rio Grande. Ah, go and see the world, lad, and forget!'

'Forget? Is it in the arms of some other woman you mean? Will that be – for I've to learn – will that be pleasuring the sight of God?'

'Ah, Amyot, don't do that! Never do that! I never thought it would be so hard to speak to you.'

'God! You needn't fear *that*. There's nothing can tempt me away from the sin *you* fear, not for ever and ever – as there's nothing can wipe out the memory of your goodness to me. I'll run up and pack my bundle at once.'

He picked up the baskets and was gone in the gathering twilight.

'Now I wonder,' thought Mrs. Bosanko, 'if I have done rightly after all!'

She went up the hill slowly, thinking how to break the news to the children.

Mary and Johnny were at play in the yard by the stable: Johnny furiously driving a new hoop and Mary, seated haughtily on the hepping-stock, timing his rounds by the second-hand of her new watch.

Mrs Bosanko halted and spent a few minutes watching them, trying to decide what to tell them at supper time. But she need not have troubled. When she got back to the house it was to find two small packets laid on the hall table with a piece of folded paper between them. She had taught Amyot to write in English script, and she noted now, even in the trouble of fore-guessing, how neatly in his hurry he had formed the words.

Dear Master and Mistress,

I have taken a few shillings with me. The rest of my wages please find in these two packets, the smaller one for Zillah. I thought it best not to say 'adieu' to her or to anyone. I could not bear it. Only to the horses did I speak. Please give my love to Miss Mary and young Master Johnny and tell them I shall think of them for ever. Also please make my excuses to the good Mr Tregentil. For your goodness to me I bless this house on its doorstep as I go, and pray the peace of God to rest on it for ever.

Amyot

Supper was laid and there were *bon-bon* crackers on the table. Mrs Bosanko had set them out with misty eyes. The children shouted with delight.

'But why is Amyot late?' demanded Johnny, when he had finished clapping his hands and jumping up and down in his chair.

His mother braced herself up for the terrible moment.

'Amyot is not here, dears. He sends you his love and wishes Mary many, many happy returns of the day. But a call has come to him and he has gone back to sea, as he came from it.'

Then, at sight of their faces, Mrs Bosanko lied for about the first time in her life.

'But he promised to come back soon, and tell you the most wonderful stories.'

And with that she broke down.

The effect upon Johnny was almost instantaneous. He had never before seen his mother crying. He jumped from his chair and ran to her. But Mary stood up and stared at them both. Like a little tragedy queen she looked. Her dry eyes met her mother's tearful ones, upraised over the nestling boy's shoulder; and as their gaze crossed Mrs Bosanko knew that she might caress a boy and be caressed, but that hereafter, or some day hereafter, she would have to deal with a woman; likewise a child of her womb – but with a woman.

It was one quick gladiatorial look; a first crossing of swords. Mary turned to her father. 'If this is your idea of a birthday, you two, then it isn't mine!' And she walked from the room.

'Where's she gone, Zillah?' asked the farmer after a while.

'I think, upstairs to her room, sir.'

But Mary had not walked upstairs. She had gone straight out into the dark; in which, later on, her father found her, seated on the top of the hepping-stock, her body rent with low strangling sobs. He held the horn stable lantern up to her face. It was tearless.

'Come in, my honey – come in, my deary—'

She let him take her hand, then snatched it away.

'Father, Father! You couldn't have been so cruel!'

He coaxed her indoors and upstairs to her bedroom.

Mrs Bosanko, who had heard their footsteps, followed after an interval and met her husband on the landing coming away.

'She is quieter,' he announced in a whisper. 'I have left her to undress.'

'I must go in and make my peace with her,' said his wife. 'Go to bed, dear. It may be late before I come to it – my child! My poor child!'

She put Johnny to bed before carrying her candle to Mary's side of the room. Below stairs Zillah had by instruction quenched the lamps over the untasted supper. An hour later the good woman, remembering that in Cornwall it is unlucky to leave a white cloth overnight on the table, crept downstairs and redded up everything, quiet as a mouse – birthday cake and crackers with the rest. She put all away carefully: so that, soon after she had closed the dining-room door and stolen back to her attic, the moon, rising and glinting through a chink of curtain, shone but on a table of polished mahogany and a bowl of perennial sunflowers.

14

Assignation at Castle Dor and its consequences

W hat had Deborah Brangwyn said to Amyot in the mowhay? She had said straightly: 'The mistress wishes a word with you. She will be at Castle Dor above here at nine o'clock. Her husband has gone to a Freemasons' dinner at St Austell. He will come back late and drunk: or, if he sleeps it off at the public there, early tomorrow. Meantime we are keeping the house by turns.'

'I think I see what you mean. But if you and she want protecting, I have only to ask leave, and I can walk home here after closing time after seeing you both safe. Only I may be a few minutes late. There is a supper tonight, in honour of Miss Mary's birthday.'

'Simpleton! Do you want to be taught *everything*? Listen: same as she, I am a woman – a Constantine, though born on the wrong side of the blanket. Lord, boy! I am her servant. Simpleton – I, even I, could have taught it to you for your asking. But the end is that she will be on Castle Dor at nine o'clock with a message: and what her meaning is 'tis not for me to know.'

Now this had passed between the woman and him, as we know, before the birthday tea party: an hour or more before

Mrs Bosanko at the end of it had given Amyot his dismissal. Until the moment of that dismissal with its reason given, he had received out of anywhere – or was it out of nowhere in the morning – that love must suffer for loving; that, the deeper planted, the more it must suffer, in that all true passion of love at its highest force inevitably ends in tragedy: that no story of love between man and woman at its highest could ever come but to a tragic end; that no ending but disillusion can be invented for the illusion which is more than half of such love; that the erosion of earth, our Mother, must take back to itself and the wind of the sky smooth over all of us with every anticipation, all regrets.

To Amyot, as to every true lad in love, the world held no foreboding at all. He was a lad out of nowhere, innocent of allegiance to the gods of our country. He only knew that the sky was clearer, every leaf brighter, every bird's note somehow acuter, more intelligible. He wondered, having broken his fiddle in surrender, why he had ever bent over its strings with his bow, trying to get something out of a hollow piece of timber, while his own living wood and field were doing their best to sing happiness around him and now his released self tingled as a bell and flung its music on the wind to the chime.

Why couldn't the whole world agree to be happy? There were brutal things in it, of course – he had known far north the brute rage of the sea, and had endured it somehow for days, clinging to his young life. There were obscene things in it too – that skipper Fouguereau, for example, But why should sorrow be always creeping in upon joy? Why should it pierce and find him out in this dear beautiful place, into which he had been wafted so mysteriously; where he had in purest kindness been nursed to health, fed, made one of the family – repaying them in all the coin he had – gratitude, devotion, service, love? Why should Mrs Bosanko, his second mother, tender to him almost almost as to her own, have dismissed him for no fault he had ever committed or thought of committing? His own mother had told him once that she had borne him in sorrow and he had been christened in sorrow. He had supposed his father to have been drowned – on some night just before he entered this world, in the *Baie des Tréspassés*. He had grown up to the name given him, had learnt a little at school and had in due course been shipped off to the Iceland fishery. Yes, then the horrors had begun: there were horrible seas all the while outside the frail bulwarks; more horrible bestial passions pent within the frail boards. Well, *le bon Dieu* knew best, and had been wonderfully provident of him for a space. He was bound for the sea again. He had been bred to the sea, and bore it no ill will.

He went up the hill, past the haystacks he had helped to pile. Their fragrance, in the July evening, reminded him of Mary and Johnny – of all the sweet innocence he had shared and was leaving; from which he was outcast, because he loved. At a turn of the climbing road he halted. A window shone, deep down in the valley; and again with a sob his heart blessed that house.

Past the field called Mark's Gate he took the shortest way to cut into the main road under Castle Dor. By the broad entrance to the earthwork he remembered Deborah's message and entered the dusking cirque. It was empty. Twice he walked the round of it, and then, through a gate, struck the high road.

Some way beyond the gate a broad ribbon of light fell across the road from the blacksmith's forge. Across that light came a figure, its shadow elongated towards a pool on its left. Always, it seemed, he saw her across fire.

In the deepening dusk she saw him by the gate.

'You came before your time.'

'By accident. I have not waited long.'

'By accident? What is that bundle you carry on that stick?'

'All I possess. I am dismissed. I must go down to Troy and, early, be at the custom-house, to ship on board a steam-packet, the *Downshire*. I think she sails some time in the forenoon – so Mrs Bosanko says, who has commanded this. So our ways

115

lie together, and I can explain as I see you home, if you will permit?'

But while he hesitated she bent her brow towards the gate and he held it open for her to pass in.

'We can talk here. She has dismissed you? Why?'

'Because—' He hesitated again and now hopelessly.

'Oh, I know! These cold dutiful women of the north! . . . so Deborah brought you my message – and you are going. Amyot!'

'Mistress!'

'It is dark and I cannot see your eyes. But look me in the face and tell me true . . . has anything happened to you of late?'

Walking side by side they had reached the edge of the cirque.

'I don't know – I don't know!'

Then in a moment his arms were around her and she slid down between them with a choking happy laugh.

'You won't go – say you'll never go! Amyot! Amyot!'

As they stood by the gate Diana shone above them, in her first quarter, clear and clean, and edged like a suspended scimitar.

An elderly woodman, tenant of a cottage above a little beach – one of a string of coast recesses to which the woodlands descend under Castle Dor – arose at four o'clock next morning from his wife's side, and pulled out to draw his nets early, between the morn and the dawn. His was a mixed employ – woodman, gardener's help, fisherman for his master's great house above. The bay had, for a week past, been teeming red mullet. There was a company of guests 'up at the mansion', and the red mullet is of all fish perhaps the most delicious at breakfast, baked, fresh out of the sea.

The fisher – by name Eli Rowe – was by no means a man to see visions, but while preoccupied with his work he heard a sudden splash on the water, close inshore – too close by the rocks to be the leap of a salmon.

No – it had been the dive of a human body: for after a moment or so there followed the swish-swish of a swimmer, of somebody swimming strongly with an overhead side-stroke that cast the water vigorously behind it. He peered. Even in the moonlight, more than three hundred yards away the swimmer's back-hand thrust threw up pools of pale phosphorescence; and in the swirl moved a man's head, dark and distinct.

Then, against the moonlight, another figure came down to the sea's edge, and it was the form of a woman, clothed. In the hush the fisherman could hear her feet softly crunching the shingle. She seemed to carry a light bundle. Then, as the swimmer turned back towards the beach, the woman's figure was lost under the cover of a far-jutting rock.

Eli saw the swimmer reach and run up shore. Well, it was a funny world, with lots of people in places where you'd least expect 'em; and this was no business of his.

But later on, having pulled to his own beach, drawn his boat up and unloaded his catch, standing by his garden gate, he seemed to see a woman's shape moving up the footway inland – as he thought, dejectedly. The other – the man – had disappeared.

Linnet and Amyot had come down to the beach through the odorous woods, by fringes planted with subtropical bushes and mats of English mints and thymes – each exhaling on the warm night, all commingling a fragrance that hung and clung about the pair as they walked down through their dream. In the hush of it little woodland creatures moved now and again, crept, stirred.

'You will not go!'

'I must – I must – I have given my word.'

'What is that? What is a word compared with love? Love is a deed – a document signed in the end.'

'It is signed, for ever and ever.'

'And *yet* you can go? You could hide, in the woods above Lantyan; no one would look for you, and we would meet.'

'I have promised. Can I break honour – and with these people so kind? But I will come back one day and meet you near Lantyan. I swear. Oh, dear love, how can I *not* come back?'

'Men always swear that, I have heard – who is *that*, moving behind the trees above us?'

'Shadows only. There is no one by.'

Later he opened a gate over the little moonlit beach, and a salt strong smell was suddenly on their faces, conquering, beating back the perfumes of bush and shrub into their fastnesses. Over the white shingle a languorous tide was feeling its way up towards high water, running and streaming, with edges yet whiter, yet more dazzling. It had covered the low-water tangle of seaweed; the scent of which, however, it retained, pushing, wafting it up the shore. They could hear it pulsing as a great bosom might heave: and over it, covering it, gently, followed the masculine breath of brine, clean-blown over far surges out in Atlantic. They descended by a low cliff track upon the shingle.

'Stay here,' commanded Amyot. 'I must swim. Can *you* swim?'

'Alas! No.'

'Some day we'll contrive that I shall teach you. Dear God, what a lesson it shall be, my hand holding up your gentle body!'

'Some day? Ah, that's long – long! It's the word that all men promise.'

But love, after the first brief stupor, had made Amyot strong: had converted him from boy into man, into master.

'Sit here,' he commanded; and she, slipping down through his arms upon the shingle, lay with head and body relaxed under his kisses, loving the new tone in his voice.

With a kiss that seemed to draw all of her out of her, he sprang away, ran down the beach, stripped under the shadow of a rock, clambered up it, dived . . .

Through a dream she heard the splash the fisherman had heard, and then the long swish-swish of his side-stroke. It died away of a sudden into silence. As a fact, he had turned on his back and lay afloat staring up into a sky lustrous, wide, widening wonderfully.

So then was silence. She, listening through all, had a fancy that he was drowning out there. The whole dreadful lesson –

that bliss is transient, that nothing perfect lasts – came on her with a prolonged run of wave and rivulets drawn ebbwise over the shingle.

She pulled off shoes and stockings. She whispered: 'Oh, my love! Are you alive? Are you there?'

She called it twice, and a third time more loudly. Then the strong arm-stroke was resumed and repeated, while he came rushing up the beach, shining, dripping.

She had waded some yards out to him.

'Love, if I could swim!'

'If so, beloved—'

'We would swim out and out side by side, breast by breast, until we reached a shore. Yes, and if we sank, far down there would be caves, hidden caves with floors of sand . . .'

She passed her hand over his naked wet shoulder. He, slipping some way down the shelve of the beach, found and kissed her white insteps.

'I will come back – I swear.'

'Don't swear it, Amyot. Don't swear it, my love! All men do that, they tell: and I want to wait and want and think of you as – as different.'

'I understood you were to be here last evening, at nine or there-abouts,' said Mr McPhail severely, when Amyot presented himself at the custom-house. 'I came down here after my supper at Mrs Bosanko's request, lit up and had your papers ready, with a boat to ship you aboard. Well, the *Downshire* has already sailed. Did Mrs Bosanko bungle my message? It's not like the good woman – leastways it's not like my notion of her.'

'No, sir. She told me the *Downshire* would sail early!'

'Did she tell you I would be here waiting?'

'I am sorry, m'sieur!'

'And you came late, I suppose: found the windows dark and the door fast, he? Maybe you had been drinking?'

'No, sir. I did not arrive until five minutes ago.'

'Well, the *Downshire* sailed at six o'clock this morning.'

'Yes.' Under the sunrise, Amyot, sitting stupefied with bliss and woe, on the beach where he had dropped, had watched a steamship in the offing shaping off the coast for a clear run down channel; the *Downshire*, no doubt.

'Did you sleep then at Lantyan?' Mr McPhail asked.

'No, m'sieur – no, sir.'

'I understand French,' said the collector. He pushed up his spectacles and eyed Amyot; pulled them down and eyed him again.

'Then belike some woman got hold of ye?' he suggested, not harshly.

Amyot winced, and then, as he took the full innuendo, threw up his chin, proud as fire.

'It was not like that, sir!'

'Ah, well: I'm no speirin'. Only knowin' a bit anent seamen and youngsters – we'll say no more about it. And now what's to be done? I like your look, lad: only you mustn't fall into a habit of missing appointments. As William Shakespeare puts it, there is a tide in the affairs o' men. I took mine at your age or thereabouts, though 'twas pretty well on the neaps, to be sure. Step into the next room there and wait while I run across to the harbour office and get latest news of likely arrivals.'

Amyot thanked him and stepped into a clean little low-browed room that had an antique bay-window almost over-hanging the water. He went to it straight, of course, by seaman's instinct, to scan the tide and the shipping across the fairway. His hands went up half way to his eyes as though to rub off a dream, an illusion – for across there, and the nearest in a tier of shipping, lay the *Jolie Brise*, laden, with flag half-masted to summon a pilot.

There was nothing wonderful in this, to be sure. The little schooner plied up the Breton coast to strike across for Troy with a mixed cargo – strawberries for jam at their season, apricots later, onions, lime – for which there was a fair demand on this side, since the kilns which formerly burned at the head of every Cornish creek had fallen into disuse.

No: there was nothing to wonder at. But Amyot's heart tightened at sight of the sweet horrible vessel, with her delicate lines. Head to sea, she lay, one anchor down, her stern moored to a large buoy in company with the hawsers of two large ships. Under the tall side of the nearer she seemed but a cork boat.

Ah, she was a beauty! But if the collector in his kindness attempted to ship *him* aboard of her, there would be murder before Ushant. Amyot had grown; suddenly he knew himself a man. If he must come out of his dream in this way . . .

Standing there by the window, he caught the sound of the collector's footsteps hurrying up the steps from the street; and close upon it the veritable voice of that infernal Fouguereau, following, bellowing.

'But he is here, here in your office, the little pig! That accursed Notary is dead, my friend, and can claim him no longer. I spied him along the street! Oh, you needn't run! I have the law and can claim him!'

Amyot had stepped forth from the inner room. He moved a little aside as the collector hurried in by the doorway. Then advancing again swiftly as Fouguereau panted on the top step, catching breath . . .

'*Vlan!*' Amyot grunted and struck.

The blow took Fouguereau on the apple of the throat: a second and fiercer one smashed on the point of the jaw, and as he turned slowly, horribly, throwing out hands, feeling for somewhere to drop, a third thudded on the nape of his neck. The giant rolled down the steps and lay at their feet, inert as a felled ox.

'My God!' cried Mr McPhail, pushing past Amyot and stooping over the body. 'Have you killed the creature?' In the act of stooping he glanced down the street and up the hill facing the steps, and he saw that the roadway on both sides was strangely, providentially empty.

Save for one guttural sob from Fouguereau, following Amyot's first blow, the affray had begun and ended in uncanny silence.

'My God!' repeated Mr McPhail. 'Have you killed him?'

'I don't know.' Amyot descended the steps slowly, breathing hard, studying his bloodied knuckles. He added: 'I don't care.'

A woman, the keeper of a small greengrocery shop half way up the short hill, had caught sight of the end of the business from her abutting shop window. She came running out and down.

'What has happened? Oh, Mr McPhail! Whatever has happened?'

'Whist, woman. Hold your speech!' the collector commanded. 'The man has had a bad fall – nothing worse. He's stunned, but breathing – and by the smell of his breath he has been drinking. He'll come to in a minute or so. If you want to be useful you might run along to North Street and fetch the inspector. No fuss, mind! Just step along briskly and say quietly that I want him at the custom-house within five minutes. Understand?'

The woman nodded and went.

'And now, lad. You just make yourself scarce, and quick about it. You can nip down the quay ladder there. Tide's out. Make along the foreshore, easy-like, to Pottery Corner and take the ladder there up into the street just as if you'd been mooring a boat. Got a handkerchief? Good. Wrap your hand up, and if you meet anyone stick it carelessly into your pocket. No, I don't take any thanks: it's unprofessional. Lucky for you I'd given my clerk leave to go off for the hour. But the Lord looks after fools.'

15

Two customers at the Rose and Anchor

Fouguereau, at the end of another two minutes or so, opened his eyes and collected some of his senses.

'What the devil!' he growled. 'Hands off, you! What are you doing to my throat?' – this in French.

Mr McPhail took his meaning. 'I was loosening your neck-cloth. You have had a pretty bad fall. Better lie still for a minute.'

The giant sat up heavily, thrust him away and gazed around. Then, pulling himself erect by the end of the handrail, he lurched against it and spat curses, at the same time feeling in his pockets.

'I haven't robbed you, if *that's* what you're thinking,' said Mr McPhail.

'Which way did the little beast run?'

'He's not a beast, and he's not little, and I can't call to mind that he ran. He left you in my charge. Attending to you, I did not notice which way he took.'

'I believe you are a liar,' observed Fouguereau, and spat.

The collector went white and shook. 'I am not a liar,' he answered, mastering his voice. 'Yet I give it you straight – if a lie would save any decent lad from the likes of you, I'd tell it.'

'But it won't, my little clerk. That boy belongs to me. He broke ship, back along, and by the law I can claim him. But yes, and I have his papers in my locker on board, and such a pretty whip coiled on top – what you call a cat of nine tails.

123

This makes twice. The first time an old dotard of a notary saved him. But he is dead, I find; therefore out of action. The dead don't count much. And this second time *you* got him away.'

'That's for you to prove.' Mr McPhail weighed his words. 'As it's for you to prove how you came at the bottom of these steps, I should guess, however – mind you, it's only my guess – that he saved himself, gave you your deserts and walked off.'

'The little rat took me unawares.'

'Oh, of course, just as you were minded to take him. Hadn't you best get aboard and to sea? The pilot's alongside.'

'To hell with the pilot and you! He can cool his heels and send in his outward bill to the agents when he's tired. I can work my tub in and out of your harbour at any state of the tide. But I'll have this fellow if I wait here a week.'

'What about demurrage?'

'To hell with demurrage! I own three-parts shares.'

'Well then – what about the harbour master? He wants your buoy cleared.'

'What you don't see is that this fellow has broken ship, and your police are bound to find him and hand him over.'

'You may put that to *them*: since here they are.'

The inspector of police came along at a measured stride, a young constable beside him. He was a grave man, tall and tolerant.

'I hear you've had some little trouble over here,' said he.

'Trouble?' snarled Fouguereau. 'There's no trouble except that a seaman of mine has broken ship, and I'll trouble you to find him for me.'

It is astonishing how some men can put themselves on the wrong side of sympathy, almost before uttering twenty words. The inspector gazed at the skipper placidly.

'Your name?'

'Fouguereau.'

'Yes, to be sure: master of the schooner *Jolie Brise* yonder, eh? Seaman's name?'

'Amyot Tristane, of Loctudy in Brittany. Either that or Tristane Amyot. A bastard, anyway.'

'Sure?'

'*Qui, diable!*—'

'It's hardly the description I can make out on a warrant and take to a magistrate to sign: let be it's no description on which to identify and arrest a man. Be a little more definite, please.' The inspector had picked up a cross-examining manner by listening to the Deputy Chief Constable at Petty Sessions and by some practice on his own in Occasional Courts. 'This man was employed by you on board your schooner. At what hour, so far as you have ascertained, did he break ship?'

Fouguereau was silent.

Mr McPhail filled up his silence with a chuckle. 'Don't be too strict with the man, inspector. Seeing that it happened the best part of a year ago, you can't expect him to tax his memory to the day and hour.'

'I have his papers, I tell you! If you will come aboard—'

'I shall not. For as it happens I have yours: and if you step along with me to the police station I can show them to you. There is information against you, drawn up by a gentleman of your country and signed by four witnesses—'

'Pah! He is dead, and it is stale.'

'It is stale, to be sure: yet not quite so stale as your claim on this young man, eh? There is also a fine packet of documents about you in French. I don't read French myself: but perhaps the collector here will come along with me and translate.'

'It is unnecessary,' said Mr McPhail.

Fouguereau cursed them and lurched away and along the street to the Rose and Anchor for a tonic. He ordered a double glass of brandy at the bar. Deborah served him, watching him in silence.

Fouguereau swallowed his brandy, then pushed the glass across the metal bar-top to be refilled. Deborah pushed it back. 'I'll not serve you another. You're drunk already.'

'Come, one small glass, that's a good girl!'

'Not a drop.'

'Eh, well!' he leered at her. 'I like spirit in a woman – with a bust like yours too. Do you know I could clear your damnable bar, glasses and all, with one sweep of this arm?'

'Of course I do.'

'And you're not afraid?'

'Of *you*. Not one little bit.'

The fellow, eyeing her, added: 'I suppose you reckon on some help you can call out of the rear of this cabaret?'

'Not at all. I should fetch in help from the neighbours or' – she glanced towards the square – 'or call the police. Shall I?'

'No: wait a bit. I'm not properly drunk as you might say: dizzy – and trying to think.'

'Well then, think.'

'That fancy lad of yours – you and Madame don't keep him anywhere on the premises – eh?'

'What are you talking about? Will you go, or shall I call down the master and fetch the police?'

'*Tiens*! Your English police are no help, any more than ours, to an honest man – I am thinking of that onion-seller of mine you snatched out of my punishment, back along – you and a nice conspiracy. Is he hereabouts?'

'No.'

'Not employed here – not on the premises – *hein*?'

'He is not,' answered Deborah. 'And what's more, if I knew where he is at this moment I shouldn't tell you. Is that enough?'

Fouguereau rose. 'It's enough: all but another glass of brandy, eh?'

'If you will promise, beast that you are, to go straight forth.'

He was served, drank the glass and lurched out.

Later that morning Mr McPhail visited the Rose and Anchor for his customary pint of cider. He preferred cider to beer 'for drinking purposes' as he put it: the cider was superlative – it had a dash of perry in it and came from Mrs Lewarne's father's orchard over the water: good clean stuff, in colour a pale amber. Daily, mid-morning, he sought the Rose and Anchor, entered the bar-parlour, struck thrice on a gong-bell, and left the rest to the intelligence of the house.

Linnet Lewarne entered, with jug, glass and spotless pewter tankard all ready on a tray. She explained, as Mr McPhail rose from his chair to acknowledge this condescension, that Deborah was out – likewise her husband's bar attendant, who had twisted an ankle the night before out walking, when he should have been abed.

'I don't see why you should apologize, ma'am,' said the collector of customs. "Tis an honour you do me. Yes, and if an elderly man may say it without offence, I never saw you looking in finer health. Marriage agrees with ye, that's certain.'

'Thank you, Mr McPhail.' Linnet compressed her lips and poured out the cider from jug to glass with a careful hand. 'Now hold it to the light. Say, before I tip it into the pewter, if I draw it as well as Deborah does?'

'Every bit, ma'am. It's clear as one of the precious stones one reads about in Revelations but seldom sees in real life.' He handed back the glass. 'Now I'm very glad you're serving me in place of the maid. For I've a pretty story to tell of something that happened earlier, and it'll interest you in a way. You remember that onion lad you rescued, back along – best part of a year ago? Take care, ma'am, and tip it quick or you'll spill some, and it's too precious to be spilt.'

'Deborah is cleverer at it than I.' Linnet commanded herself and tipped the liquor swiftly.

'That's right – well, he came to my office this morning; and there, if you'll believe it he happened on that fellow Fouguereau – or rather, Fouguereau happened up Fore Street in chase of him. And the lad gave him three of the prettiest rat-tats . . .'

Mr McPhail recounted the story, now and then withdrawing

his nose from the pewter. Linnet listened, feeling back with hot hands behind her for the door jamb to steady herself.

'But where is he?'

'The skipper? Well, by rights he should be in hospital at this moment. But that kind of animal – once at school, I read about a Greek fellow who could kill an ox at a blow. I didn't believe it then, and I believe it less now. Terrible liars, all the Greeks I've met.'

'No, no! I mean Amyot!'

Mr McPhail gazed at her searchingly over his pewter.

'I'm not a policeman. You mean the Breton lad? I didn't happen to look which way he went. Perhaps up river . . .'

The *Jolie Brise* sailed on the evening tide, the mate at the helm, the skipper below in the cabin. He lay stretched on his bunk, hot and flushed, his breathing heavy – the bottle of brandy on the table was untouched.

16

Rewards and fairies

The morrow of Amyot's flitting from Lantyan, Johnny Bosanko awoke with a bright sense of expectancy, and gradually realized desolation. There was no Mary in the opposite bed to chitter to in the dawn and conspire with. Mary had been taken to her mother's room (to sob herself asleep, still upbraiding). Amyot, their adored, had gone and so had his, Johnny's, little prospect of happiness.

But he was a child of pluck and resource. Since the skies had fallen all about him and Mary, it was up to him to act. He crept downstairs in the half-light to his mother's drawing-room, found a sheet of notepaper and wrote:

Dear Fairies,

Will you please find Amyot and bring him back. My sister Mary is disconsolate about his going, and I am feeling very poorly about her.

Dear frends, if you only new what a sikening bisness it is for both of us.

Yours respectfully

J. Bosanko

This letter he addressed:

To the Fairies
anywhere near Lantyan
Lostwithiel

and sent it up the kitchen chimney, as he was wont to send to Santa Claus at Christmas.

Then, when the household was up and about, Johnny coaxed his sister out to the woods to pick whortleberries. Their mother packed up some provender for them in a basket, and told them to bring it back filled. 'Fair exchange is no robbery, and there's nothing your father fancies more than whortleberry pie.' The weather was torrid, and in the woods they would be out of reach of sunstroke.

'But it's all spoilt now!' Mary lamented.

'You bet it ain't,' asserted Johnny stoutly.

'I don't suppose there's anything in the world so – so *callous* as boys.'

'If you mean that I'm unfeelin' you just wait till I find you something.'

'What?'

'Guess!'

'You're very mysterious this morning.'

'And you're very full of fine words. I heard Father say, one time, that fine words buttered no parsnips. Don't know what he meant, but it's something you oughtn't to get into the habit of.'

'Well, what is it you're promising to find?'

Johnny hesitated, but remembered Mary's once having said that fairies were an exploded something-or-other. It meant that she didn't believe in them, and he in turn had stared at her, asking himself if she were sickening for something-or-other.

'I don't *promise* to find anything. Suppose it's a curlew's nest—' He had blundered again. The rooks, about which Mr Tregentil was so curious, built in trees, their nests plain to see: but of all nests the curlew's is about the hardest to find. 'His call is everywhere, his nest nowhere.' Amyot had said once that he wouldn't be content until he had found a curlew's nest for them some day.

Mary choked back her grief. They started to pick whortle-berries – 'arts', Johnny called them.

When they had picked enough to fill a pie-dish, and had stained their own mouths in no small measure, 'just to sample 'em', as Johnny put it, they went down to the river shore by Woodget Pyll, and – so well as they could – washed their faces in the brackish water. Wandering up the Pyll they came on a ruined cottage, backed by a deserted orchard. They found a space within the nettle-grown enclosure, and there ate their meal. Johnny, though he could not of course have put any of the feeling into words, was conscious for the first time in his life of that joy which requires a background of sorrow. Mary and he had lost their beloved Amyot, and the world was desolate therefore. But, apart from the romance of their expeditions and the holiday meal, his heart swelled up with its first instinct of manhood. Mary had cried against his shoulder. It meant, though superior in age and knowledge, she was that funny thing, a girl: and it was up to him to comfort, protect: some precocious surmise of man's job in life. All the morning he had walked with a growing sense of self-importance. Also he had faith.

He said as Mary tidied up: 'Now I shouldn't be surprised if this was just the place to find a curlew's nest – on top of this wall, say.'

'You'll break your neck,' commanded Mary as he started to climb. 'I forbid you! And who's talking of curlews' eggs at this time of year?'

'I wasn't talking of curlews' eggs. I was talking of *nests*.'

He climbed to the top of the mud wall, and after a brief inspection slithered down. 'No nests there,' he announced.

'I knew there wouldn't be.'

'But there's a fine tree of summer apples up the hill – hidden

131

so you can't see it from the shore below. You just pack up and wait! They're either White Quarrendens or Polly Whetters by the looks.'

He was gone for the minute or so, and came back treading softly, mysteriously. But his face was radiant.

'I knew it all the time,' he announced in a whisper. 'I knew—'

'But – what is it?'

'It ain't any *it* at all. It's *him*. Guess, guess! No, I can't wait. It's Amyot.'

'Maybe, miss,' – Johnny even in his excitement could not forbear – 'maybe, next time, you won't be so cocksure about there being no such things as fairies.'

'What are you telling?'

'As it happens, I took and wrote to 'em. Wrote and posted the letter up the chimney, I did.'

'What? You've got a heat stroke! – Amyot?'

'Didn't I promise to find you something? Well, I climbed that tree to the second fork, but I wasn't really looking for the apples. I was really looking for Amyot while you were packing up, and now you'd best unpack again and see if there's anything left; for by the looks of him he's hungry. When he lifted his head out of the grass where he'd been sleeping—'

'But where is he?'

Johnny stepped around the ruinated doorway and called, 'Amyot!'

Three seconds later Amyot entered; worn, dishevelled, faint, just strong enough to fold Mary in his arms, staggering a little as she ran into them, rapturous.

'I heard your voices – then I tumbled down and slept, I think. Yet I heard your voices—'

'Amyot!'

They pressed the remains of their food on him. He ate ravenously, mechanically, with a sort of tender madness in his eyes, gazing all the while from the open doorway upon the peaceful woods and the river slowly ebbing at their feet.

'We will fetch you more. Oh, sit here while we run and tell mother!'

The children left him and ran. A pathway led up through the close sapling oaks, and almost at the top of the ascent they encountered Mrs Lewarne – Linnet. She too had a basket on her arm. Now Johnny might believe in fairies and suchlike, but to Mary Mrs Lewarne was a vision of all things desirable in grown-up life – beauty, grace, carriage, a sweet commanding voice, the true accent, clothes, and all delicate appanages of wealth – everything in short that her own little soul aspired after. And yet not too proud to carry a basket!

'Such a fine afternoon,' said this lovely lady. 'I thought you might be picnicking this way. And I thought—'

'Yes, yes – we have found Amyot! He is down in the cottage below. We were fetching food for him. Shall we tell mother we have met you?'

Linnet Lewarne paused. Then of a sudden she put her fingers to her lips. 'Wait,' she said. 'Let us consult, the three of us.'

She smiled mysteriously, and, beckoning to the children, led the way to a small dell beneath the oaks, and sat herself down, patting the ground on either side of her. The children followed her example, agog with curiosity.

'I take it you wish no harm to come to Amyot?' The question, flung at them so sharply, startled the children.

'Of course not,' said Mary, and Johnny added stoutly: 'I'd fight for him if need be, and if it's that French skipper that's after him you've only to tell Father . . .'

But Mrs Lewarne shook her head solemnly. 'That's just it,' she replied, 'your father could do nothing. It would be his duty to give Amyot up to the police. That French brute *did* come back, and Amyot fought him and knocked him down, which means he is liable to be arrested and charged with assault – and you know what that means.'

'Prison?' breathed Mary, turning pale.

Linnet nodded. 'Six months or more,' she said. 'Just think of it. Breaking stones or sewing mailbags, and he might try to escape, and then they'd send the bloodhounds after him.'

The children stared back at her in horror. 'Then what can we do?' cried Johnny. 'If the police find out he's here they'll come and put the handcuffs on him, and take him before the magistrate.'

'Exactly,' said Linnet. 'They must *not* find out. And that is why you cannot tell your father, or your mother, he is here. It would not be fair to them.'

Mary and Johnny looked grave. They had been brought up to bring all their troubles to their parents. If they had to return home and tell lies it would not do at all. Linnet Lewarne, watching their faces, guessed something of the turmoil within.

'I don't ask you to deceive them,' she said softly, 'just not to mention that you found him. They'll not question you – they think he's far away at sea by now, and if the police should come to Lantyan making inquiries – well, we can cross that hurdle when we come to it.'

Mary, with the memory of her birthday spoilt, was the first to succumb to temptation. 'No one's going to go looking for him here,' she declared, 'and it will be easy enough for Johnny and me to bring him bread and eggs, and bits we'll keep back from our own breakfast and dinner.'

'Oh, as to that,' announced a casual Linnet, 'I can always manage to come over. My movements won't be questioned. All I want to make sure of is that you two will not betray him.'

'Betray Amyot?' said Mary fiercely. 'Never in this world!'

'Cross our hearts and swear to die,' vowed Johnny.

They were rewarded by a brilliant smile, and then, more embarrassing, a kiss. The temptress rose to her feet.

'So,' she said, 'we are agreed. Amyot's hiding-place is a secret, known only to the three of us. And now supposing you both wander back to Lantyan – taking your time about it, very naturally – while I see to the replenishing of our – our pris-oner's larder?'

It was really something, so both the children decided after-wards, to share a secret with Mrs Lewarne. Being grown up and married meant, of course, that she knew what she was about. She would never have suggested the secret had it been wrong.

'We mustn't forget our whortleberries,' said Mary. 'There's a basketful down by the creek.'

'And Amyot can have a quarter of 'em,' added Johnny. 'If we gave him more than a quarter, Mother might be suspicious, or accuse us of eating 'em ourselves.'

They made their way back to the shore, but this time with stealth, exchanging conspiratorial glances, and all the glad delight with which they had discovered Amyot was now, somehow, over-shadowed by anxiety. A secret was exciting, but it was a burden too. Even the bright day had lost something of its splen-dour; mackerel clouds, foretelling change, were gathering in the west. A flock of black-headed gulls, harbingers of autumn, rose from the mudflats bounding the creek, and with a single cry, warning and shrill, skimmed the shore downstream to join the parent river. A solitary heron, disturbed in his quiet search for food, flapped his way after them.

There was no sign of Amyot, but Linnet, glancing towards the ruined cottage and its gaping doorway, smiled, and said:

'You'd best go now, children. I can take care of him.'

She made a brusque gesture with her hand, turning from them, and Johnny and Mary, sensing themselves dismissed, picked up the basket of whortleberries without a word, and made their way up towards the wood without a backward glance.

They had gone some few hundred yards when Johnny halted, saying: 'We've forgotten to give any of these to Amyot.' He pointed to the basket. 'Shall I run down with them?'

Mary shook her head. 'They don't want us,' she said briefly, 'nor the whortleberries neither.'

They plodded home in silence. The very wood encompassing them seemed heavy with the secret, and a brooding stillness filled the air. Down in the lush creek nothing stirred. The cottage, desolate now for so many months and years, slumbered away the afternoon, while now and again a robin uttered his plaintive song from the deserted orchard, whose apples would never more be gathered up and stored.

17

Doctor Carfax disturbed

D octor Carfax, having lunched late after completing his morning rounds, and with no message to take him out again before evening surgery, had promised himself an afternoon of comparative tranquillity in his garden; or, to be more precise, in the small wooden hut he had built for himself at the end of the path beside his well-kept lawn. The coming and going of vessels and pleasure boats, the whole life of a busy seaport, afforded endless amusement to anyone with a good spy-glass, while the fascinating world of his own dust heap, placed in the twenty-foot drop immediately beneath the wooden hut, and supplied with droppings from the gardener's fork, induced in Doctor Carfax food for philosophical thought, such as the temporary nature of all things vegetable and animal – animal in particular when the spy-glass revealed an encounter to the death between two stray earwigs and a colony of ants.

Therefore, on this particular July afternoon, the doctor was considerably irritated when Mona, the good woman who 'did' for him (Mrs Welch to everyone but the doctor himself) thrust her round face in at the window of the hut and announced the fact that the front-door bell had rung.

'Let it continue to do so,' replied her master in no uncertain fashion. 'The Roberts baby is not due for another two weeks, I bandaged Ned Varcoe's ankle for him this morning and left him comfortable, and Eliza Hocken has enough tablets for her indigestion to kill her, if she cares to do so – besides, if any of my patients want me they know to come to the surgery entrance. For goodness' sake, woman, go away and let me be.'

Mona stood her ground. The jangle of the front-door bell had disturbed her in the middle of her afternoon ablutions, as sacred to her as her master's meditation was to him, and the pair of them must suffer for it in consequence.

'It's not a bit of use ranting at me, doctor,' she said. 'By the time I'd got myself as far as the front door he'd walked inside, and I couldn't deny you was here seeing as he'd watched you go to the hut from over the garden wall.'

'Confound it!' Doctor Carfax exploded like a Fifth of November firework. 'Before I know where I am they'll be thrusting their miserable faces through the kitchen window and telling you to call me from my dinner. It's a mistake to have a house right on the street and a garden wall so low that a body can't seize two minutes' sunshine without all his patients knowing it. One of these days I'll decamp, I swear it, and build myself an eyrie on Bodmin moors and those who want physic can ride through the bogs to get it.'

'Yes, doctor,' sighed Mona, who had heard all this a dozen times before. 'Meanwhile he's let himself into the library without asking my leave, and if I know anything of his ways he's sitting in your own armchair from which I removed the covers this very morning, not expecting company.'

'The devil he is,' returned the doctor, with a further series of cracker-like detonations unsuited to the gentle ears of his housekeeper. 'And who, pray, is this ill-bred intruder, who thrusts his way into my private apartments which, as everyone knows, are sternly forbidden to all my patients?'

'It's Mr Lewarne, sir, from the Rose and Anchor.'

'*Lewarne?*'

Anger turned to astonishment, and the November squib to

a whistle of surprise. 'And what in the world would he want with me? He's not even one of my patients.'

'I couldn't say, doctor. He asked for you, walked straight past me and that was that. But I couldn't help noticing he looked uncommon whisht.'

'H'mph.'

Carfax had no great use for the landlord of the Rose and Anchor, who had bought his way into prominence through the years and was both bully and boaster combined. Indeed, if it was not for the fact that Lewarne kept an uncommonly good cellar, and had the good fortune to be married to the loveliest young woman in Troy, the doctor would have barely exchanged ordinary civilities with the fellow. True the cellar had been bequeathed by a predecessor, or rather sold with the establishment, and Linnet Constantine offered up as a bargain by an impecunious father – Lewarne had shown discernment in purchasing both – nevertheless there was something distasteful about a man who could not tell one vintage from another, possessing a wife with the bloom of maidenhood still upon her cheeks.

'So he did not state his business,' said the doctor thoughtfully, turning his back upon the dust heap and the harbour, and setting off down the garden path, a sudden curiosity overcoming his desire for philosophy and solitude. 'Well, we shall soon see,' – this remark to himself rather than to Mona. But the good woman trotting behind his elbow took it for conversation, and, being endowed with a certain amount of perspicacity as was only befitting in a housekeeper to a medical man, she seized the opportunity of suggesting that Mrs Lewarne was expecting at last.

The 'at last', reflected the doctor, was a hint to the effect that Troy gossip had already busied itself with Nature's delay in providing the patter of little feet under the roof of the Rose and Anchor, which delay would soon be translated, if he judged his Trojans correctly, into whispers of open breach between man and wife. Wisely he made no comment, but let the suggestion go. Then rounding the wall of his house, he climbed the few garden steps, and entered his library by the bow window, with the intention of startling his man and throwing the daylight upon his face at the same time. His intention succeeded. Mark Lewarne lumbered to his feet without the time to compose his features had he been able to do so. Mona was right. The man was indeed 'whisht'. A sorry spectacle, with head poking between slack shoulders, sick-dog eyes and hands clamped awkwardly to his sides.

'Well, Lewarne, and what can I do for you? I take it you're not ill, or you'd have found out my surgery hour is from six to seven.'

Doctor Carfax was brusque. Courtesy was hardly due to a fellow who plainly, by his behaviour, had no manners himself.

The landlord shuffled his feet. 'I'm sorry to disturb you, doctor,' he said, 'but it's a personal matter, nothing to do with my health, that is, nothing directly, though what with worry and loss of sleep I shouldn't wonder if I'd dropped a bit of weight.'

'No harm if you did,' snapped the doctor. 'More men of your age die of overweight than from any other cause. Come to the point, man. What's the trouble?'

Mark Lewarne looked first at the ceiling, then at the floor, then finally, in despair, at his interlocutor.

'It's the wife,' he said; 'she's breaking my heart.'

Doctor Carfax moved from the bow window to the hearth-rug, and standing with his back to the empty grate fumbled in his coat pocket for pipe and matches. This gave himself time to think, and the unwelcome intruder an opportunity to recover equilibrium. 'Many years ago,' he said at last, between puffs, the pipe in question being slow to draw, 'I wrote a paper, being a student at the time, on the nature and function of the heart. I can assure you, and my opinion is backed by the highest medical authority, that the organ in question is so constructed that the possibility of its ever breaking can be discounted. Or, if you happen to be a gambler, the odds would be a million to one against such an eventuality.'

This statement appeared in no way to reassure the landlord.

'That's as may be, doctor,' he replied doggedly. 'I'm not talking of the medical side of it. I'm thinking of the mental stress. I'm at the end of my tether.'

Doctor Carfax sighed. The afternoon meditation, spy-glass in hand, seemed infinitely remote. He was used to confidences, and this one had all the appearance of becoming prolonged.

'Sit down then,' he said, pushing forward a chair, 'and if you want to smoke by all means do so.'

Mark Lewarne shook his head. He lowered himself into the proffered chair, and stared earnestly at the doctor.

'She'll hearken to you,' he declared, 'that's what I tell myself. She thinks the world of your opinion. And a word from you as to her conduct would set all to rights. She'd never dare go against it.' He slapped his knee in emphasis, and the listener, unperturbed, continued to puff at his pipe.

'Are you complaining of your wife's behaviour,' asked the doctor, 'or merely that she is following some course of treatment that might prove injurious to her health?'

It took the landlord a moment or two for the question to penetrate. 'Her health's all right,' he answered, frowning. 'Never looked better. It's the way she treats her husband goes against nature.'

'Ah!' It was not the first time, by any manner of means, that Troy's senior medical man had heard similar complaints from irate or disappointed bridegrooms, and the solution was not always easy to find, delicacy and tact being essential to the matter. 'She sends you packing, I take it, at those times when you most desire to pay her compliments?'

'Packing?' echoed the landlord. 'I tell you, doctor, she'll have none of me. She'll hardly speak to me civil. And haven't I given her the best in the world, a good home, gowns, and fal-lals, anything she cares to ask for? I don't know another woman in Troy enjoys such a position. And all I get for it is cold looks and a sarcastic tongue. Not only alone, mind, but before company. Soon I'll be the laughing-stock of all my customers, and won't dare show my face in my own bar.'

The discomfiture of the man was such that tears were starting up in his eyes which he had not the pride to wipe away. Doctor Carfax considered his reply, and, shifting position, stared out through the bow window, from where he could see the ferryman, his boat loaded, plying his industrious way to the opposite shore. Linnet Lewarne was at fault no doubt. She had no business to treat her man thus, whether alone or before the world. She had made her vows and must put a good face on it. As to her husband, the fellow was a fool in the first place to marry a girl young enough to be his granddaughter.

'Now listen here, Lewarne,' he began, 'I've never played go-between yet and I don't intend to begin now. Get that into your head right away. What goes wrong with you and your wife is your business, not mine. I may have brought her into the world, and seen her through a number of childish complaints, but that doesn't put me in the place of father confessor. If you want me to diagnose your trouble I can do so but you won't thank me for it. It's this: there's more than forty years between you.' Having delivered his verdict the doctor proceeded to relight his pipe, which had gone out. The land-lord continued to stare at him beseechingly.

'I've told myself that a score of times,' he said, 'but she was as sweet as honey when we were first wed. I thought myself the luckiest man alive. No, I tell you what it is, doctor' – Lewarne leaned forward and lowered his voice – 'there's someone else, and if I knew who it was I'd wring his neck.'

So that was the lay, mused Carfax. Well, well . . . it only proved his diagnosis the more correct. 'And what do you expect me to do about it?' he said aloud. 'Gain your wife's confidence and then betray it to you?'

'No, doctor,' returned the landlord, 'I've others who'll do that for me. I want you to put the fear of the Almighty into her, so she sees the error of her ways before it's too late.'

'God bless my soul!' Carfax rose from his chair in disgust. What a nerve the fellow had! To thrust his way into the house unasked, not even one of his patients, and then demand that he, Carfax, should turn preacher and reprimand an erring young woman with whom, if the truth were known, he had every sympathy. It was too much.

'I'm sorry, Lewarne,' he said shortly, 'but it's none of my business. Your wife is old enough to know what she's about, and if she misbehaves you must deal with her yourself. Good afternoon.' He walked pointedly towards the door and threw it open. The landlord of the Rose and Anchor watched him in dismay.

'But how am I to handle it, doctor?' he cried. 'She swears one thing and acts another. She's been out walking in the moonlight with some chap or other – my own barman declares he spotted her last night, and me out at a Masonic dinner, but when I taxed her with it this morning she laughed me to scorn.'

Carfax knit his brows. A husband who listened to gossip got what he deserved. So that was how Ned Varcoe came by his twisted ankle; playing spy on his employer's wife. Lewarne, unable to ignore the open door, rose to his feet reluctantly. 'Very well, doctor,' he said, 'if you won't speak to her I can't make you. But her quick tongue wouldn't get the better of you as it does me. "Oh yes," she tells me, "of course I've lain in another man's arms. I fell off the hay wagon at Mr Bosanko's and if the farm-hand hadn't caught me I'd have broken my ribs, so I can't swear no one's touched me but you can I?" And with that she laughs and shuts the door in my face. How would you answer that one, doctor?'

'Good afternoon, Lewarne,' repeated Carfax grimly. The landlord hesitated, half offered his hand, then withdrew it again. A moment later he was through the hall and out of the house, and the doctor, uttering a 'Pheugh!' of disgust, threw open the bow window of his library to cleanse the air. He retraced his steps towards the garden hut, but already in the brief time he had absented himself the sky had grown overcast, and his mind, disturbed by the unwelcome visitor, could no longer drift into pleasant reverie. 'Oh, damnation,' he muttered in irritation, brushing off from his spy-glass a spider which, on any other occasion than the present, would have called for interested investigation. 'Linnet Lewarne must manage her own affairs.' Nevertheless the landlord's parting speech had recalled a certain incident in the hayfield, when Linnet as Harvest Queen had tumbled so suddenly from the wagon, and might in truth have had a nasty fall but for the resourceful arms of the Breton lad who stood near by.

'Intent or accident, it was neatly done,' remembered the doctor, and then on the instant he stood motionless, struck by a sudden memory. Had not he described just such a tumble a year ago to poor Ledru? Did not a queen, centuries past, cover her guilt in the selfsame fashion?

'Well, I'll be—' The doctor, cutting short his own condemnation to perdition, turned on his heel and hurried towards the house. It was only when he reached his bookshelves that he remembered that all the volumes relating to the incident in question, which certainly never took place on any hay wagon, had been in the care of Mr Tregentil of Penquite for several months.

It was obvious what had happened. Tregentil, like other patients who found a tonic to their liking, had exceeded his dose of research into manor rolls and tithe maps, by perusing the Tristan legends, and what was more unethical still, must have related them afterwards with gusto to his innocent pupil. *Robinson Crusoe* was one thing, twelfth-century couplets were another. It would serve Tregentil right if he was put on to a different course of treatment altogether. A fish diet, with milk and soda to take the place of Graves. Be that as it may, the English lessons must be nipped in the bud before further translation by

144

master and pupil was thoughtlessly discussed in the presence of the romantic-minded hostess of the Rose and Anchor. As he proceeded up the hill towards the stables Doctor Carfax wondered who would be the more put out by this sudden unexpected outing at three o'clock of the afternoon following upon a busy morning – himself or his mare Cassandra.

18

Duet of passion

Thou art the grave where buried love doth live,
Hung with the trophies of my lovers gone.

'Tell me; tell me the first moment when—'
'When . . . ?'
'When it first happened to you – the very first.'
Asked the inevitable question, old as love itself, or but a few minutes younger, Amyot lay back, his shoulders crushing the bracken, his eyes half closed, watching the spirals of a lark that sang in the dazzle above. The bird dropped.

'There was no first – oh yes, there was! But a thrill only, when you touched me, that day, sponging my hurt back.'

'Yes, yes.' Linnet leaned over him and nodded. She took the hand he was passing over his forehead and drew it to her: but he pulled it away.

'Let me think . . . and then afterwards, when Monsieur Ledru pointed from the ridge, something seemed to break here.' He touched his forehead again. 'It was just – how shall I say? – just as if someone had broken a bottle of essences: but the scent was all of the thyme our feet had been treading, and there was music with it, and a touch on my face and hair just as if fingers were playing the music. And with that the word sprang out of me.'

'What word?'

'A name. I had never heard it before.'

'Mine?'

'No, not yours. The name of a place: of the very woods above us. Lantyan.'

Linnet was silent for a while. 'That was a wonder,' she mused, scarcely aloud: and then quite aloud she said: 'But I can beat it. Before ever I saw you, a minute or so before, I heard a name spoken; and it was yours – Amyot. It floated in by an old window I had just opened. No: now that I come to think it did not float – it twanged rather, it throbbed, just like one of those chords you used to pluck from your fiddle. My heart throbbed to it, and sooner than you – yes, sooner than you – I awoke and was alive; yes, sooner than my fingers ever touched you, over the sponge – sooner than ever I saw you. But tell me what happened next.'

'What happened was that the moment the word sprang out of me I saw a carriage coming down the road at speed; and I was running and screaming. Such a scream too! I did not know it for my own voice.'

'No! That is because in that moment you were born again: born from a boy into a man. Of a sudden, eh? – you could master horses.'

'I never shall know how that happened. You see, I was bred up on a tiny island where there was never a horse: and across the traject – how do you call it? – the ferry over from Loctudy – but a few poor beasts that brought down our fish carts.'

'Yet in that instant you knew yourself a master of horses!'

'I did not know it – I just screamed. But I will tell you that since then I have had a command over horses – I who had never bestridden one. I doubt if even now I could ride well a horse of any mettle. But I could command one, I know. I have only to whisper. Mr Bosanko will tell you. It is all a puzzle to me.'

They were silent for a moment, then Linnet turned again to her lover. 'Listen. Lay your head back here in the nook of my arm and listen, while I tell you in my turn. When that carriage was swaying and the mad pair plunging right on top of you I was expecting death. I caught at the rail before me and held it: I was being shot out of all things known to me into nothingness. I heard your scream: I saw a figure – you – standing black against the shine of the road. They say that in the last instant of drowning all kinds of memories crowd into the mind. Amyot, look up and answer. Have you ever thought that you and I have lived before – perhaps many times, to be born again, to kiss, to drain one another's heart out through the lips, to possess, to die? Think, my love, and help me if you can.'

'I cannot think, Linnet, with my head on your breast. I wonder only, and dream.'

'Dream a little while only; for I have much to tell you – much more. You remember that afterwards you lay in the road with me bending over and trying to awake you, the blood from my cut eyebrow dripping on you, faster even than the rain could wash it away – and over us the cloud as it pelted was drawn like a cloth – and I was leaning over you, touching you, taking your head between my hands. But actually – yes, to me, actually – I was sitting far above, as in a tier of a theatre; and you lying naked, breast and thighs all stark, laid bare under the shadow of that curtain. It was on sand you lay stretched – bloodied sand. Then it was over, and we were back again at Castle Dor, and Doctor Carfax was coming to bandage you. But that night I dreamt of you, and woke all of a sudden in a fever. I dreamt I was crossing to you across a bridge of burning plates, and somehow the way was barred to me. I could not reach you. I believe I cried out in my anguish – then I was wide awake, with an old man alongside me, and his feet were the burning plates.'

She bent over him, touching his lips, and he drew her beside him, gazing in wonder at her troubled eyes, marvelling that she should suffer for his sake in dreams.

'It was not so with me,' he said. 'I slept like one dead, and have done so ever since that day. But waking you are with me: no matter where I am or what I am doing, there is no one but you, smiling at me, as you did across the fire. We drank together, do you remember, and I broke my fiddle across my knee, knowing that from henceforth I had all the strength of all the world and that it came in some mysterious way from you alone. No man, no woman, no beast, has any power over me – I sensed that when I hit Fouguereau – it's as though when we drank something magic had entered into me, and because of the magic we live, you and I. Without it we'd be just common mortals, blind and deaf and dumb. Kiss me again, Linnet.'

'I assure you I did not deviate from your instructions in the very slightest,' said the approaching voice of Mr Tregentil from the Penquite side of the creek, and its tone was high-pitched and querulous. 'I kept most faithfully to *Robinson Crusoe*, and it would never have entered my head to read your notes to the young man, or the volumes you lent me, far less discuss their contents. Besides, he would not have had the wit to understand them.' He was plainly addressing Doctor Carfax. 'As to the young woman you mention, I have barely addressed two words to her. In all events your prescription has come to an end, as I understand Amyot has been discharged by Bosanko and sailed from Troy this very morning; but I hardly see why that should be a reason for you to put me on boiled fish and milk and soda. It is all very annoying, and just when the rooks and jack-daws are so busy congregating and I was counting on him to separate, if he could, their food-searching activities. Mind your feet, there is a sudden dip here, where we cross the stream. Ah! Mistress Lewarne!'

Amyot had dived away, deep into the undergrowth. Linnet sat on a knoll of the clearing, pale, collected, defiant, her arms carelessly enfolding her drawn-up knees.

19

An encounter at Penquite

'Now did I not know Tregentil to be morally and consti-
tutionally incapable of carrying on a clandestine love
affair', thought Doctor Carfax, 'I would say to myself
I had caught him red-handed.' For indeed the owner of Penquite
had turned remarkably pink for a man suffering with a long-
standing liver complaint, and the lovely young hostess of the
Rose and Anchor was far enough distant from her duties in
the Troy hostelry as to suggest she had come to this remote
spot for a deliberate purpose: indeed anyone with a grain of
perception would think it an assignation.

Doctor Carfax had driven an irate Cassandra the two and a
half miles to Penquite at a steady jog-trot, and on arriving at
the house had been told that its owner was out walking in the
grounds, and had last been seen making his way downhill towards
Woodget Pyll. The doctor left horse and trap in the care of
Dingle the coachman, and set off on foot in pursuit of his patient,
whom he finally discovered at the bottom of the field about to
cross over from the path to the head of the creek itself.

Mr Tregentil, supposing his visitor had ambled over for a
pleasant afternoon's bird-watching, followed by a cup of tea,
was surprised and considerably put out to find himself the
instant object of attack, for the medical man was not one to
mince matters; and, outraged, his patient had only just finished

declaring his innocence, when they had the ill fortune to stumble upon the very young woman whose name had been both upon their lips. To be accused of showing the doctor's private notes and papers to the lad from Brittany was bad enough, but to have the accusation followed up with the suggestion that he had discussed the reprehensible amours of the long-dead Tristan and Iseult with the wife of the innkeeper was an insult to Mr Tregentil's sense of dignity. Small wonder he changed colour, and, with the doctor's eye upon him, proceeded to bluster his way out of the dilemma.

'What a pleasant surprise! So unusual to find anyone in Woodget Pyll – everything very overgrown – so many nettles and brambles. But the blackberries are profuse this year – I see you have brought a basket, doubtless you intend to fill it directly. Well, well, who would have thought it? I was only saying to Doctor Carfax ...' Mr Tregentil left the remainder of his sentence unfinished, fearing that whatever he said now would only serve to incriminate him the further, and with a fine show of action he began to hack at the undergrowth with his stick. This enabled him to turn his back upon both Carfax and the young woman, so sparing his blushes and atoning for centuries of neglect at the same time.

Linnet Lewarne, with a fine disdain, looked away from Doctor Carfax's patient, slashing with such sudden fury at the offending brambles to the tall figure of Doctor Carfax himself, whose quizzical expression reminded her only too plainly of the time long since when she had endeavoured to hide from him a childish rash, which rash – so she insisted – came from eating strawberries, though both knew well she had developed measles.

'A fine afternoon for meditation,' said the doctor, glancing about him, 'and nothing like a muddied creek for giving man, or woman for that matter, a sense of proportion. The ebbing tide uncovers the waste places, and betrays to view all the hidden ugly things one believed forgotten and dead. I see no boat and no horse; therefore you came on foot. You enjoy walking?'

Linnet understood the inflection in his voice. If it was not war it was something near it. Doctor Carfax was suspicious — but of what?

'As a matter of fact I do,' she replied coolly, 'and having called on the folk who live at my birth-place, the forge at Castle Dor, I decided to come on here. As you say, it's a fine afternoon for meditation.'

'Though likely to rain,' observed her antagonist, 'before night-fall. In which case you would do well to walk back with us to Penquite, and accept a lift in my trap.'

Linnet hesitated, glancing almost imperceptibly at the tumble-down cottage in the background, and the doctor, whose keen eyes missed nothing, wondered why the solitude of the almost ruined dwelling, charming though it was in its romantic setting, should be preferred to his company in the dogcart. Possibly he was right after all, and although Tregentil could be counted out of the business, she had come here to meet another.

Linnet must have guessed his thought, for slowly she rose to her feet, picked up her basket, and brushed the leaves from her gown. 'Thank you,' she said, casually enough, and then, raising her voice, possibly to attract the attention of Mr Tregentil still labouring amongst the brambles: 'Perhaps it might be prudent to do as you suggest and drive home with you to Troy. I can pick my blackberries tomorrow if it's fine.'

So saying she turned to the stepping-stone at the head of the stream, and her voice had certainly carried, for Mr Tregentil, darting a look of discomfiture at the doctor, emerged from the tangle of nettles and thorn that encompassed him, and pointed the way through the hedge to his own domain.

'Have a care,' he said nervously. 'The bank is somewhat steep; pray take my arm.' But Linnet was up and into the field before Mr Tregentil could do anything to help her. She waited for both men to join her and then, ignoring the doctor, flashed upon his patient a smile both warm and inviting.

'How remote you are here from all the trials and turmoil of

the world!' she exclaimed. 'I don't wonder you seldom move beyond it. But are you never lonely?'

Such waves of sympathy, reflected the doctor, would melt the heart of the firmest misogynist on earth, and what the devil was she about, wasting her powers on Tregentil unless there was some purpose behind it?

'Lonely! Dear me, no – that is to say, very seldom. I have so many hobbies,' flustered Carfax's patient, uncertain whether to lead the way up to the field or hover beside his unexpected visitor, unaccustomed as he was to entertaining members of the opposite sex, with the exception of Mrs Bosanko. 'What with bird-watching, butterflies and bookbinding – three Bs I have you note – and now these papers of Doctor Carfax's to sort – at least, that is beside the point – in other words, I am fully occupied from morning till night.'

Mr Tregentil glanced anxiously at the doctor, realizing that he had, from excess of nerves, touched upon the subject most taboo; indeed it was on account of the papers that his medical adviser had descended upon him in wrath scarce ten minutes ago. Carfax said nothing, nor could anything be learnt from his expression, Mistress Lewarne, on the contrary, was as quick on the scent as a greyhound after a hare.

'Sorting papers?' she asked. 'There is nothing I like so well. We used to have many such at home in the old days, which might have been destroyed but for me. If you are in need of help, Mr Tregentil, I should be delighted to offer myself as assistant librarian, for to tell you the truth time often hangs heavy on my hands at the Rose and Anchor, especially during the afternoons when the bar is closed.'

A somewhat unmelodious sound from the rear informed both Linnet and her host that Doctor Carfax was humming a tune under his breath, a habit of his when deep in thought, and frequently indulged in when the condition of a patient required a drastic change in treatment. Mr Tregentil recognised the signal, and with all the horror of a milk-and-soda diet threatening his immediate future, he struggled manfully to combine firmness with courtesy.

'Most kind of you – most kind – I'm overwhelmed,' he faltered, his already green complexion turning a shade more olive. 'The fact is I have my own system of filing – years of experience in India – no one but myself would understand it.' Baring his long teeth in what he vainly imagined was a smile of apology, Doctor Carfax's patient had all the appearance of a gaunt wolf at bay.

'Besides,' he added, 'the bees may swarm. They sometimes do, you know, as late as August – granted a sunny spell. If the bees swarm I drop everything else and run – and it would not be safe. Even the people at the lodge shut themselves indoors on such an occasion.'

The humming from the rear had turned to a snort, and Linnet, looking over her shoulder suspiciously at the man who had brought her into the world, observed that he was having trouble with his bootlace and was bending to tie it. When he raised his head she caught his eye. It was sufficiently suffused as to suggest a paroxysm of mirth unbecoming in a man of his years.

'We used to keep bees too,' she said steadily, without taking her eyes off the doctor. 'I still have my veil and gloves at the Rose and Anchor. My father was stung several times, but I – never.'

Mr Tregentil led the way in silence up the field, and his two visitors had difficulty in keeping pace with his loping stride. He had but one thought in his head, which was to bid his adieux to Mistress Lewarne before she could trick him into an invitation inside his house. If she should achieve that, in front of the doctor, he would be put on prison fare for at least three weeks. When they arrived before the somewhat forbidding façade of Penquite, the superb view from its main rooms some- what spoiled by the fact that they faced due north and were perpetually in shadow, Mr Tregentil ignored the open window of his drawing-room, which might have suggested the comforts of easy chairs and a table laid for tea, and hurried to the front drive where Cassandra patiently awaited her master. His visitors had perforce to follow him.

'Thank you, Dingle, thank you,' said the master of Penquite to his coachman. 'Doctor Carfax and Mistress Lewarne are about to leave. Indeed' – turning to the latter – 'we are likely to have rain within the hour, setting in for the evening – it would be best to lose no time at all.' And giving his hand to Linnet she had no choice but to accept it and mount the doctor's dogcart.

'Not so fast, Tregentil,' called his medical adviser. 'There is the little matter of your treatment to discuss. I am thinking of changing the prescription.'

'Of course, of course!' The patient looked wildly about him. 'Mrs Lewarne will excuse us, I'm sure, for a few minutes – my wretched health . . .' And with lowered head Mr Tregentil charged his front porch as though a swarm of his own bees were after him. Once in the safety of his study he collapsed in the first chair to hand, groaning, his hand to his heart. 'You see how it is,' he gasped, 'I am really most unwell. Your accusations have upset me, and that young woman had no business to be lurking down in the Pyll picking blackberries – I assure you I was astonished to find her there. As to helping me sort the books and papers – what an appalling prospect; I am most unnerved – please, Carfax, take her away from here at once before she causes further trouble.'

Doctor Carfax paid no attention to his patient. He had crossed over to the table on which were piled a number of papers and documents along with a heap of assorted Celtic and Breton journals. He picked up one at random and began to turn the pages.

'H'm,' he observed, 'Penquite, Penquoit, the early form of Pencoose, or "the end of the wood", as used in east Cornwall. There must be at least a dozen places so named between here and Truro. This could well be the boundary of a forest stretching in those days from the River Fal to the River Fowey. What do my notes from Béroul tell me? That the lovers hid in the forest of Morroi or Morrois – yes, I dare say, and the old name of St Clements on the Fal was Moresk. Rather far-fetched possibly to have one forest Morroi covering eight and twenty miles, terminating here – I wonder.'

His patient, seizing upon the fact that the doctor's mind had strayed and was no longer bent upon milk and soda and the loathed boiled fish, forgot the pain in his side and leapt to his feet.

'Excuse me, Carfax,' he interrupted, 'I took the liberty of noting down the discrepancies in the various journals here. There is much confusion between Welsh, Cornish and Breton names, and as to the Tristan and Iseult story in which, from your papers, you appear interested, why, there are so many versions that it is quite impossible to disentangle one from the other! I admit myself baffled.'

Doctor Carfax laid down the volume he had taken from the table, and felt in his breast pocket for the dreaded notebook and pencil.

'You are not the first,' he said drily. 'The puzzle has led men astray for centuries. Let me see now, nerves on edge, shortness of breath, twenty-four hours in bed will do you no harm, and we'll forget about the fish. A wing of chicken won't hurt you and a lemon soufflé – can your cook make a soufflé? No coffee, of course, drink what you please, but to take your mind off your own ills I suggest you carry some of this paraphernalia upstairs; write out for me the main differences between Gottfried von Strassburg's version of Thomas's poem and the poem by Béroul; it's all there, somewhere in my notes.'

'Yes, yes, anything you say,' agreed the patient eagerly. 'You mentioned the forest of Morrois just now, Béroul has the forest, but in Gottfried's version the queen and her paramour hide in a cave in mountainous country, Wales in all probability, and this follows upon the lady's shameful oath—'

'I know, I know.' The doctor sounded impatient. He glanced at his watch. 'Note down as many discrepancies as you please, but spare me your own deductions.' He moved towards the hall. 'In one version – I forget which – Tristan slays a giant,' he added, 'and in the other it is the dwarf who gets killed – Frocin, if I remember rightly.'

Mr Tregentil, who could hardly believe he had escaped the dreaded régime, was once again master of himself and delighted to speed the parting guests. He was also proud of his new-found knowledge.

'Béroul called the dwarf Frocin,' he announced, as they crossed the drive to the dogcart, 'but in the Gottfried version the name was Melot. Obviously one or the other is at fault. One thing is certain enough. The lovers were seen walking together by moonlight, and' – he lowered his high-pitched voice a little late – 'the man who betrayed them to the lady's husband was a servant. —Mistress Lewarne, I fear we have kept you waiting.'

The eyes that had looked upon him too warmly before were now cold as ice. 'It's of no consequence,' she said, staring straight ahead. Doctor Carfax mounted beside her and took the reins.

'Don't forget, Tregentil,' he said. 'Bed for twenty-four hours. Good-day to you.'

Cassandra was off and away down the drive as though a whip had been laid about her ears, the coachman having not as much as offered her a lump of sugar. It was not until they had turned into the road, and had left all gates behind them, that Doctor Carfax realized his companion was unusually silent. Glancing down at her he saw that her face was pale, her lips set.

'Is anything the matter?' he asked.

It was then that Linnet turned upon him, her eyes blazing. 'How dare you discuss my private affairs with Mr Tregentil?' she said.

20

Thunder at Castle Dor

Doctor Carfax, whose unorthodox methods of treatment so often shocked his patients into instant cure, especially when they were malingerers, was now hoist with his own petard, and indeed too shaken by surprise with the sudden attack made upon him to realize that Cassandra, irritated by her long wait without sustenance before the front door of Penquite, had taken the bit between her teeth and, instead of turning into the lane, as she should have done, thus bringing her master and passenger home by the direct though more laborious route, was bolting along the road to Castle Dor. She did this with deliberate intent, or, as the old fellow who cleaned out her stable would have said, 'a-purpose', for she knew full well that the blacksmith at the top of the hill kept a store of juicy apples for such animals as herself who might be in need of attention, and whose afternoon had been unwarrantably tedious.

It was some few minutes before her master had her in hand again, but by that time the damage was done; the unmistakable 'clip-clop' of her near fore suggested she was about to cast a shoe. The doctor swore under his breath. 'Nothing for it but to go to the forge,' he said grimly. 'If I apologize for that exhibition of temper on the part of my animal, perhaps you will have the decency to do the same, and retract the remark you made before Cassandra bolted.'

Linnet Lewarne continued to stare in front of her. Cassandra's gallop had brought the colour back to her cheeks but had in no way disturbed her composure.

'I retract nothing,' she said, 'unless you explain.'

'Explain!' thundered the doctor in a voice calculated to make Cassandra lay back her ears. 'Explain what, in Heaven's name?'

'Oh, come, doctor,' said Linnet, with a half-shrug, 'it's no use pretending you don't know what I mean. I could not help over-hearing Mr Tregentil just now, although he tried to lower his voice. I knew Troy was a hot-bed for gossip but I must admit surprise and disgust to learn my own affairs are discussed so freely out in the country here.'

Doctor Carfax reined Cassandra to a slow walk, and for a moment or two he did not reply. Tregentil surely had been murmuring something about the dwarf Frocin, or Melot, or whatever he was named, he who had betrayed Iseult and Tristan to the king; and so far had both his patient and himself been from present-day matters and Troy chit-chat that they had not once mentioned a living soul. Unless . . .

'I suppose you were called in to look at Ned Varcoe's twisted ankle,' continued Linnet with scorn, 'and he had the impudence to tell you, as he did my husband, that he saw me walking at midnight under the stars. The next time that hunch-backed bartender chooses to play the spy when it is not his business, I trust he breaks his neck and not his ankle.'

The doctor, a man of equanimity of temperament unless crossed, and not one to experience swift changes of mood, was aware of sudden chill. He was reminded of a time, some years past, in his younger days, when he had made a grave error in diagnosis. The patient, a seaman, much addicted to the bottle, with all his customary symptoms after a 'booze' ashore, had been bidden somewhat curtly to nurse his raging head and sleep it off. It turned out he had a tumour on the brain, and the best surgeon in Plymouth had not saved him. Carfax now found himself troubled with the same sense of consternation and dismay that he knew then. But there all resemblance ceased. What he appeared to be stumbling upon now had no name in the world of medicine, but belonged surely to some other dimension outside time itself, and as a scientist he refused to credit it.

'Yes, the cap fits,' he said at last. 'I was a fool not to see it in the first place. Ned Varcoe has been misshapen from birth, wretched fellow, and never grew after he was ten years old. No doubt that makes him bitter.'

The hostess of the Rose and Anchor drew her shawl more closely around her. Perhaps she too felt the chill air descending upon them from Castle Dor.

'So you admit it?' she asked. 'You were breaking all your professional rules and discussing the incident with a patient?'

Doctor Carfax flicked the reins gently. Cassandra needed as tactful handling as Linnet herself.

'My dear,' he replied, 'if I told you that Tregentil and I were talking of a queen who has been dead some thirteen hundred years, probably longer, you would not believe me. Oh yes, I was guilty of unprofessional conduct all right. We were most certainly discussing your affairs. But I assure you I did not hear the tale from Ned Varcoe.'

'Who then?' flared Linnet.

The doctor considered. It has been a misunderstanding, of course, that had brought him driving post-haste to Penquite in the first place. Possibly the time had come to turn the tables on the young woman who had caused the misunderstanding.

'Do you remember the harvest tea at Lantyan?' he ventured.

'Very well,' she answered.

'Then perhaps you will tell me why you fell so deliberately from the wagon into the arms of that Breton lad of Bosanko's?' returned the doctor.

Touché. The silence that followed proved the shaft had struck home. They were nearing the top of the hill as the doctor asked his question, and Cassandra quickened her pace, recognizing familiar landmarks. The forge lay to the right, and the dogcart

161

was alongside it before Linnet had time to frame an answer. The blacksmith was standing outside the forge, as it so happened, looking along the road towards Lostwithiel after a departing cob newly shod before next marketday, and at the sound of the doctor's wheels he turned, and lifting his hand in greeting came to meet the trap.

'Good day to you, doctor. Cassandra in trouble, I see. Steady then, there'll be an apple for 'ee direckly. Good day, ma'am. You'm a proper stranger. I was only saying to missus yesterday it's some time since we saw Mrs Lewarne. The pity of it she's gone to St Austell today and won't be back till evening.'

The doctor was careful not to look at his companion while she murmured her regrets. The assertion that she had already called at the forge that afternoon was therefore untrue. Oh, what a tangled web we weave, he mused, as he helped Linnet descend from the dogcart, and watched while the blacksmith and his lad led a willing Cassandra inside the forge for attention.

Linnet followed them, and stood for a moment or two in the doorway, her eyes drawn to the sudden flare of the fire, and father and son in their leather aprons moving in the half-light like strange demons, the sparks almost singeing their hair. Even Cassandra, contentedly munching her first apple, had become a ghost horse in this setting, her harness the trappings of a palfrey, and the ring of metal and the acrid smell suggested violence; not the homely atmosphere of a blacksmith's shop.

Doctor Carfax moved forward to chat with the smith, who already had Cassandra's hoof tucked in position and was removing the offending shoe, when glancing over his shoulder he perceived that the shadow had gone from the entrance to the smithy. Linnet had vanished.

The doctor muttered an excuse to the blacksmith and strode out into the road. His companion was not there. He looked to right and to left and called aloud, but had no answer. He went to the back premises of the forge in case she had decided to wait within, but there was no sign of her.

'Now what the devil!' he said to himself, looking upward at the sky, for the clouds were gathering fast, and here on the high ground the wind was already rustling the hedgerow. Away to the west the white peaks of the china-clay district were hidden in a pall of rain.

'She's out yonder!' The grimy face of one of the blacksmith's brood stared at him from an upper window of the forge. The child pointed across a field. 'I seen her this instant, where the pigs are to.'

Swearing in irritation, the doctor opened a gate and proceeded to tramp in the direction signalled by the grinning urchin at the window. He had no stick, and there was little Carfax disliked more than having to pick his way across country, especially on uneven ground, without his favourite cherry-wood. God damn it, there she was, some few hundred yards ahead of him, making for the tangled undergrowth of the old camp. He put his hands to his mouth and shouted: 'Linnet – Linnet Lewarne, come back!'

She had the decency to turn and stare, but instead of obeying the command waved him on. Then the rain began to fall: the first few drops a warning only, but swiftly gathering momentum, coming thick and fast from a travelling cloud that trailed a ragged hem beneath it, smoky black. A single clap of thunder split the air. Instinct bade Carfax run. Cursing and stumbling, half blinded by the rain, he caught up with Linnet as she flung herself, breath-less, into the outer ditch of the old encampment, huddling for shelter against the dipping holly whose straggling branches trailed in a host of brambles. Carfax bent to protect her, his arms outstretched, and they crouched there together in the ditch while the rain fell slantways, blotting out the countryside.

'What made you do it?' cried the doctor. 'Are you out of your mind?'

She looked up at him, laughing, face and hair streaming wet with the rain. 'I've been out of my mind since I jumped from the hay wagon,' she said, 'and I don't care if you know it. You always saw too much anyway.'

A second clap of thunder sounded to the left of them, and Linnet, instead of diving instinctively into the spreading mass of holly, moved forward so that the teeming rain fell on her upturned face.

'May it flood his cellars and drown the pair of them,' she said, 'then I'd be quit of trouble in all conscience.'

Whether she addressed the remark to him he could not tell, but her sudden rage matched the weather. Dragging her back into shelter against the bank, Carfax dislodged a shower of earth and stones, and catching at the holly's root the rubble of centuries was about them, a broken piece of pottery, rotting timber, and the moulded edge of a long-buried bone.

'Had I known you were to develop so savage a character,' he said, 'I would never have slapped the life into you some twenty years ago.'

'It's a pity you did,' she answered, 'seeing I bring trouble wherever I go. Hark at that thunder; they'll be awash down at Lantyan, with the rain coursing downhill to meet the river.'

The callous note in her voice stung him to anger, for why should it delight her that the Bosanko's farmstead should be flooded and the good people themselves distressed who had often treated her with kindness?

'As to your husband,' he said, 'drown him if you wish, and his servants too. But spare your friends.'

At this she turned on him in a rage and struck his shoulder.

'I have no friends,' she cried; 'they are all spies, every one of them. They set traps to catch us, but they won't succeed. And you: you're as bad as the rest. Mark sent you after me today and you can't deny it.'

'He did no such thing,' said Carfax, seizing her wrist, 'though he complained to me of your conduct, and I can't say I blame him now I hear you raving.'

All at once he leant forward, straining his ears to catch an echo through the wind and rain. 'What was that, did you hear it?'

'I heard nothing. The thunder's passing.'

'It sounded like a horn – yes, there it is again!' and distinctly to his ears came the thin reedy note: not a bugle call, nor any known summons from the high road beyond the encampment, but as if someone above them on a ridge of land unseen put a horn to his lips and blew. Carfax was aware of mounting anger of so ungovernable a nature that he could not recognize it as his own, for to be made a fool of by this child and her lover seemed suddenly beyond all reason damnable. He still held her wrist, and now forced it upward, so that she cried in pain. 'You're tricking me,' he shouted, 'there's some game on to make me as big a laughing-stock as your husband. Confess now!'

But even as he threatened her the sensation came to him, unbelievable and horrible, that what was happening now had happened a hundred times before; that the scene between them was a sickening repetition of others known too well; that he was in fact that very husband whose disparity in years between him and his bride was bringing him through jealous rage to the border line of madness. Not once, twice, thrice, but a dozen times had she been unfaithful to him, yet always the proof of guilt was turned, and he, the accuser, made to seem accused.

'Who wouldn't play tricks on an old man?' she cried with contempt. 'When a woman is young she loves by instinct, not by duty. And the first trick was the best yet, when my own maid took my place on my wedding night, and lay between the sheets with the groom who was so drunk he never knew the difference between us. And now I know what love is I'll continue to trick you and the whole world to keep what I've won, no matter what it costs me.'

Then, as suddenly as it had started, the rain ceased. The mist cleared. All was silent. Carfax released Linnet's wrist, wondering in confused fashion why he was holding it, and the ringing in his ears warned him that the second clap of thunder must have been uncomfortably close, for it had made him temporarily

165

deaf. Linnet fumbled with her streaming hair, which had escaped its pins.

'We had a lucky escape,' said the doctor. 'It's never been a desire of mine to be caught out in the countryside in a thunderstorm.'

'I'm sorry,' answered Linnet. 'I don't know what came over me in the forge, but the smell of the fire and the metal turned my stomach; I felt I must have air or I should die. I love this spot. You can breathe here when you stifle in the valley.'

They stepped out from the cover of the holly, and Linnet, stirring the rubble at their feet, bent to pick up something.

'Look,' she said, 'what a strange stone. It's all worn through the centre, like a ring.'

Carfax took the object from her, and turned it over in his hand.

'It's an armlet,' he said slowly. 'Shale, by the look of it, and centuries old. It may have been worked here on this very site. I'll have it examined by an expert and discover the date.'

'No!' Linnet almost snatched it from him. 'What does the date matter? I prefer to keep it. It would fit a man's arm today.'

They climbed out of the ditch into the field, and the steam from the soaking grass rose in their faces. Away towards Liskeard the storm rumbled its indefinite way. Carfax shook his head, endeavouring to clear his ears. He was still confused. 'Cassandra dislikes thunder as much as I do,' he said as they picked their passage across the field towards the forge. 'I only hope they were able to hold her. What were we discussing before all this happened?'

'Nothing of any consequence,' shrugged Linnet. 'I had a headache, but it has passed, just like the thunder.'

When they arrived at the forge they found Cassandra had been duly shod, and the apples had calmed any tendency to nerves. As to the blacksmith and his son, they took it for granted that Doctor Carfax and his companion had been taking shelter in the homestead at the back.

The drive along the high road to Troy was uneventful. Linnet prattled of childhood days at the farm across the water, and the doctor did not bring up the subject of present-day marital difficulties. They parted at Cassandra's stables, the doctor to see his animal bedded down for the night before returning in time to prepare for evening surgery, and the hostess of the Rose and Anchor to take up her duties in the bar.

'Let me know,' said the medical man, whose afternoon of meditation had been so rudely interrupted for her sake, 'if there is anything I can do for you at any time.' She gave him her hand and smiled. 'As to that,' she rejoined, 'I'm seldom ill, but if I should be I'd rather be in your hands than in another's.' With which parting invitation she was away down the hill, with the doctor gazing after her, nonplussed.

Carfax let himself in at his front door some thirty minutes later to discover two visitors waiting for him in the hall. They were the collector of customs and the police inspector.

'Good evening to you both,' said the doctor. 'What ill wind blows you here at such a time? Some law-breaker broken his neck trying to dodge Her Majesty's government?'

Both men rose to their feet. 'In a manner of speaking, yes!' replied the inspector. 'But it wasn't his neck, it was his jaw. It's the skipper of the schooner *Jolie Brise*, who got himself in a fight first thing this morning, and sailed on the afternoon's tide, and to tell you the truth he was an awkward fellow; we were glad to be rid of him. But the point is, his crew have brought the vessel back themselves an hour ago with the skipper dead. And I want the death certificate out of you, sir, if you will come aboard and sign it.'

It was a day to try one. Carfax took up his hat, which he had laid down on the hall settle.

'Did he die from the blow he received?' he asked.

'It would seem so,' returned the inspector, 'but that's for you to judge. In all events, according to the crew, he never recovered. The trouble is, the young fellow who did it is still at large, and had Mr McPhail known it was to turn out this way he'd never have let him go. It's the Breton lad who worked in the *Jolie Brise* some months back.'

Doctor Carfax knitted his brows. 'The Breton lad?' he repeated. 'But I have it on good authority he sailed on the *Downshire* and should be away down channel and half way to the bay by now.'

The collector of customs shook his head and smiled somewhat sheepishly.

'Not so, doctor,' he said. 'The *Downshire* sailed without him. The lad came here to report too late. It was then he fell to fighting with the skipper, and it was like David setting about Goliath: the big fellow dropped like an ox. I see now I did wrong in letting the lad slip away, because, now the skipper's dead—' he glanced at the inspector – 'well, the lad will be wanted for murder, won't he?'

Mr Tregentil, propped up in bed with pillows, a wineglass and a bottle of Graves on the table beside him, consulted a sheaf of notes strewn upon the counterpane, and proceeded to summarize their contents on a piece of foolscap, in a thin spidery hand.

'According to Gottfried von Strassburg,' he wrote, 'Tristan encountered the giant Urgan li vilus upon a bridge, having previously cut off his hand, and after blinding him in both eyes flung him over the bridge to the rocks below, and so to his death. In recompense for ridding the country of such a monster, his friend Gilan bestowed upon him the gift of the fairy dog Peticru, which Tristan straightway took to his loved lady, the Queen Iseult. It was after this exploit that King Mark, almost mad with jealousy, banished the lovers. The poet Béroul', he added in a footnote, 'makes no mention of the incident with the giant, nor the gift of the dog, but describes flight of the lovers to the forest of Morrois where they find shelter in the domain of a hermit, Ogrin. There would seem to be confusion of the names between

Urgan and Ogrin. It is significant that the poem by Béroul contains portions of so primitive and barbaric a nature – Tristan in one case scalping an opponent – as to suggest that the so-called medieval romance of Tristan and Iseult was based upon a far older, ruder story, having its origins in prehistoric times.'

21

'My hand the Hairy Urgan slew'

For the sole sake of Peticru
My hand the Hairy Urgan slew.

'The children were unaccountably quiet tonight,' remarked Mr Bosanko to his wife, as candlestick in hand he led the way upstairs to bed. 'If it wasn't for the fact that we've had thunder and lightning here a score of times before, I'd say the storms earlier on had upset them.'

He had no reply for a moment or two, for Mrs Bosanko had paused to listen outside the children's door, then hearing no movement followed her husband into their own room.

'It's because of Amyot,' she said quietly; 'they're fretting after him.'

The farmer scratched his jaw and frowned. 'That's all very well,' he replied. 'I was fond of the lad myself, but I never thought we had him for good. He'd have taken himself off sooner or later, even if there'd been no fancy nonsense 'twixt him and Mrs Lewarne, like you said. And if he was inclined to sentiment – and most Frenchies are in my opinion – then it's just as well he is out of the way, with our little maid growing apace.'

Mrs Bosanko stared at her husband, shocked. 'Why, Gabriel,' she chided, 'what an idea, and Mary only just turned fourteen, and still playing with dolls.'

'That's as may be, dear, that's as may be.' Mr Bosanko set down the candle on the dressing-table. 'But if you'd seen her sobbing her heart out in the stable as I did last night you'd have said she was sixteen past and in all the woes of first love. 'Tis a queer thing, a woman will get all sorts of strange notions about wrong looks passing between folk who should know better, and be as blind as a bat where her own datty's concerned.'

Mrs Bosanko, wrestling with the stubborn hooks of a bodice, remained silent. She was thinking of Mary's face, pressed to the window as the rain fell and the lightning flashed, and the funny, strained way she had asked: 'Have many people lost their lives in a thunderstorm?'

She had been thinking of Amyot sure enough, but the *Downshire* would be many miles out to sea by now, please the Lord, and running into fine weather. The bedroom across the landing may have been quiet, but despite Mrs Bosanko's reassurance, silence did not mean her children were asleep. Far from it. They were packing a basket with preserves from their mother's larder.

'If we're questioned,' whispered Mary, with a shamelessness hitherto unknown to her, 'we'll have to make out there's a thief at large.'

'I'm quite happy to go hungry,' said Johnny, who had drawn aside the blind to look up at the sky. 'Half of my supper went in my pockets anyhow. Look, it's clearing, and the stars are out. I vote we go now while we have the chance.'

'Best wait for the dawn,' suggested his more practical sister, 'then if things should go amiss, and they find we've gone, we can say we got up early to go mushrooming.'

And to prove that she needed no clock to awaken her, Mary tied a piece of string round her toe, and so to the bedpost; thus if she turned in bed the pain of it would do the trick. Could her father have seen her, his theory of first love would have been proven to the hilt.

It was Johnny, without benefit of string, who opened his eyes to find the pale dawn creeping through the window, and, slipping out of bed to look at Mary's birthday watch, he saw that it wanted a few minutes to five. He glanced from the loaded basket to his sister's sleeping face; and the plan, half formed in his mind the night before and now fully shaped through the dream that had awakened him, had all the majesty and splendour of high adventure. It was neither more nor less than that he and Amyot should escape together and seek their fortunes. Amyot would be the knight, and he the squire, and the pair of them would roam the forests of Cornwall – well, if there were no forests, at least the moors up by Brown Willy – and they'd live by hunting game, and trapping wild birds even if it was cruel, and catching trout in the little moorland streams; none of which would be possible if Mary accompanied them, it being a known thing that girls were an encumbrance on these occasions. The only permissible girl was a damsel in distress, and Mary was not as yet a damsel, nor was she in distress.

Johnny dressed swiftly and silently, and, stealing from the room with the basket over his arm, he was soon down by the stairs, carrying his shoes, and so out of the back door and into the sharp cool air, with the first light throwing a pallor on to the trees behind the farmhouse. The fact that he did not immediately strike up the lane and so to the woods which would being him eventually to Woodget and to his friend, but instead turned softly across the farmyard and opened the door of a disused pigsty, and darted down on his knees into the fresh straw, was a further part of his scheme; one which was so interwoven with his dream that he only knew he followed an impulse stronger than any known command. He gathered an object from the straw – not without difficulty – and burdening himself with this new hazard, as well as with the laden basket, set forth on his lonely mission to succour Amyot Tristane.

'It's queer,' he thought to himself, 'that I'm not frightened. For anyone could be, alone like this in the lane and nothing astir. I might be but for the dream.' And so vividly did the picture present itself of him and Amyot fighting side by side, laughing, with the three wicked barons riding at them, all killed by one thrust of Johnny's sword, the barons bearing an unmistakeable likeness to Mr McPhail, the collector of customs in Troy, the police inspector and his junior, that had they in truth come out of the undergrowth now, flourishing spears and battleaxes, he would have cared nothing for them. How crowded the trees were in this dawn light, their branches interwoven and interlaced, more like a forest than a wood, with great crowned heads reaching to the sky – they had not been so yesterday. A badger's trail lay to the left, or could it be a bear? But that was nonsense – there were no bears left in England, nor dragons either, though no one could say what had happened to all the bodies; buried perhaps under the roots of trees, or deep down in undiscovered caves. Where had they all gone to, he wondered, the long two-handled swords, and the gold, and the rings from ladies' fingers, and the bracelets, and the gems? So much brightness vanished. No one, not even his father, knew the answer.

'Now that's queer,' breathed Johnny as he reach high ground, and looked westward through a gate to the rolling hills beyond. 'You'd say there were camp-fires yonder, up towards Castle Dor, and horsemen riding, and hounds as big as stags following.' But it was the trick of the light of course, with day coming on, turning the few stunted trees on the sky-line to unlikely shapes. He cut downwards through the woods to the head of the Pyll, and already he could see the gleam of water and a white mist shrouding the valley. The world was still asleep and Johnny alone had life, or so it seemed, threading his way through the sapling oaks, his feet noiseless as they trod the soaking leaves of last night's storm. Then, coming at last to the tumbled cottage bathed in mist, he caught his breath in wonder; for surely it was a man there in the creek, poling a flat-bottomed boat to the grass verge, his arms and his legs bare, his long hair streaming to his shoulders?

'Amyot!' called Johnny, 'Amyot!' and began to run, forgetting he was heavy laden, and so caught his foot in a root that stretched across the path, and crashed headlong into a pit of brambles. The jagged edge that caught his temple was not a stone but the cracked lip of an old earthenware pot, cast away Heaven knows how many centuries ago, and left to moulder, unseen and unlamented, until so intrepid and unwary a traveller in time as Johnny Bosanko should chance to fall upon it and lie strangely still.

Linnet Lewarne was also astir betimes that morning. In truth she had scarcely slept for the night. The talk in the bar had all been of the return of the *Jolie Brise* to harbour with the dead skipper aboard.

''Twas the blow that did it,' pronounced Tim Udy, with all the authority of a man whose eldest son licked stamps in the customs office. 'Proper stunned, the fellow was, and never recovered. He was half blind by all accounts when he sailed from Troy, with the blood congealing in his brain.'

'Half blind maybe,' retorted Deborah, placing a mug of beer on the counter, 'and if he was, it was the liquor did it, and not from here neither, but from the King of Prussia on the quay. He got short shrift from me.'

She shot a glance at her mistress who, standing proudly aloof between bar and private saloon, was taking no part in the proceedings. The landlord, on the contrary, turned upon Deborah with interest.

'So you served him, did you?' he inquired, 'and after he'd had the blow? If I'm not mistaken the law will be after you for witness.'

Deborah shrugged. 'I'll be ready for them, and swear the skipper was fighting fit into the bargain.'

'That's all very well,' pursued Mark Lewarne. 'He may have seemed fit to you, but the skipper was suffering from delayed action by all accounts. It's mighty queer he should be taken ill sudden and die within a few hours. Make no mistake about it,

175

they'll arrest the man that did it, and he'll have to stand trial for manslaughter, if nothing worse.'

At this Linnet stepped forward, regardless of the company, all of whom could perceive her flashing eye and heightened colour.

'And what makes you so mighty sure of your facts?' she demanded. 'If you studied for the law in your younger days it's the first I've heard of it. They'll be making you a Justice of the Peace before we know where we are.' A titter rose from the back of the room, quickly stifled when the landlord turned a baleful glance on the offender.

'They might do worse,' he said slowly, staring at his wife. 'I'd see justice was done anyhow. There's folk get away with things these days that have no right to do so.'

Interest stirred. All eyes were upon them. It would not only be the death of the skipper that would be discussed that night after closing time, as customers walked home to bed, but the fact that the landlord of the Rose and Anchor and his young beauty of a wife had shown fight in public.

Ben Tabb, coxswain of the lifeboat for near on twenty years, and a peaceable man by nature, sought to throw oil on the troubled waters.

'Ah well,' he said, 'it's natural for women to champion a lad in trouble. The skipper of the *Jolie Brise* is no great loss, rest his soul, and I daresay 'twas all done in provocation-like. Don't fret, missus, they'll acquit him.'

'Acquit him?' repeated Linnet, raising her eyebrows: 'They'll have to find him first,' and with that she swung through the door with a rustle of petticoats, leaving them to continue the argument, but not before she had caught the speculative look in her husband's eye, and the sly smile on the pinched face of little Ned Varcoe, who, nursing his injured ankle, was polishing glasses at the farther end of the bar.

Her burst of temper had done no good to Amyot or to herself. Suspicion and surmise bred certainty, and a name might now be put upon the supposed lover said to wander with her in the moonlight. Whether this should come about or not, one thing was very plain; Amyot was in danger; not from her husband Mark Lewarne, not from his spy Ned Varcoe, but from the mustered forces of the law itself. The final piece of information came from Deborah, who, just before closing time, ran upstairs to tell her mistress what a late-comer to the bar, the younger of the two Troy constables, had let slip in a moment of indiscretion.

'There's a party of them setting out for Lantyan first thing in the morning,' she whispered through the bedroom door. 'If Mr Bosanko can't give them news they'll search the neighbourhood. They're going by road of course, and intend to be there before seven o'clock.'

Linnet thought rapidly. This meant they wanted to hold Amyot for questioning, and the reason for doing so was that the cause of the skipper's death had been the blow on the head after all.

'What time is high water?' she whispered back.

'Somewhere near seven, mistress. Have no fear, I know what you want me to do. There'll be a boat at the steps for you by five.'

And so it was that shortly before Johnny Bosanko crept from his bed at Lantyan, two young women were rowing steadily in the half-light up Troy harbour; past the mortuary where the evening before the post mortem, conducted by Doctor Carfax, upon one Fouguereau, had set the forces of the law in motion; past the silent ships waiting their turn at the jetties, and so up river with the flood tide to a sleeping countryside shrouded in mist, the waist-high bracken dipping to the water's edge.

It took them an hour and a half, even with the tide, to reach Woodget Pyll, and by then a pale sun was struggling to break the leaden sky, and Penquite, on the hill, with windows shuttered, had all the appearance of a fortress set on a summit to keep silent watch upon the creek below.

Linnet and Deborah, resting on their paddles, let the boat drift with the current, away from the main river, and so between marshy banks to the head of the creek. A wisp of smoke coming from the direction of the cottage gave warning that a fire was alight, and Amyot was drying the clothes he had soaked in last night's storm.

'Here,' commanded Linnet, pulling her oar so that the bows of the boat just touched the jutting shore, 'wait for my return, and if there are two of us you know where to land us across the river. Then you can hold your tongue, and hang the consequences.'

Deborah Brangwyn regarded her mistress gravely.

'You've thought what it means,' she said, 'once it comes out that you've gone with him, and the police on your heels? There'll be no hushing of it up. It will be in the newspapers and all, and you a marked woman.'

'I don't care,' replied Linnet. 'If he has to suffer for what he's done I'll suffer with him. There's no going back on it.'

'Love's one thing when it's secret meetings and the world unknowing,' demurred Deborah, 'and another when you've no money, and no roof to your head, and folk pointing at you and calling you adulteress.'

'They can call me what they like,' said Linnet; 'we're bound together, he and I, till the end of our days, and the world can know it.'

She gathered her skirts together and sprang ashore, while a pair of swans, preening their feathers on a strip of grass on the farther bank, hissed at the intrusion, then, followed by their brood of seven, slid into the water silently, and so downstream.

Linnet plunged through undergrowth, heedless of brambles, and came upon Amyot crouching on the strand beneath the cottage, turning the sticks of his smouldering fire. He was stripped to the waist, his shirt, coat and socks spread on the bracken, drying as best they could by the feeble flame.

'Amyot,' she called softly. 'Amyot, my love.'

As he leapt to his feet and came towards her, bare-foot,

178

throwing aside the bent spike with which he had stirred the fire, it seemed to Linnet that his very nakedness made him taller, more remote, and his uncombed hair gave him a wild look altogether unexpected and forbidding; while the very spike thrown heedlessly over his shoulder might have been a spear, not rusted from disuse, but stained with the dried blood of a slain enemy. In a moment they were in each other's arms, and the way he kissed her and held her to him proved he was indeed the Amyot she knew and loved, and no stranger.

'Your husband has been ill treating you, is that it?' asked Amyot. 'And you've come to me for protection? I'm ready for him if he follows you here.'

Linnet put her hand over his mouth. 'Hush! Not so loud. No, dearest one, it's not for my sake I've come, but for yours. The skipper of the *Jolie Brise* is dead. He died because of the blow you gave him. The police are coming this very morning to look for you at Lantyan. There's not a moment to lose.'

Amyot stared down at her in perplexity. 'Fouguereau dead!' he repeated. 'Even if he is I never intended it. I'll tell them all they want to know and willingly.'

'You don't understand,' said Linnet urgently. 'The English law can hold you pending arrest. Once they get you they may not let you go. If the worst should happen they could try you for manslaughter. You might have months, years, in prison – I don't know, I'm not acquainted with the law. All I know is you must leave here instantly, and I'll come with you.'

Already she had left his arms, and was gathering up the clothes spread to dry, then kicking at the smouldering fire to deaden it.

'If what you say is true,' said Amyot, 'we'll be fugitives from justice, and I with a price on my head. God knows I shall want you with me, but I'm well-nigh penniless.'

'I've money enough for the pair of us,' she told him. 'No need to worry on that score. And as to being fugitives, we'll take train and be lost in London, where many a hunted man has found sanctuary before now.'

She had it all planned, she said, how they'd make their way across country, hailing the first carrier's cart on the road to Liskeard, and catch the mid-morning train to Plymouth and beyond. The hue and cry would not be raised until they were many miles away. If she knew anything of Troy police methods they'd still be discussing the case over breakfast at Farmer Bosanko's, when she and Amyot were boarding the train at Liskeard.

'Stay,' said Linnet, as he struggled into his still-damp shirt. 'This is for you. It came into my hands last night – I'll tell you about it presently.'

She burrowed into the depths of the purse-bag at her waist and brought out the armlet. 'You see?' She smiled, slipping it up his forearm. 'It fits you perfectly. If we're ever separated by force of circumstances, you can send it to me, and I'll come to you. It binds us together like a ring does married folk, but there's no church oath with this one.'

He took her face between his hands and kissed her lips.

'We don't need vows, you and I,' he said, 'nor gold nor metal. What we are to each other lasts to the grave and beyond.'

They were about to hail the boat and the waiting Deborah when Amyot turned his head to the woodland path above the ruined cottage.

'Did you hear that?' he asked. 'It sounded like a call for help.'

'It's nothing,' said Linnet impatiently, 'a lamb perhaps, strayed from the flock. What does it matter?'

The sound came again, and unmistakably: no lamb's bleat, but the feeble cry of a child. 'Amyot! Oh, Amyot!'

Linnet's lover struggled from the arms that strove to hold him back.

'It's Johnny,' he said, 'I'd swear to his voice anywhere. He's up there in the woods, and maybe come to harm. We must go to him.'

Linnet, in a fever to be gone, looked over her shoulder towards the already ebbing tide. 'I'll call Deborah,' she said.

'Deborah can go to him and take him back to Lantyan, and we'll take the boat across the river to the opposite shore at St Winnow and be on our way.'

'No,' said Amyot. 'No . . .'

He pulled himself free, and began running up the path through the woods in the direction of the cry. Linnet followed him, half sobbing in vexation, for if they delayed much longer her plan would be spoilt, people would be astir, and the tide would not wait for them.

She climbed half way up the wooded hill and came upon Amyot kneeling beside a dip in the path, and he held the limp form of Johnny Bosanko on his arms. Blood was running from a cut on the child's forehead, and his face and his lips were blue. 'He's badly hurt,' said Amyot. 'We must take him home.'

There was an upturned basket beside the path, its contents scattered on the ground. 'Don't you see?' said Amyot. 'He was bringing me food. He came here alone for my sake. God knows how long he's lain here.'

Something stirred in the undergrowth hard by. A faint yelp, like an echo to the boy's cry, came from the midst of it. A small object struggled out, shook itself, and pattered towards them, tail erect. It was surely the smallest dog Linnet had ever set eyes upon, and what part he had played in the accident that had befallen Johnny Bosanko no one was likely to answer.

Linnet stooped down, her heart grown heavy and dull within her, and mechanically she put back the packages, one by one, in the upturned basket.

'You know what it means,' she said. 'It's over for you now. There's no escape.'

'I know,' said Amyot. 'They'll come for me at Lantyan. And if they put me in prison I shall deserve it. Not for what I did to Fouguereau, but for what I've done to Johnny.'

He looked down at the boy in his arms, and as he spoke his name Johnny opened his eyes for the first time and smiled at Amyot in recognition.

'I brought the pup for you,' he murmured. 'You picked him, don't you remember? The smallest of the litter, but the best.'

Amyot tried to staunch the blood that was trickling down the boy's cheek.

'Yes,' he said gently, 'I remember.'

The puppy began to play with Linnet's skirt, and setting down the basket, she let him straddle across her hand and bite her fingers.

'He'll never harm no one,' whispered Johnny. 'He's a magic dog and brings good luck. And he's Cornish through and through, 'cos Father mated Bessie with a pure-bred terrier down to Gerran's bay.'

He smiled once more at Amyot before closing his eyes.

'I'm glad you fought that giant,' he said. 'I hope you scalped him good and proper. I forgot to say – the pup's name is Pettigrew.'

Already there came a sound of voices, and footsteps were crashing through the undergrowth towards them.

BOOK THREE

Yet well I know that few there be
Who Tristan's tale alright have read.

22

'. . . none can part the love of us'

Needs must our bodies sunder thus,
But none can part the love of us.

Doctor Carfax, returning from Bodmin Assizes in October with Mr McPhail as fellow passenger, had not proved himself a particularly lively companion. The collector of customs decided that the medical man was beginning to show his age, and if the somewhat testy manner in which he had given evidence during the hearing of the case against the young foreign seaman; Amyot Trestane, was anything to go by, he was getting short in temper too. Anyone would think that the doctor had taken it as a personal affront for the skipper of the *Jolie Brise* to have died as he had done, and so obliged him to certify the cause of death as cerebral haemorrhage due to a fall. True the doctor was only doing his duty by signing the death certificate, and he, McPhail, had reluctantly done the same as witness of the fight on the steps of his customs office, and of that fatal blow which was certainly unprovoked and therefore inexcusable by law; but the whole business, from the post mortem nearly three months ago to the preliminary hearing before the magistrates, who had found that there was a case to answer and committed young Trestane to stand for his trial for manslaughter at the next assizes, seemed to have aged Doctor Carfax in a remarkable manner.

'It's a funny thing,' McPhail had said to his wife at the time, 'that Doctor Carfax must have seen hundreds of chaps stretched out from one cause and another, men who have been his patients, too, and well known to him, yet a Frenchman from a dirty schooner gets his deserts from another Froggie half his size, and our doctor makes a tragedy out of it.'

Mrs McPhail, woman-like, professed herself in sympathy with the doctor. 'If it's his word sends the young man to prison you can hardly wonder at it,' she replied, 'a nice young man too, and well spoken, I remember, for I bought a load of onions off him some time back, at quarter the price they charge in the town. Still, duty is duty, just as you said, and we can't all be murdered in our beds.'

Her husband had never suggested such a likelihood, but he had been reminded of his wife's random remark when one of the original magistrates, after the preliminary hearing, had been heard to observe: 'We can't have foreigners treating our respectable towns as they would their own back streets and let them get away with it. A line must be drawn somewhere.'

The line had been drawn with Amyot Trestane, and so he had been remanded in custody for the space of ten weeks, during which period he would, presumably, have ample time to reflect upon the grave consequences of losing his temper and causing the death of a fellow countryman. Those good people of Troy whose attention had been temporarily aroused by a common seaman's brawl, ending in disaster to one of the participants, were inclined to agree with official opinion.

'They should make an example of 'un, that's what I say.'

'Send him back where he belongs to be. We don't want him and his kind creating under our windows. 'Twill be knives and all sorts next.'

'The young fellow's a proper heathen by all accounts. Living on berries he was, when they caught him, and hiding in trees. Good job they've got him under lock and key.'

It said much for the discretion of the police inspector of Troy and his young subordinate that no word filtered back into the town of the inexplicable presence of the hostess of the Rose and Anchor in Lantyan woods on that morning they arrested Amyot Trestane. It was assumed, if not stated in so many words, that Mistress Lewarne and her maid Deborah Brangwyn had risen early with the idea of picking blackberries, or mushrooms, or both, and their attention had been drawn to a child's cry in the woods. The fact that they stumbled upon the fugitive carrying the child to Lantyan was pure coincidence.

One thing was certain, and this was grudgingly admitted by those disciplinarians amongst the citizens of Troy who were all for the culprit being shipped off to Devil's Island: the young seaman did not attempt to evade arrest. Indeed by bearing the child home to its parents he deliberately walked into the arms of the law. It was this mitigating fact, insisted upon most warmly and fervently by Farmer Bosanko from Lantyan, that saved the day for Amyot Trestane at Bodmin Assizes.

'So, doctor,' said Mr McPhail, determined to break the silence which threatened to reign the full ten miles from Bodmin to Troy, 'all's well that ends well, and I dare say you are as glad as I am to see that young fellow freed, and to know he won't have to serve a long prison sentence after all.'

Doctor Carfax, who had been navigating Cassandra under difficulties until she was free of the narrow town and out on to the open highway, grunted in reply, then whipped Cassandra to a smarter pace.

'I hesitate to make a pronouncement on any subject unless sure of my facts,' he said at last, 'for how do we know that all has ended well? Young Trestane is at liberty, to be sure, but bound over to keep the peace, and until we see how he conducts himself hereafter we cannot say for certain that all is well.'

'Oh, come, doctor!' objected the collector of customs. 'Such a thing as causing another man's death is not likely to happen again. The fellow has learnt his lesson. And you heard what Mr Bosanko said. He has made himself responsible for young Trestane.'

This remark produced no more than a non-committal 'H'mph'

from the driver of the dogcart, which dubious sound was followed in a moment or two by an observation of so unsympathetic a nature that Mr McPhail was quite taken by surprise.

'It would be better for Amyot Trestane and everyone concerned,' declared Doctor Carfax, 'if he had been deported.' And as though he must emphasize this statement with a show of force, he cracked his whip, causing Cassandra to kick up her heels and gallop. The collector of customs, rudely shaken, was obliged to hold on to his hat with one hand, and to the rail of the dogcart with the other.

'Do you mean you think he has criminal tendencies?' he gasped, when he had sufficiently recovered his breath to make speech possible.

'No,' snapped the doctor, 'I do not.'

'Well then?'

'There is no "Well then" about it. The young man would be better employed in his own country, where he might marry amongst his kith and kin and settle down, than presume on the good nature of Mr and Mrs Bosanko. That sort of thing just does not do, and they'll come to regret it.'

Which went to show, so Mr McPhail told his wife later that evening, how easy it was to misjudge a man's character; for there was Doctor Carfax, who had shown himself so full of concern for the prisoner's fate before Bodmin Assizes that anyone would think the young man was his own nephew, turning round, after his name had been cleared, and declaring he should have been deported.

'The old devil is as hard as flint and no mistake about it,' decided the collector of customs over a steaming glass of grog, for the wind had been keen coming over the high ground by Castle Dor, and the passage in the dogcart rough enough in all conscience, 'and if you or I are taken ill this coming winter, my dear, I vote we call in that new young chap down to St Blazey, who's as gentle as a lamb, so they tell me, and never gainsays a patient.'

Doctor Carfax, unaware that his shortness of temper might have reduced his enormously long list of prospective sick by two, did not immediately walk home after leaving the stable, but turned instead downhill into the town. He had a disagreeable mission to perform, and it was possibly the thought of this that had made him such an indifferent companion during the drive from Bodmin to Troy.

The October spring tides had clashed with a sou'west gale of some ferocity, and descending the path through the churchyard the doctor became aware by the excited knots of people, and the laughter of the young in the slowly gathering dusk, that the town quay must be flooded, and the water making its way into Church Square and down into Fore Street. The more adventurous were already wading knee-deep, and screams of delighted laughter greeted one young woman who was obliged to lift her skirts to unprecedented heights, displaying a pair of remarkably good legs in the process.

'Pull 'un up higher, Deb!' shouted an onlooker, male, needless to say, who had taken his stance with a bunch of cronies on a vantage point on the churchyard wall. We'm all waitin' breathless for what's comin' next,' but the young woman, undeterred held her petticoats with one hand and sent a shower of water in the direction of her mocking audience with the other.

'If it's salt water you're asking for there's plenty of it here,' she called in return, 'and a ducking's no more than you deserve, the whole bunch of you.'

Whoops of joy greeted her arrival on dry land beside the Rose and Anchor, and as she darted in at the back door of the hostelry she collided with no less a person than Doctor Carfax himself, who, for reasons of his own, was relieved to find his presence on the scene had escaped general notice.

'Why, doctor,' exclaimed Deborah, 'I didn't see it was you, with so many down under gaping at me!'

He drew aside to let her pass, inquiring after her mistress at the same time. 'She was upstairs when last I saw her, sir; I just slipped out to hear if there was any news, and—' Deborah checked herself, for the only news that was likely to interest the hostess of the Rose and Anchor that evening was what had happened at Bodmin Assizes.

'And became very wet by so doing,' the doctor continued for her. 'If you have some sense go and change immediately, but first conduct me upstairs to your mistress, for I have a message for her.'

'Yes, doctor.'

Deborah led the way to the best bedroom overlooking the square – that same room where the unfortunate Notary Ledru had breathed his last a year ago – and knocking on the door announced: 'Here's Doctor Carfax to see you, ma'am,' and then withdrew, but not before the caller had noticed a lightning exchange of glances between the two young women, and an almost imperceptible nod on the part of the maid. It was simple enough to guess question and answer. The nod intimated that Amyot Trestane had been set free.

'Good evening to you, Linnet,' said the doctor. 'I apologize for this somewhat brusque intrusion, but knowing your husband is generally occupied in the bar at this time I thought I might catch you alone.'

Linnet advanced from the window, from where she had been watching the scene below, and in the half-light it seemed to the doctor that her beauty, of which he was always well aware, had for the first time a curiously uncanny quality, like a vision seen in a dream and scarce remembered, while the faintly mocking smile with which she greeted him brought a disquiet and discomfort too.

'You chose your moment well,' she replied, the inflection in her voice as mocking as the smile. 'No one will disturb us here with all this nonsense going on below. Why must men behave like children just because the water they see every day of their lives chooses to wet their ankles once in a while?'

Yes, thought the doctor, and if it rose to the height of the window-sill, and they were struggling for their lives, I can see you throwing open the lattice and laughing for the sport of it, casting a wager on him who swam the best.

Then he noticed she was carrying in one hand the smallest of dogs, a pup with an absurd bell about its neck, which she set down on the floor while she proceeded to light the lamp.

'That's a new pet, isn't it?' he asked.

'Not so new,' she answered. 'I've had him these ten weeks or more.'

Now, shielding her face from the flame as she trimmed the lamp, he saw that she was very pale, and he was shocked, too, to remark how thin she had grown since he had seen her last.

'We have so little company these days I've come to use this room as my own,' she told him. 'I slept badly where I was before. Sit yourself down.' No sign of Lewarne's belongings about the room either, noticed the doctor, which suggested – well, exactly what it did suggest.

'I'll come to the point of my visit at once,' he began, 'I'm here on behalf of Mrs Bosanko. I was at Bodmin Assizes, and she wishes you to know that young Amyot Trestane has been acquitted of manslaughter. He is bound over to keep the peace, and Bosanko stands surety for him.'

'Yes,' said Linnet. He could sense the triumph in her voice.

'This means for at least six months he will remain under the direct eye of both Bosanko and his wife,' continued the doctor, 'without the right to move outside the farmhouse itself unless he has their permission. Mrs Bosanko thought you would like to hear the exact terms of his release.'

The silence that greeted his announcement was proof of its significance to the listener. No doubt she had put a very different interpretation on the word freedom.

'I had a few words with the young man,' added the doctor, 'who realized that but for his employers' intervention he might have been deported. He assured me, with tears in his eyes, he would do all he could to make up to the Bosankos for the trouble he has caused them. I rather think they would have spared their pains but for the children.'

Linnet had stooped once more to pick up the dog, who was now nestling close to her, with ears pricked, and sharp eyes fixed on the visitor.

'Amyot blamed himself for Johnny's accident,' she said. 'There might have been none of this bother had he run for it at the time.'

'And caused a second death,' put in the doctor drily. 'Johnny Bosanko would have bled to death had he been left to lie there in the woods. As it is, he has a scar on his temple which will mark him for life. Amyot Trestane will do well to spend the next few months devoting himself to that boy and his parents.'

Cries of merriment rose from the square below as the water swept in from the quay and doused the onlookers, but there was silence within the guest-room of the Rose and Anchor. Doctor Carfax rose to his feet.

'I won't detain you any longer,' he said, 'except to pass a final message from Mrs Bosanko to say that in the present circumstances she regrets she cannot offer you the hospitality of Lantyan.'

Linnet Lewarne moved to the door, but before she opened it, paused for a moment, looking at the doctor with an expression so inscrutable that he could not tell whether she accepted him as enemy or friend.

'I ask hospitality of no one,' she said, 'least of all Mrs Bosanko. But I tell you this. Anyone who tries to come between me and the man I love will suffer for it.'

The church clock was striking seven as Doctor Carfax, buttoning his coat against the weather, left the comparative shelter of the Rose and Anchor and made his way home uphill, the excited cries of those watching the rising tide sounding like an echo to the chimes, and the image of the young woman he had just quitted leaving as ruthless an impression on his mind as those seas now pounding and sweeping the deserted quay.

23

Mary finds a champion, and
Mr Tregentil takes tea at Lantyan

'Johnny, will you get down from off that wall?'

'No, miss, I will not.'

'Johnny, if you don't obey me, you will fall and cut your head again, and this time I shall be blamed, worse than before, and sent away for good to an improving school.'

Here was a threat causing Johnny Bosanko to pause in his scramble between cow shed and barn in an endeavour to scatter seed through the gap in the slate roof, and on to the bald head of his father's cowman; so swinging his legs reluctantly some twelve inches nearer the ground and safety, he regarded his sister in lofty condescension.

'All right,' he said, 'but I'm too high now to jump, so Amyot must come and lift me down.' From which it will be clear that Johnny, far from being humbled by the accident that had befallen him in July, was now, through a certain amount of injudicious spoiling on the part of his parents, in a fair way to becoming a tyrant. Mary, shrugging her shoulders, went off to summon Amyot, knowing very well that he was bedding down Lion and Pleasant after a hard day's work with the plough.

The sound of stamping from within the stables proved her right, and she leant to watch over the open hatch, while her favourite tossed hay into Lion's manger, singing softly to the horse as he did so: a queer, catchy refrain in French, which Mary had heard often before.

'You'd better come,' she said darkly; 'he's at it again.'

Amyot turned, surprised, then seeing Mary, smiled and laid aside his fork.

'You startled me,' he said. 'I was many miles away just then.'

'In Brittany?' she asked, her pleasure damped for no good reason.

'Neither Brittany nor Cornwall, but some dream world between the two,' he answered. 'That's what comes of all those weeks of idleness. Too much time and not enough hard work. What's the trouble? Is it Johnny?'

She nodded, noticing not for the first time that since he had come back to them from Bodmin he had dropped the 'miss' and 'master', at any rate when the three of them were alone together, and this gave her a pleasant feeling of equality. He followed her to the spot where her brother, cocky and triumphant, sat drumming his feet upon the ten-foot wall. Amyot, without a word, put up his hands and turned his back, and the boy slid on to his shoulders.

'Now, sirrah, gallop,' commanded Johnny, with all the authority of a near-invalid whose instant word is law; but Amyot, to the secret satisfaction of Mary, only smiled and put the boy to the ground.

'No,' he said, 'you work for me, not I for you. Come feed the horses, and later you shall help polish the brass. Brothers in arms must keep their weapons bright.'

It was strange, pondered Mary, what understanding he had of her brother and his childish games, almost as though he himself believed in them, when, as all grown people knew, heroes and knights and battles belonged to a world of fancy, having little to do with the hard facts of life.

The accident, which had marked her brother's face but not his nature, had exercised a more profound effect upon

194

fourteen-year-old Mary who, keenly sensitive, and a prey to all new emotions, blamed herself for the whole affair. If she had not slept so soundly on that fatal morning she could have prevented the tumble, and Amyot's arrest into the bargain. As it was, not even Johnny's recovery, and Amyot's release, could wipe out the memory of that first morning's anguish, when her stout avowal that Johnny 'must have gone out early to pick mushrooms' was proved so swiftly a lie with the arrival of the police in search of Amyot, their setting forth through the woods, her father as guide, and the disastrous return, Johnny unconscious in the arms of a stricken Amyot. What had seemed daring and exciting the night before had turned to a near tragedy, and her mother's cry at the sight of the bleeding Johnny: 'Is he dead? Ah, God, is he dead?' was so poignant a revelation of adult helplessness in the face of danger – and on the part of one who had seemed to hold all security within her sure hands – that to the watching daughter the supremacy of the grown-up world was instantly vanquished.

The people who had hitherto wielded power and were beloved were seen to be as vulnerable as herself; even so commanding and confident a person as Mrs Lewarne, who, by some manner or means happened to be on the spot at the same time as everybody else, lost all poise and assurance. She hardly spoke, never as much as glanced at Mary who had been her ally the previous night, and stood white and tense in the background, holding Bess's smallest pup tight in her arms.

Instinctively Mary felt Mrs Lewarne had done wrong to visit Amyot in the woods, that it would do his cause no good, that somehow the secret of his presence hidden in Woodget Pyll, known to the three of them, had become tainted overnight; the motives for his hiding were suddenly mixed, his abrupt departure from the farm in the first place was connected with it, and perhaps the police thought to accuse Amyot not only of killing a man but of other deceits as well. She could confide in no one. Her mother, at Johnny's bedside, had thought only

195

for him, and her father, appalled that the lad he had befriended must be tried for manslaughter, was too preoccupied with his own feelings to heed his daughter. So Mary Bosanko kept her own counsel, grown older and wiser through experience; and when Amyot, freed, returned to Lantyan, her joy at his home-coming was tempered by a determination to keep him out of further trouble; which trouble, though hardly acknowledged even to herself, meant Mrs Lewarne.

This afternoon she followed Amyot and her brother back to the stable, and seated on the ladder 'twixt floor and loft watched the pair of them finish seeing to the horses, and so on to the cleaning of harness.

'And now, sir,' said Johnny, with all of a child's unconscious ingenuity in seizing upon a ticklish subject, 'we're ready, the pair of us to ride forth and defend our honour 'gainst the might of the enemy.'

He laid aside a leather strap on which he had been spitting with much relish. 'The thing is, whose champion would you best like to be? Mary's here, or Mrs Lewarne's, over to Troy?'

Mary, scarlet with embarrassment not only for her own sake but for Amyot's as well, hurriedly interposed with: 'Don't be so daft, Johnny. Amyot doesn't want to be anyone's champion,' and proceeded to jump off the ladder, brushing the wisps of hay from her skirt.

'But you do, don't you, Amyot?' urged the irrepressible boy, turning to his friend. 'All knights swear fidelity to some lady or other, and wear their ribbon as a favour; it's partly the reason they fight.'

Amyot, to Mary's great relief, smiled at Johnny composedly. 'To be sure they do,' he said, 'but in the heat of battle they don't always remember it. If Mary will have me, I'll be glad to be her champion.'

'Then that's settled,' cried the delighted Johnny. 'Give him a piece of your ribbon, Mary, to twist in his coat button,' and nothing would content him but that his sister should hand over the half of her scarlet hair-ribbon, snippered in two by Amyot's own clasp knife. The champion placed the ribbon in the top buttonhole of his jacket with suitable gravity.

'It's only in play of course,' whispered Mary hurriedly, desirous of proving to Amyot, above all persons, that she had reached the age where such games were considered folly; but either he misunderstood her purpose or thought to pacify her brother, for he looked at her in all seriousness and said: 'I would willingly lay down my life for you both, that's understood between the three of us.'

Just then her mother's voice could be heard calling from the house to say Mr Tregentil had walked over to tea, and would they please come in and wash their hands and faces, and Amyot too if his work was done. Johnny was gone in a flash, for since the accident the owner of Penquite had developed a pleasant habit of bringing with him small tokens of sympathy when visiting the farmhouse: a clutch of eggs, believed to be those of the lesser spotted woodpecker, blown by himself in youth and greatly prized; two butterflies, a Comma and a Painted Lady, not thought to cross the Tamar but pinned many years ago when his eyes were keener; and finally, a ship in a bottle, fully rigged, that had occupied Mr Tregentil's horny fingers for many a long evening in days gone by when sitting on the veranda of his Indian bungalow.

'We don't matter any more,' laughed Amyot; 'today's present is more important than tomorrow's battles. But I shall wear my favour just the same.' And he touched the ribbon in his buttonhole.

There was the trouble, thought Mary, washing her hands; however could you tell whether Amyot, who seemed a boy like Johnny one minute, and a grown man the next, really meant what he said? The piece of ribbon was a joke, as she had told him, and perhaps the wearer had already forgotten what it was meant to represent, but Mary's consciousness of Amyot's buttonhole was so acute that the ribbon seemed to her the size of a banner as she slipped into the kitchen and took her place at the table.

'. . . so it would seem I am perfectly right in my conjectures, and you are descended from a long line of kings,' Mr Tregentil was in the midst of announcing triumphantly, a spot of colour on his high cheek-bones, and his eyes widening in appreciation at the large slice of home-baked saffron cake that had just been laid upon his plate.

'My dear life,' said Mrs Bosanko with some complacency, as usual paying more attention to her guest's possible appetite than to his conversation, for Mr Tregentil, walking in unexpectedly like this, must perforce make do with what was going and not expect drawing-room tea. Thank goodness Gabriel, and Amyot too, had their jackets on, and Johnny was so engaged with the little carved figure the visitor had brought him that he did not try to feed the kitten with crumbs from the table.

'My dear life,' she repeated, 'whatever next. The large pink cup for Mr Tregentil, Mary: not the one with the crack in it. Well, I'm sure we must all be very flattered and must mend our manners accordingly. Gabriel, you might make a start by not pouring your tea into a saucer and blowing on it.' This with nods and frowns in the direction of the unheeding guest. 'My dear,' replied her husband, 'I've poured my tea into a saucer for forty years at least, and won't change the habit now, for all the blue blood in Christendom. You'll pardon me, Mr Tregentil, but what 'zactly is it that you've discovered about my forbears?'

'Why, just what I was endeavouring to explain to your wife as we sat down to tea,' replied the visitor, between mouthfuls of cake; 'four lumps if you please, Mrs Bosanko, and plenty of milk if not too creamy; I cannot digest cream – my researches into your ancestry prove that your mother having been a Hoel, Bosanko, then you are in all likelihood descended from Hoel the First, King of Little Britain.'

The farmer considered the astonishing piece of news with the same equanimity as his wife. 'You'll pardon my ignorance, sir, but my knowledge of history don't go back much beyond William the Conqueror, though I know about Alfred and the cakes and our own King Arthur. But as for your Hoel or Howl, I never as much heard of him.'

Mr Tregentil stirred his tea and regarded his host with an air of authority. The task he had undertaken, at behest of Doctor Carfax, had turned out to be of so absorbing a nature that he no longer considered it part of his medical treatment, but a hobby that threatened to swamp him to the exclusion of any other. The sixth century AD was now his period, and woe betide anyone who thought to argue with him on the subject.

'Hoel the First,' he declared, clearing his throat as though preparatory to a lecture, 'was a contemporary of King Arthur. You must understand that in 530 or so AD the country was split up into small kingdoms, and my researches lead me to believe that Little Britain was not Brittany at all, as had been hitherto supposed, but an area stretching roughly from the Dodman to the Fal estuary. King Hoel held court at Karahes, or Carhayes, as we call it, not to be confused with Carhaix in Brittany.'

He was pleased to see he had the attention of the table. Everyone knew the Dodman, the headland some ten miles to the west of Troy, and the beach below Carhayes Castle was a favourite spot for Sunday-school outings.

'Why, bless my soul,' murmured Mr Bosanko, 'that's something my mother never knew at all events. She was plain Mary Hoel of Portloe, and never set foot in Carhayes Castle to my knowledge.'

His visitor could not forbear smiling in superior fashion.

'I am speaking of Carhayes as it was in the sixth century AD, my good Bosanko. A castle in those days would be more of a hill fortress than anything else, and King Hoel something of a barbarian in all probability. I can't promise you an ancestor with fine feelings or fine manners.'

'Well, but would he wear a crown, sir? That's what these children will want to know. Aren't I right, Johnny?'

The farmer winked at his young son as if the whole conversation was in the nature of a tremendous joke, but both Johnny and Mary were as serious as the lecturer himself. Mr Tregentil, suspecting that the older members of the party were not sufficiently impressed, stiffened somewhat, and declined a second piece of saffron cake.

'A crown? I hardly think so,' he replied, gesturing, hand in air, to dismiss so childish a notion. 'Some distinctive headgear to signal him apart from his ruder followers in all probability, but no more than that.' Mary, who was so easily hurt herself these days, perceived that Mr Tregentil was put out, and being her mother's daughter, wished intuitively to set the guest at ease.

'Was your ancestor also a king, Mr Tregentil?' she inquired politely. 'And did he reign over his subjects at Penquite?'

Now it so happened that Mr Tregentil's father had been a man of modest background who had made a small fortune in tin, and his only son, on retiring after thirty years as a tea planter in India, was enabled to enjoy the fruits of the father's industry by taking a long lease of the mansion in which he now dwelt. No amount of research had yet resulted in him claiming kinship with the ancient family of de Pencoit, now extant. This was a disappointment to Mr Tregentil, and Mary unwittingly had touched a sore point. However, the child had shown interest, which was more than her parents had done, and deserved an answer for her pains.

'The Tregentils were never river folk,' he replied grandly; 'they came from the hills.' He waved his hand in a northerly direction. 'They held manor lands at one time near St Columb, and although the exact locality is hard to trace, I propose making an expedition to that neighbourhood in the near future. It may well turn out that the Tregentils had seignorial rights to Castle-an-Dinas itself.'

He paused for the information to take its proper effect. Johnny, whose eyes had never left Mr Tregentil's face since he had mentioned Hoel the First, found curiosity too much for him.

'And what might that be, if you please?' he demanded.

The visitor sat bolt upright. 'The greatest earthwork in the whole of Cornwall,' he replied. Johnny gasped. There came to his mind an instant vision of Mr Tregentil, standing upon mighty ramparts, with ten thousand men-at-arms behind him, obeying his every whim.

'I'd dearly like to see it,' he said daringly.

Greatly to the surprise of Johnny's parents, Mr Tregentil, instead of allowing the request to pass unheeded, appeared to show pleasure at the prospect. 'Indeed, why not?' he said at last. 'Nothing would be simpler. A survey of Castle-an-Dinas should be part of the education of every Cornish boy.'

Johnny was not slow to seize his advantage. 'And Mary must come too,' he insisted, 'and Amyot, 'cos of being Mary's champion. We must all go.'

'My dear, steady now,' interposed Mrs Bosanko. 'Mr Tregentil has other things to do than to escort a great party on to the moors this time of year, with the days drawing in, and one thing and another.'

She had noticed the red hair-ribbon in Amyot's buttonhole, and hoped it did not mean that despite her care Mary was getting foolish ideas into her head.

'I assure you, Mrs Bosanko,' said her guest earnestly, 'nothing would delight me more than to escort your family to Castle-an-Dinas, if Amyot here will accompany them. We can choose our day, and, by starting early, be back before nightfall. It is not often one sees young people with such enthusiasm for things historical.'

So the farmer's wife allowed herself to be persuaded. After all, the idea might come to nothing, and turn out to be one of Mr Tregentil's fads, like her husband's descent from King Heol. Next week he would develop another craze, and kings and castles be forgotten.

Mary and Johnny, once the visitor had departed, could talk of little else. Winter treats were few and far between, and a visit to what they understood must be Mr Tregentil's ancestral home would be the best thing that could happen between now and Christmas. Only Amyot remained silent, and Mr Bosanko, laying a hand on his shoulder, said kindly: 'What ails you lad? Have you no wish to go gallivanting across the moors in search of castles?' Amyot started. He had been staring out of the open door, deep in thought.

'Why, sir, I'll be glad to go,' he answered 'it's just I was puzzling where I had heard the name before. I could swear I knew a man called Dinas once, but who it was, and when it was, I cannot tell.'

Mr Tregentil, loping briskly along the high lane to reach Penquite before darkness overtook him, came to the conclusion that Farmer Bosanko had very little historical sense. The news about Hoel the First had meant nothing to him. It would have meant even less, in all probability, had he proceeded further with his dissertation and informed the good man that Hoel the First was father to the young knight Kaerdin and Iseult of the White Hands, the unfortunate maiden who endeavoured to console the legendary Tristan when parted from her namesake, Iseult the Blonde, queen to King Mark. True, Gottfried von Strassburg gave the father's name as Jovelin and made him Duke of Arundel, but that was plainly an error.

However, Doctor Carfax had bidden his patient stick to facts, and Mr Tregentil, turning the matter over in his mind, decided not to trouble his medical adviser with so small a matter as Gabriel Bosanko's descent from Hoel the First, but to insert the information in a footnote when he returned the doctor's books and papers.

24

Plot and counterplot

An epidemic of colds and coughs, coming before due season had kept Doctor Carfax busy in Troy since the Assizes, and so it happened he had not driven out lately 'into the country', as the immediate neighbourhood within a mile or so of town was styled by Troy's inhabitants, to pay his customary call either upon Mr Tregentil of Penquite or the Bosanko family at Lantyan.

When last heard of, the retired tea planter had been in the best of health, hard at work on his new craze for etymology which had led him so far beyond his original task of sorting the doctor's papers, that the latter had demanded the whole bundle be posted back to him; while Johnny Bosanko, the scar on his forehead luckily all that remained of what might have been a serious injury, had more need of a schoolmaster's cane than the doctor's physic.

One evening towards the end of the month, dismissing the last of his surgery patients, and wandering into the dining room to await his dinner and read his post, Doctor Carfax found a note from Mrs Bosanko asking his blessing on a proposed expedition to Castle-an-Dinas.

'Dear Doctor,' she wrote, 'Mr Tregentil has very kindly offered to take the children to see the big earth-castle near St Columb, where it seems his ancestors lived centuries ago, and would it be too much for Johnny, and should they wait until spring? I don't want to disappoint them, and if you say they can go, then go they shall. I am pleased to tell you Johnny seems entirely recovered. Yours sincerely, Alice Bosanko.'

The doctor, with a quiet chuckle, laid the letter aside. The idea that his patient's researches had brought him to the point of claiming kinship with the unknown dwellers on Castle-an-Dinas – for such was obviously the earth-castle near St Columb mentioned by Mrs Bosanko – was the best piece of news he had heard that day. Tregentil would be claiming descent next from the virgin Columba herself, which would upset a great many people, especially those who paid their devotions to the saint in St Columb Church; though possibly the realization that the manor of Tresaddern, west of the earthwork, was so named because it was one Tre-saddarne, the god Saturn's town, would shock them even more.

As far as the children were concerned, nothing would be better for them than a day's outing on high ground and out of the valley, except to extend the time to a couple of days or even more.

'Mona,' he remarked to his housekeeper, as she bore in the evening meal, a plump pheasant shot on a nearby estate and sent as token of esteem by the owner, 'Mona, does your good sister at Tresaddern Farm still take in visitors?'

'She does indeed, doctor,' said Mona, 'and had a house full of them all summer. Though what they find to do but walk, and fish in the stream a mile away, I could not tell you. Some folk have odd ideas of spending a holiday.'

Doctor Carfax, noting with relief that his housekeeper had not forgotten the breadcrumbs, carved wing and breast from the succulent bird and sat himself down at the table.

'Do you think she would have room for Mr Tregentil and the Bosanko children, if they halted there for a couple of days to give young Johnny a change of air, and Mr Tregentil a chance to seek his forbears?' he inquired.

'I feel certain she would, sir,' replied the housekeeper. 'She lives in but half the house as it is, and any visitors would be gone by now. I'll write and make sure if you wish me to.'

The doctor considered. 'Then do that, Mona,' he said, 'and I tell you what, in addition. If the party cares to make the expedition next Friday, staying over Saturday, we'll let them have half of that excellent Spanish ham that Mr McPhail sent along yesterday from the customs office. If you sister is half as good a cook as you are, Mr Tregentil will forget about his doubtful ancestry, and give himself up to the delights of Epicurus.'

'Yes, sir,' agreed Mona, pleased with the compliment paid to herself and her family, for although totally unacquainted with Greek philosophy, she knew enough of her master's ways to take his point.

She wrote off post-haste to her sister Mrs Polwhele at Tresaddern Farm, asking for rooms for 'a wealthy patient of dear doctor's and two well-behaved children,' and received a reply by return that 'the whole of Tresaddern would be put at the disposal of Doctor Carfax's party.'

So far so good. Notes were duly dispatched to Mrs Bosanko and Mr Tregentil from the doctor, explaining that he had taken it upon himself to arrange accommodation for the explorers on the Friday and the Saturday of the coming week with Mrs Polwhele of Tresaddern, sister to his own housekeeper, and as Tresaddern was in the immediate vicinity of Castle-an-Dinas the expedition could be made in perfect comfort. It would also afford him the greatest pleasure, added the doctor in the note to Mr Tregentil, to provide the party with a certain addition to the Saturday dinner, which, if eaten with moderation and at least four hours before retiring to bed, would do none of them any harm.

Missives expressing the warmest thanks from both Lantyan and Penquite found their way to the doctor's house within twenty-four hours.

'All fears as to the advisability of the expedition so late in the year are now laid at rest,' declared Mrs Bosanko, while Mr Tregentil, who had been in some anxiety about the discomfort of sitting in the entrenchment of Castle-an-Dinas eating a cold pasty on an empty stomach, admitted 'the knowledge that a warm bed and a delicious meal await us at the conclusion of a long day, with the possibility that Tresaddern Farm may prove to be on the site of the long vanished Tregentil manor, has added enormously to the pleasure of the instigator of the plan.'

Neither Mrs Bosanko nor Mr Tregentil thought it necessary, nor indeed of interest, to add that Amyot Trestane, with the consent of his employer Gabriel Bosanko, would accompany the party to Tresaddern at the special request of Mary and Johnny.

Now if Mrs Bosanko had let well alone, and not thought it necessary to take young Johnny into Troy to buy a warm overcoat at the draper's shop opposite the Rose and Anchor, it is very possible that word of the proposed expedition would never have reached the ear of one who, in the opinion of Johnny's mother, was least suitable to hear it. Johnny's old overcoat was still perfectly wearable, if indeed a little short and slightly gone at the elbows, but with so much talk of Mr Tregentil's ancestral home, Mrs Bosanko had decided that nothing would do but that her son must have a new garment. She bustled into the draper's shop in Trafalgar Square on the Wednesday morning, her eye already caught by the smart little model, shaped like a sailor's pea-jacket, displayed in the window, and so intent was she upon her purchase that she did not notice that Johnny himself had lingered on the doorstep, and was waving a cheerful hand to Deborah Brangwyn, herself shaking a duster out of an upper window of the Rose and Anchor.

'We're off to Castle-an-Dinas on Friday,' he called, 'Amyot and Mary and me. We're going for two nights, all on our own, without Father or Mother.' The boast held all the bravado of one temporarily freed from parental supervision. 'Is that so?' returned Deborah. 'Well, you are a lucky boy. And who owns Castle-an-Dinas, if you please? The fairies, I suppose.'

'No, they don't,' replied Johnny. 'They've got nothing to do with it. Both Castle-an-Dinas and Tresaddern Farm, where we're to sleep, is Mr Tregentil's seignorial rights.'

It was at this moment that Mrs Bosanko summoned her son inside the draper's shop to try on the overcoat, and Deborah was left to make what she could of the latter part of Johnny's sentence. Her mistress should know of it, at all events, for since an embargo had been placed upon visits between the Rose and Anchor and Lantyan, news of the Bosanko household had been scarce.

If the Bosanko children were setting forth on some jaunt, accompanied only by the young man lately acquitted of manslaughter, then a letter from Deborah's mistress to Tresaddern Farm, wherever that might be, could be dispatched in safety. It did not occur to Deborah that the hostess of the Rose and Anchor would have further ideas on the subject.

A little later in the day, when the landlord was safely below in the bar saloon, the maid slipped along to deliver her news. Linnet Lewarne, sorting linen for want of a better occupation, and forbearing to scold Pettigrew who was licking his minute paws on a patchwork quilt, listened intently, then cast an eye upon the almanack hanging on the wall.

'Saturday next is the thirty-first,' she said to Deborah. 'Does the date suggest anything in particular to you?'

'Only that it is All Hallows' E'en,' replied Deborah promptly, 'and those who wish to learn their fate must look into a mirror holding a lighted candle.'

Her mistress laughed scornfully. 'I did that twenty times as a girl, and look what it brought me,' she answered. 'No, the dead may rise from their graves and the saints look down from heaven for all I care. But if I'm not mistaken, next Saturday the thirty-first is the day the licensees and publicans hold their annual dinner and Mr Lewarne is bidden to it.'

Deborah, seizing a pile of linen from the bed, stared thought-fully at her mistress. 'It could be so,' she replied, after a moment, 'but that doesn't mean it would be right for you to go tearing off in the opposite direction the instant he's away.'

Linnet smiled. It was fortunate that only Deborah could see the smile, for it savoured of triumph.

'There'll be no need,' she said. 'The dinner this year is at the Indian Queen. Landlords are asked to bring their wives.'

Tresaddern – Castle-an-Dinas – these were names that conveyed little to Deborah, but like anyone else who helped serve in a bar, and listened to alehouse talk, she had heard of the Indian Queen, a lonely inn set somewhere in wild country on the high road between Bodmin and Truro, and a famous place for brawls by all accounts.

'If it's noise and excitement and drinking you are after, you'll find it there,' she told her mistress, 'But what a dinner at the Indian Queen has to do with the Bosanko children and Someone Else I can't for the life of me see.'

'You will if you look at a map,' replied Linnet, and seizing Pettigrew in her arms she left the room and made her way downstairs to the saloon. No, she had not been mistaken. The old map hanging on the wall told her all she desired to know. The Indian Queen, some few miles from St Columb, stood at equal distance from the hill fortress marked Castle-an-Dinas; as to Tresaddern Farm, anyone in the district would inform her of its whereabouts. She looked across at her husband. He was sitting, as was his wont these days, in a state of dejection, his chin supported by his hand, his eyes staring down at the empty glass in front of him.

'You are not well, it seems,' said Linnet, moving softly to his side and removing the glass. 'That's what comes of sitting within doors all day and drinking more than your customers.'

Her husband glanced up at her and sighed. 'If I do,' he answered, 'you know whose fault it is.'

'Oh come,' said Linnet, 'it's the way of husbands to blame their own sullen temper on their wives. To tell you the truth, I've been out of sorts myself these past weeks and could do with a change.'

The landlord seized her hand. 'I'll take you anywhere you want to go,' he said, with an eagerness born of despair. 'You've only to say the word.'

His wife shrugged. 'It's too late in the year,' she replied. 'Where in the world could we go, the pair of us, and not be bored to tears?' She paused, and feigned to sweep the table clean in front of him. 'What's this dinner you have to attend this coming Saturday?' she asked casually.

'The publicans' annual, up at the Indian Queen,' he told her. 'We're both bidden for the night, but I accepted only for myself.'

Linnet wrinkled her nose, in part disgust, in part consideration. 'It would mean a drive at all events,' she said with pretended disdain, 'and a chance to wear a new dress. I suppose you refused for me because you prefer to drink with your friends?'

'Nay, Linnet, you know that isn't true.' Mark Lewarne clung to his wife. 'Why, if you'd care to come with me you would make me the proudest man in Cornwall. I never for a moment thought it possible.'

Linnet, with one of her rare gestures of conciliation, bent over her seated husband and touched him lightly on the brow.

'Mind you, I don't promise,' she told him, 'but if the weather looks settled Friday we might set out that day, and shop and sleep in St Austell, so that we could make an early start Saturday and arrive at the Indian Queen before midday. That way I could walk and see something of the countryside before it's time to change for the dinner, and you' – she paused – 'you could greet your publican friends sober for a change.'

A letter addressed to Amyot Trestane, Tresaddern Farm, near St Columb, was handed in to the postmaster's office across the way by Deborah some twenty minutes later.

The evening of Friday, the 30th of October, Doctor Carfax, turning out of Fore Street into Trafalgar Square, after visiting a patient at the other end of town, perceived the carrier Bill Pherris, who the preceding day, at his instructions, had delivered a half-ham wrapped in butter muslin to Mr Tregentil at Penquite. Bill Pherris, at the sight of the doctor, looked sheepish, and slapped his hand on his pocket.

'Dang me if it hadn't slipped my memory,' he apologised. 'Here I've been carrying this around, doctor, since yesterday forenoon.'

He bared his head and handed over a letter, which the doctor took from his with pretended gravity. 'It won't do, Bill,' he said, shaking his head. 'Suppose Mr Tregentil at Penquite had been seized with a heart attack, and had trusted you to be his messenger? No, I was only joking. Run along in to the Rose and Anchor and have your pint.'

The carrier grinned and disappeared, and Doctor Carfax, aware that stout Mrs McPhail, who once engaged in conversation kept at it for a full ten minutes – for he had timed her before now by the church clock – was approaching him from the direction of the churchyard, altered his course like a tacking yacht and dived into the front entrance of the Rose and Anchor to avoid her. The word would go round of course. Doctor Carfax has to have his nip. No matter, gossip was preferable to Mrs McPhail's chatter. He seized the opportunity, while safe under cover, of glancing through the note just handed to him by the carrier. A rapid reading produced an explosion which, had Mrs McPhail been near to hear it, would have sent her to tell all Troy that Doctor Carfax's temper had become so violent that he was no longer to be trusted by his patients.

'Now if this doesn't beat all!' exclaimed the doctor, stamping his foot with such vigour that Ned Varcoe, left on duty within the bar, could hear him from the other end of the passage, and limped along to the front entrance to see who was disturbing the peace.

'Dear Carfax,' ran the note, 'my warm thanks for the welcome haunch of venison that has just arrived. It will be given to your housekeeper's sister the instant we descend at Tresaddern, and as the four of us, young Amyot, the children, and myself, expect to have hearty appetites, we shall look forward to an excellent stew for Saturday's dinner. We intend to leave in the brougham at crack of dawn Friday. Sincerely, E. Tregentil.'

Venison! The half of the Spanish ham dubbed venison! To be stewed for Saturday's dinner! The very word was sacrilege. And to take Amyot Trestane, of all men, to wander at will on Castle-an-Dinas, haunted as it was by – but a voice close behind him put a stop to further hurried reflection.

'Can I do anything for you, doctor?'

Little Ned Varcoe, who barely reached his hip, was standing in the passage.

'No, thank you, Ned. I was merely – h'm – giving utterance to my feelings. How is your mistress? Well, I trust, and the landlord too?'

The crippled barman nodded. 'Well enough when they set out midday,' he answered, 'but how long their tempers agree I don't prophesy. They'll be away till Sunday, master reckoned, staying for the dinner Saturday at the Indian Queen.'

'The Indian Queen?'

'That's right, doctor. Master was going anyway, and the mistress, she suddenly took it into her head she wanted a change of air.'

Little doubt of it. And the Indian Queen not three miles distant from Castle-an-Dinas. That fool Tregentil – that double-dyed fool.

Doctor Carfax bade the bartender a curt good night, and stepped across the road to the postmaster's office. He was used to making quick decisions – it was part of his profession – and a moment's calculation told him that the goods train carrying minerals on the special branch line between St Blazey and Roche left betimes on a Saturday morning. It was a lucky thing that he had safely delivered the engine-driver's wife of twins not two weeks since. The train, forbidden by law to carry passengers, would carry him. He would be at Castle-an-Dinas by noon if all went well, and in time to prevent mischief: and at

211

the worst, disaster. As for his patients, they must take care of themselves for twenty-four hours. Or call in young Tehidy.

A telegram, addressed 'Tregentil, Tresaddern, St Columb', was handed in to the care of the postmaster within a few minutes of Doctor Carfax's decision, and ran as follows:

KEEP AN EYE ON YOUNG AMYOT INTEND JOINING YOU BY MIDDAY SATURDAY ON NO ACCOUNT HASH HAM

REGARDS CARFAX

25

Castle-an-Dinas

Mr Tregentil, being an uncommonly poor whip, had no intention of driving the party to Castle-an-Dinas. Open dogcarts were suited to hardy persons such as his medical adviser, but to set forth the last two days of October for a distance of some eighteen miles, a close vehicle was imperative, with coachman Dingle taking the reins. The children and Amyot could sit in turn upon the box, and if anyone felt sick within the brougham the windows let down with the greatest ease.

The plan was for Mr Tregentil to leave in the brougham from Penquite at eight o'clock in the morning, and to pick up his little party on the high road by Lantyan turning some twenty minutes later. They would proceed on to the main Bodmin-Truro road by way of Lanlivery, and all being well should reach the right-hand turn to Castle-an-Dinas within two hours and a half. A halt for picnic luncheon would be made beside the rough track leading up to the earthwork, and then, if it continued fine, the party of four would walk up the hill to explore the castle. Dingle would deliver their belongings to Mrs Polwhele at Tresaddern Farm, and continue with the brougham the two miles on to St Columb, where he would put up at the Red Lion Hotel.

Friday dawned fine if somewhat chill, with all proceeding

according to plan: Johnny, 'lording it' upon the box, wearing his new overcoat, and Mary seated in style like a true lady beside her host, with Amyot on the opposite seat.

Mr Tregentil, wrapped in a carriage rug to his chin, his feet in a muff, wore a Tyrolean hat pierced with a rook's feather, the whole harmonizing ill with his olive complexion. It gave the wearer, nevertheless, a distinct air of an explorer: one who might at any moment climb a precipice and shoot a chamois. Amyot, fitted up by Mr Bosanko in breeches, gaiters and jacket, still sported Mary's hair-ribbon in his buttonhole; a piece of childish nonsense which Mrs Bosanko feigned to ignore when she bid her daughter farewell after breakfast.

Mary, relaxing in the brougham with half-closed eyes, torn between a desire to laugh at Mr Tregentil, whose long nose peaked over the carriage rug like a rook itself, and a fear that she might yet be sick if the window was not opened wider, found ultimate solace in Amyot's smile of understanding, his surreptitious raising of the sash, and the occasional proximity of his knee beneath the second carriage rug.

Johnny was in heaven: or, to be more correct, in that soaring world of childhood where, seated on a brougham box, he found with every turn in the road a fresh wonder and a new delight. The trees were golden, the hedgerows russet brown, bright now and again with rose-hip berries, and as they left Lanlivery behind them, and the great mass of Helmen Tor showed beyond them to the right, it seemed to Johnny that his heart must surely burst with excitement, for the familiar wooded valley of his home was lost behind him, and he was now entering the wild hunting ground of fighting men long dead.

Stately Captain, Mr Tregentil's carriage bay, breasted the hills like a war-horse, and when, after some twisting and turning for five miles or more the brougham emerged on to the great high road from Bodmin to Truro, with the country rolling away to north and west and the coast in the far distance, Johnny leapt up and down on the box urging Mr Dingle the coachman to greater speed. This Mr Dingle was not prepared to do, the truth being that he disapproved of the whole expedition. An excursion was all very well in late spring or early summer, with a two-hour wait for horse or horses near a shady grove or a convenient inn; but to take an animal out for some eighteen miles or more in late autumn, to a part of the country where no civilized being went, and expect horse and coachman to spend two nights away from their own comfortable quarters at home, in a strange hostelry at St Columb, was, in Mr Dingle's opinion, a little short of murder. It would do the brougham no good: the springs would go. They would probably lose a wheel. The horse would become overheated and take chill. The bedding at St Columb would be damp. All these fears, and more besides, he expressed to Johnny in tones of resigned gloom, punctuating each sentence with: 'I don't hold with it. 'Tis no time o' year to be taking the the horse on the road. If we come to a sudden descent I can't hold 'im'.

There was no sudden descent. The great high road spanned the country like a ribbon, and, as Johnny was quick to point out, the surface was much better than that between St Sampson's and Troy, to which Captain was accustomed. 'Maybe today,' the coachman grudgingly allowed, 'but come a bit of frost, and poor Captain's feet would go from under him.'

'There'll be no frost,' promised Johnny. 'Father's barometer is set fair, and not too high. We may have showers and them not heavy.'

Mr Dingle grunted. ''Tis diff'rent up here to what 'tis back home,' he muttered; 'a shower up here's a proper cloudburst. A road will run water in less than no time, and we'll have Captain slathering to his withers.'

A rattle from the window below and the sound of his master's voice made the coachman draw rein and pause in his tale of foreboding.

'Bear right soon after we pass the turning to Roche, Dingle,' called Mr Tregentil, 'but do not take the turning to Withiel or

215

St Wenn. Our road should be marked St Columb, and we should be able to see Castle-an-Dinas standing high on the hill long before we come to it.'

'Yes, sir,' replied the coachman saluting with his whip, but when his master's head was withdrawn he repeated, for perhaps the tenth time: 'I don't hold with it.'

Mr Dingle, expecting a turreted battlement albeit in ruins, was more convinced than ever of the folly of the expedition when, after some further half-hour's driving, Johnny called excitedly: 'Look, I think that's it, away yonder, like a hump on the skyline, that's Castle-an-Dinas.'

The coachman, shocked into momentary silence, followed the line of Johnny's pointing finger. 'Is that what we've come for?' he asked incredulously. 'Poor Captain's pulled the brougham some fifteen mile to see that old hillock? If Mr Tregentil had any sense he'd bid me turn right round and go home again.'

'Hush,' whispered Johnny. 'Mr Tregentil's ancestors lived there.'

'I dare say they did,' observed the disgusted coachman. 'Savages in skins, mos' likely. No proper gentleman would stand it.'

Mary, within the brougham, pressed to the window by her enthusiastic host, was of much the same opinion as Mr Dingle. Castle-an-Dinas was nothing but a hill, ringed with furze bushes. It was no better than Castle Dor, where she and Johnny used to play hide-and-seek when waiting for the horses to be shod. It did not really matter of course. The excitement lay in staying away from home and being with Amyot.

'It – it must have a very fine view,' she said politely.

Mr Tregentil, busy with a map, brushed the remark aside. 'It commanded the whole of Cornwall, and was obviously quite impregnable,' he told her, with pardonable exaggeration. 'See, Amyot. You have nothing so fine in Britanny, I'll be bound.'

Amyot, after a quick glance at their distant objective, resumed his seat. He was looking a little pale. The result, so Mary thought with sympathy, of sitting with his back to the horse. It would

216

not be long now before they reached their halting-place and could all get out.

There was no mistaking the turning and the sign 'St Columb'. The coachman continued along the side-road until further shouting from within the brougham warned him they had reached the first stage of his two-day purgatory.

'Eleven-thirty. Excellent time. I congratulate you, Dingle,' cried his master. The coachman touched his hat in silence, and proceeded to sit in a posture of resignation, while Amyot helped the party to descend.

'It won't do, sir,' Dingle said in sepulchral tones, 'to keep Captain standing long. He'll take chill, seeing how hot he is, an' the distance he's been.'

'No, no, of course not. Quick with the hamper, Amyot; we'll eat here, and let Dingle and the brougham go.' Mr Tregentil, always a little apprehensive in the presence of his coachman, flustered around giving directions. 'Spread the rugs, that's it, Mary, we mustn't get damp ourselves – very unwise. Dingle, don't waste another minute, proceed down the lane to the right, into the valley, and leave our things with Mrs Polwhele at Tresaddern, and then do you go on with the horse and brougham to St Columb as arranged. Be back for us on Sunday morning at half past eight.'

A few minutes later the coachman, head bowed, shoulders hunched, disappeared from view, for all the world like a mourner conducting a hearse.

'Can't we eat up at the castle?' begged Johnny. 'It's easy to carry the things. Please, Mr Tregentil.'

This was agreed upon after some little demur, and Amyot, shouldering rugs and luncheon basket, led the way up the rough path towards the encampment.

'Stay, Amyot,' called Mr Tregentil. 'Let me consult the map to find the entrance. We can't leap ditches, laden as we are.'

'It's to the right, sir,' said Amyot; 'the east gate is nearest to us.' He pointed with confidence greatly to the surprise of Mr Tregentil, and continued to lead the way at a bounding pace.

'Most unusual,' murmured Mr Tregentil. 'He never as much as glanced at the map.'

When he and Mary topped the rise they found Amyot and Johnny waiting for them by the outer perimeter of the earthwork, and there was the entrance, just as Amyot had said, breeching one ditch and then a second, until it finally opened on to the centre of the encampment itself, which, overgrown with bracken and furze, covered some acre and a half of land.

'Come,' said Mr Tregentil, surveying the scene with satisfaction, 'let us unpack the hamper, eat and then explore.'

Amyot, the basket still on his shoulder, intervened. 'You'll find it drier, sir, across the centre, overlooking the northern rampart.'

Mary, puzzled, stared at Amyot. Why did he use the word 'rampart', and how did he know it would be drier there? Anyone would think it was Amyot's ancestors who had lived at Castle-an-Dinas, and not Mr Tregentil's at all.

'We'll soon have a fire lighted, and can boil the kettle,' continued Amyot. 'Johnny, you'll find a pool of water to the right there, good for drinking. The sheep and cattle that graze here won't have fouled it.'

It was curious. He seemed to be in charge. He spoke faster than usual, and with authority.

Somewhat perplexed, Mr Tregentil followed Amyot to the piece of ground designated, and yes, it was exceedingly dry, with granite slabs to sit upon, while below to the right lay the dewpond, sure enough, towards which Johnny was clambering, kettle in hand.

Amyot stood motionless. He set down hamper and rugs, and stared about him.

'Dinas,' he said, as though to himself, 'Dinas . . .'

'Correctly spoken,' agreed Mr Tregentil. 'Dinas, the Cornish for hill-fort.'

'Oh no, sir,' disputed Amyot. 'It's a man's name by rights, and he my friend.'

218

Mary, of a sudden, felt uncomfortable. It was all very well for Amyot to play these games with Johnny, but it hardly did to make fun of Mr Tregentil. She turned away, and began gathering sticks for the fire to hide her confusion. Johnny came running up, the kettle filled with water. 'It's fresh as anything,' he cried. 'I tasted some of it.'

'Why, naturally,' said Amyot, 'with some hundreds of men and horses depending upon it, and no spring or river near. Climb the inner rampart there, Johnny, and see how stoutly it's built against attack.'

Mr Tregentil was a little put out. Amyot had been brought to fetch and carry, not to air his uneducated opinion upon the finest earthwork in all Cornwall. This was the prerogative of Mr Tregentil himself.

'You must know, children,' he announced, with an eye upon Amyot, 'there are other fortresses so named. There are two on the south coast, near St Antony. Dinas . . . Dinan . . . Dennis . . . all these words mean fortress.'

'And he who mans them a chieftain, serving the great king,' said Amyot to Johnny, who smiled and nodded.

Mary, her face scarlet, pressed a pasty, wrapped in a napkin, upon Mr Tregentil. He took up his stance beside her on the rug, and during the picnic and luncheon addressed his remarks upon the structure of hill fortresses strictly to Mary, who understood no word of it. Later, when the crumbs were gathered, the napkins folded and the embers of the fire trodden underfoot, Mr Tregentil ensconced himself on the highest perimeter complete with map and field-glasses, while Johnny, brandishing a new-peeled stick to serve as sword, stood on sentry-go beneath him.

'Amyot,' said Mary, as he helped her fasten the hamper, 'it was not very polite of you and Johnny to make mock of Mr Tregentil.'

Amyot looked at her in amazement, 'I make mock of him?' he repeated. 'If I did so I had no intention of it, and I'm very sorry.'

They finished packing in silence. The air was oddly still, a different stillness, thought Mary, from the woods at home, or down by the river shore. High up here, under the sky, it was as though she and Amyot and Mr Tregentil and Johnny had in some way trespassed on forbidden ground. Those great banks were treacherous, making the circle seem a prison; she could think of no worse fate than to twist an ankle and lie alone here, staring at the sky.

'I wonder what manner of folk it was who really lived here?' she said to Amyot.

He did not answer, and looking up at him she saw his face was pale again, as it had been in the brougham, and his eyes were troubled.

'Rough men if you like,' he said, 'but all my friends, and Dinas the wisest and the best, bearing me here to die. The causeway's yonder, beneath the grass under the westward gate, and that was the way she rode, when Dinas brought her to my side.'

Then suddenly he leapt to his feet, waving his hand to her brother. 'Come, Johnny,' he said, 'I'll defend the fortress and you shall storm it,' and it was all play after all, the nonsense they shared together; yet Mary stood there watching them, anxious for no good reason.

Presently, laughing and breathless, they flung themselves down in the bracken beside Mr Tregentil, and, with a warning glance at Johnny, Amyot respectfully begged their host to conduct them round the encampment.

Later, when the afternoon turned chill, Mr Tregentil decided it was time to descend to the valley, and find their quarters at Tresaddern Farm. Passing through the western entrance they made their way down the slope, but not before Mary, bringing up the rear, had stopped to touch the grass. Amyot was right. It had been a causeway once. She could feel the stones.

Down in the valley, sheltered by a cluster of trees, stood the comforting grey farm-house, reminding Mary of all the scents and sounds she had left behind her at Lantyan; a fat sow snuf-fled in the mud, young turkeys ran in the midden and a smiling broadhipped Mrs Polwhele waited at the door to greet them. She curtsied low at sight of her guests, declaring in strident tones – a habit of hers when nervous – that it was the greatest honour to receive such a nobleman as Mr Tregentil under her humble roof, bringing his handsome family with him, and wasn't the eldest young gentleman the image of his father. The compli-ment was well intended, but unfortunate. Mr Tregentil, who had been on his feet since before seven that morning, felt a prick of irritation.

'You are under a misapprehension, my good woman,' he said. 'These young people are the children of a neighbouring farmer, and this is their French attendant. What is that I see, a telegram?'

Mrs Polwhele, profuse in her apologies, dipping to the ground with every word that passed her lips, proffered him Doctor Carfax's telegram on a silver salver. 'There's a letter too, sir,' she said, her voice rising in excitement. 'It must be for – for the foreign gentleman – Mr Trestane, I think it is.'

She hurriedly produced a second salver, and the envelope bearing Linnet's bold handwriting upon it was handed with another curtsy to the astonished Amyot. Mr Tregentil, intent upon his telegram, had turned his back. Johnny, forgetting his manners, was already half way to the kitchen. Amyot, with a quick glance at the handwriting, thrust the letter in his pocket. Mary alone was seized with apprehension.

'It's from Mrs Lewarne,' she thought. 'That's why he hasn't said a word.' Her day, that had dawned so fair, was suddenly doomed. She walked slowly with sinking heart to the bright parlour.

26

Doctor Carfax sets forth

It was raw and foggy when Doctor Carfax alighted at Roche station on the Saturday morning at the uncomfortable hour of half past seven. He decided to have breakfast at the adjoining inn, and there see if he could hire a conveyance to take him on to Tresaddern, failing which, he must rely on his own two feet. The prospect did not daunt him, for the farm was only a few miles distant, and providing he stuck to the road, and the fog did not thicken, the walk would serve to clear his head, reeling as it was at the moment from the roar of the engine, the hiss of steam, and the loquacity of the engine-driver.

The ride up through Luxilian valley, had it been done in summer, on a fine morning, would have proved instructive – even amusing; as it was – to stamp up and down St Blazey platform in the small hours, collar turned up, hands in pockets, and then hail his acquaintance the engine-driver with a trumped-up tale of a patient in distress, and beg a lift in the draughty cabin, one moment face ablaze with the roar of the fire and the next half jerked off his feet by the motion of the engine, was not Doctor Carfax's idea of how best to spend a few hours away from duty. Nevertheless the strange feeling of compulsion that had been with him ever since he had heard that Amyot Trestane was to form one of the party visiting Castle-an-Dinas, coupled as it was with the information that Linnet Lewarne would also be in the neighbourhood, had driven him to take this extreme measure of leaving his house like a thief in the night and boarding the train. What he intended to do was not yet clear, except at all costs to keep Linnet and her lover apart.

He had taken the opportunity after dinner, before snatching a few hours' sleep, of reading through the mass of notes compiled by his patient Tregentil, with the result that he had been more profoundly disturbed than ever. Tregentil had done his work well: too well for Carfax's comfort. His industrious patient, blissfully unaware of any deeper implications, had drawn up a *résumé* of every known legend that had any bearing on the strange history of Tristan and Iseult, and the pattern of events, curiously intermingled as they were, followed a course uncannily similar to that which was happening on the same terrain today. Thought transference seemed the only possible explanation. He, Carfax, and poor Ledru, and then Tregentil, had in some way set the appalling thing in motion, while the impressionable lad from Brittany and the impulsive young woman born at Castle Dor, had acted as mediums to a source of power which, if tapped, might revolutionize the whole conception of time in its relation to the unconscious mind. If a man, standing under the stars, could be so imbued with the spirit of a place that in delivering a child he breathed into her his own sense of haunting tragedy, dooming her to unwilling repetition of a story that was not hers, why then, good heavens! the sooner he gave up private practice the better, and his colleagues too; so that girl-children might be born in hospitals and turn to nursing when they came of age, which would be a very good thing for the country. If only poor Ledru had lived, what a *compagnon de voyage* he would have made on this particular expedition!

The recollection of the last night they had spent together, following so swiftly upon his turning over of Tregentil's notes, made Doctor Carfax stir still more uneasily in his chair.

It had been heart of course; he had conducted the post mortem himself, and yet – what was it the poet Béroul called

224

the potion that Iseult had given to her lover, and then herself? He searched the notes . . . ah, here it was, the 'lovendrant'; Tregentil had written beside it 'love-potion, in ancient English'. Linnet Lewarne had offered them a strange brew indeed that evening a year ago in the Rose and Anchor. If she had the bottle still, an analyst might show— Nonsense! he was letting his imagination run away with him, and that was fatal. He had nearly made a fool of himself once before, at Castle Dor, and would not do so again. Curious that Béroul's story broke off before the finish, and Gottfried von Strassburg's too: the last just after the lovers had parted; and Tristan, in Brittany, tried to console himself by marrying the sister of his friend Kaedin. Only one other manuscript, and the French romance in prose, gave the alternative ending, with the wounding of Tristan by Mark, and his death at the fortress of his friend Dinas. No one was likely to discover now which of the legends was true. It would certainly make for peace of mind, though, if young Amyot Trestane, unconscious participant in a struggle he did not understand, could be shipped off to his native land and find a bride. Doctor Carfax, weary of his patient Tregentil's spidery handwriting, had removed his spectacles, pushed aside the papers and yawned his way to bed, to snatch what sleep he could before setting forth at an intolerable hour of the morning. Now, next day, as he sat over eggs and bacon at the Roche inn, he seemed to remember Tregentil's having been in some exceitement over the discovery that the Cornish King Hoel, and not Duke Jovelin of Brittany, had been the father of young Kaedin, and Tristan's bride Iseult of the White Hands, namesake to the queen. Which would suggest that Tristan, in parting from the queen, never crossed the sea at all, but merely passed into another Cornish kingdom.

Well, it was of little consequence. Doctor Carfax called for his bill, and learnt, without much suprise, that it would take some little time to find him a vehicle; the butcher down in Roche would be going his rounds at ten and not before; and so without more ado he decided to walk.

It was years since he had travelled this part of the country. What an increase of building, away to the south in the clay country! Hamlets that had barely existed save for a cottage or two were now ugly villages linked together; and topping them everywhere were the great white clay peaks themselves, turning the moorland landscape into an unlikely range of mountains. Here was Tristan's 'Blanche Lande' come to life indeed, the deep lakes sunk beside the peaks; the River Par; even the Fal itself chalky white these days near to the source.

Tresaddern, if Mona had described it correctly, lay at the foot of Castle-an-Dinas to the west; a signpost turning from the St Columb road should point the way. The fog was patchy. Clear when he had set out from Roche, now it seemed to close in once more – wreaths of drifting mist, passing in front of him some fifty yards ahead, obliterating the scene on either side. It had been all moorland once, of course, stretching from Dartmoor across the Tamar to the high ground here, forming the backbone of all Cornwall, with the rest vast forest. Hardly a country for perfect knights and gentlemen. What hunting, though, amidst the heather and the granite; what savagery, what wild descents for plunder to the shore! A fire signal lit by Seneschal Dinas at his fortress here to his overlord King Mark at Castle Dor would warn him of approaching danger.

Castle-an-Dinas . . . Castle Dor . . . once bastions filled with men commanding this whole wilderness now grass mounds, sleeping under a quiet sky. Doctor Carfax left the high road for the St Columb turning, and presently, having passed some cottages, became aware of rising ground to the right of him, and despite the mist knew instinctively that the fortress lay above. Had the morning been clear, and he not pressed for time, it would have been pleasant to wander there on the summit and make comparison with the smaller Castle Dor near home. As it was he must continue on his way, and leaving an old tin mine to the left of him, he reached the valley and Tresaddern Farm in another half-mile's walk.

Tregentil might do worse than pick upon this spot for an ancestral home. The wall encompassing the piece of orchard there must be centuries old, and the farmhouse itself a manor in days gone by, rugged, strong, with space enough once for seigneur and his family and a pack of servants besides. Mona's sister had done well for herself, with this snug holding, deep enough in the sheltered valley to withstand wind and weather.

The party must be astir, for the curtains were pulled, the windows open, and there was young Johnny Bosanko himself running through the strip of front garden to the gate, a collie pup at his heels.

'Hallo, doctor,' he shouted. 'We didn't expect you till this afternoon, and Mr Tregentil said if it was misty you wouldn't come at all.'

He unlatched the gate, while the dog leapt up to paw the stranger.

'Well, Johnny, Mr Tregentil was at fault,' replied the doctor. 'I travelled somewhat rapidly as it happened. Have you long breakfasted?'

'Yes, rather,' said Johnny, 'and now I'm hungry again. Mrs Polwhele says it's the change of air. You'd best come inside, sir, out of the damp, and wait for Mr Tregentil to return.'

Doctor Carfax paused on the threshold of the house.

'Back?' he asked. 'Why, where has he gone?'

'To St Columb,' answered the boy, 'not quarter of an hour ago, he and Amyot and Mary. They've all three walked in to St Columb to look at the church, 'cos Mr Tregentil thinks his ancestors are buried there. Mind the step, sir, and there's a fire in the parlour, and here's Mrs Polwhele herself to bid you welcome.'

Doctor Carfax, remembering the courtesy due to his house-keeper's sister, removed his hat with a flourish, and although glad enough of the parlour fire, and the easy chair, and the cup of tea and cake she pressed upon him, he could have done without the life history of herself and Mona, which naturally enough he had heard a dozen times before. Curtsies, gestures, coupled with side-issues, such as her husband's series of operations during the past few years, kept Mrs Polwhele busy in a non-stop flow of conversation, while her visitor nodded politely, interposing a remark now and again, and thankful that the doubtful interest of Tregentil tombs – if they existed – would keep Amyot Trestane at Tregentil's heels within St Columb church for the remainder of the morning.

A smell of burning fat, a wild exclamation at the passing of time, recalled Mrs Polwhele to her duties in the kitchen, and the guest relaxed with a sigh, to light his first pipe since breakfasting at Roche.

'And so,' he said to Johnny, between puffs, 'you didn't please to go to the church. Why was that?'

'Because it's dull,' returned Johnny promptly, 'and if you ask me Mr Tregentil hasn't got any ancestors at all. And as to Castle-an-Dinas, why Amyot knew more about it than he did.'

'I dare say,' grunted the doctor, 'and what exactly did Amyot know?'

Johnny, who had felt in the visitor's overcoat pocket to see if he carried the usual box of cough lozenges, and was disappointed to find it empty, proceeded to climb the furniture by way of diversion.

'Well, he knew the way for one thing,' he answered, 'and where the gates were, and the pool for drinking-water, and when the others were talking he pointed out where the horses used to parade up and down before Dinas mounted them.'

Doctor Carfax grunted once again, then cocked an eye on the boy.

'Dinas?' he said cautiously. 'I thought that was the name of the castle?'

'Perhaps so,' shrugged Johnny, 'but it was the name of the owner too who served the king. And talking of kings, I've got one for an ancestor and so has Mary. Mr Tregentil discovered them in a book.'

'Get along with you,' said the doctor.

'But it's true, sir, I promise you. His name was King Heol, and he loved at Carhayes, years and years ago. And Father knew nothing about it, 'cept that Granny was a Miss Hoel before she became Bosanko. We've great-uncles and aunts living down there still, between Portloe and Gerran's Bay.'

Doctor Carfax groaned. What in the world had Tregentil been up to now? Hoel and Bosanko – as if the whole situation was not complicated enough without dragging poor Bosanko into it.

'If I were you,' he said testily, 'I should take what Mr Tregentil says with a pinch of salt.'

'Yes, sir,' agreed Johnny. 'He might be 'saggerating about the king, but Father says there've been Hoels there for generations. It's from one of the great-uncle's terrier dogs we bred Pettigrew.'

'You bred what?' said the doctor, startled.

'Why, the smallest pup in the world, that Amyot loved. He wears a bell round his neck, and is as spoilt as anything, and lives with Mrs Lewarne.'

Doctor Carfax, staring at the fire in front of him, hardly noticed when the boy ran whistling from the room. Hours later, or so it seemed, he heard the sound of carriage wheels, and rousing himself from the deep speculation into which he had been inadvertently plunged, he left his chair and went to the window. The brougham had drawn up outside the farm-house, and an agitated Tregentil was descending from it alone.

Black as thunder, Carfax strode to the door, and met his patient as he crossed the threshold.

'Where is Amyot?' he demanded.

Mr Tregentil, rook's feather askew in his hat, was visibly put out.

'He's given me the slip,' he fluttered. 'Mary too. I was in a dark corner of the church, peering at the lettering on a tomb – unfortunately not a Tregentil, none are to be found there, I was misinformed – when suddenly Mary exclaimed, "Amyot's gone, I'm after him," and before I reached the entrance both had vanished. I searched high and low, questioned passers-by, not a trace of either. I concluded the best thing to do was to fetch Dingle and the brougham, and hope to pass them on the road. But we have seen no one. We had better return to St Columb forthwith.'

Doctor Carfax, looking upward, saw that the mist was once more closing in upon the trees about Tresaddern.

'A fruitless journey,' he said grimly. 'We can spare ourselves the trouble.'

'But why, in heaven's name? Where else can they be?' asked Mr Tregentil.

The doctor, seeing young Johnny, that sprig of the line of vanished Hoels, marching up and down by a tumbled barn, stick on shoulder serving for a sword, unconscious of any adult eye upon him, turned suddenly to his older patient, and pushed him within the house.

'Not in your world, Tregentil, nor in mine,' he answered, 'but in some borderland of buried kings and lovers. Haply, on the high road to the Indian Queen. Come and eat, for we may have to travel with them before nightfall.'

27

'Now let us trick her . . .'

The night before Linnet Lewarne and her husband set forth on their two-day holiday, when the bar was closed, the shutters put up, and landlord and wife gone upstairs to bed, Deborah Brangwyn waited until the church clock struck eleven and all was still, then slipped along the passage to her master's room and softly tapped upon the door.

A hoarse voice bade her enter. The landlord was sitting humped on one side of the great brass bedstead, not yet undressed, the candlelight throwing a monstrous shadow of him on the wall behind his head.

'What's wrong?' he asked. 'Is your mistress ill?'

Deborah shook her head, motioning him to silence, then closed the door behind her.

'No, sir,' she whispered, 'but I must speak to you, and there may not be another chance.'

The landlord glowered. 'Can't be so urgent you have to disturb me in my bed,' he muttered. 'Well, what is it? Out with it.'

Deborah set down the candle and stood with folded arms.

'You must know my mistress has deceived you, and has done so this long while,' she said.

Mark Lewarne made as though to rise, the bed creaking

under him; then he sat down again, heavily, and stretched out his hand for the tumbler of whisky beside him.

'I don't want that gossip,' he said harshly. 'I've had more than enough of it from Ned. You can shut your trap.'

He swallowed down the whisky, and the hand that replaced the glass was trembling.

'If I speak it's for her sake I do it, not for yours,' said Deborah. 'She has a good home here, and all she needs, with you dying a wealthy man; and that before long if you continue the way you do. Be angry if you like, I don't care. When you're dead and gone she must do as she pleases. But to run off now with a penniless farm-labourer, and he a foreigner who's barely escaped prison, will ruin her life for ever, as well as yours and mine.'

The landlord stared: his head, for all the whisky he had taken, strangely clear. 'So it was true,' he said slowly. 'The Breton lad – Ned swore it was he and I wouldn't believe him. They met and kissed in the moonlight, but that was in summer. Why, he was shut up and waiting trial for several weeks, wasn't he? And now he's back at Bosanko's, sworn to good behaviour?'

'That's so,' Deborah nodded, 'but nothing will keep them from running off if once they meet. Mistress wrote him two days ago – I posted the letter. Not to Lantyan – he isn't there. He's gone with the Bosanko children to a farm called Tresaddern, not a few miles from the Indian Queen. Now you see why she's so eager to go with you. It's not for the dinner, nor your sweet company, but for his bright eyes she's doing it, and so to seize her chance and be gone.'

Deborah snapped her fingers, and in the brief gesture the landlord saw the destruction of all his hopes and dreams, nurtured, despite his fears, during the past months. They were away, without thought or care, a pair of lovers blinded to all sense of duty, taking ship and sailing out of his life for ever, gone without recall, Linnet and the Breton lad, with a snap of Deborah's angers.

'I'll waken her,' he said. 'I'll go and wake her now and tax her with it.'

'No,' said Deborah swiftly, 'you'll never stop her that way, it would madden her the more. Listen, while I tell you . . .'

She drew near, sinking her voice to a whisper, and now their two shadows merged together on the wall, out of all proportion, menacing, grotesque.

Never, thought Mark Lewarne, when he and his wife set forth next day to St Austell, driven by Tim Udy in the barouche, had Linnet appeared so beautiful; never, in the bare two years of their wedded life, so carefree, or so gay.

She even smiled upon Ned Varcoe, whom she so much despised, bidding him see that the hostelry did not burn down in their absence, and then kissing the top of her dog's head, which was no larger than a man's fist, gave him into the charge of Deborah, with instructions to feed him upon stewed rabbit. 'You may eat cold meat yourselves,' she said, 'but Pettigrew must have the best.' So saying, she stepped into the carriage like a queen, hands enfolded in a warm muff, the blue stuff of her coat matching her eyes.

They put up at the White Hart, and she insisted that her husband should go shopping with her, and buy her gloves and a new hat, the flightiest hat you ever did see, made of velvet and ribbon – joking the while with the shop assistant as she chose it, declaring she would wear it at the dinner, for she, and none other, was the Indian Queen. They left the shop, Linnet with the hat set jauntily upon her head, her arm linked in her husband's, and surely, thought Mark Lewarne, she has not only me bewitched but the town as well, for everyone they passed stared at her, glancing back in admiration, while at the White Hart his acquaintance, the landlord, treated her more like royalty than the wife of a fellow publican.

It can't be true, Mark Lewarne told himself, when she toasted him at dinner, it can't be true what Deborah said, she does not mean to deceive me; no woman with a lie on her conscience could show herself so artless and so free from guilt.

233

'It was a holiday I needed,' she told him. 'I've been fretting this long while for a change of air. I feel a different being already'; going willingly to his arms, for the first time in months, when they came to share the room put at their disposal.

She slept beside him like an innocent child, who for too long had slammed her door in his face when he dared approach it, or even locked it to insult him more. What if it had been jealousy and spite that had driven Deborah to make her accusation? Women did such things after a tiff. Linnet had not ridden abroad or visited Lantyan since August to his certain knowledge. She had spent most of her days sitting up in the big guest-chamber, with that ridiculous dog on her knees, cold and sulky it was true, but perhaps for the very reason she had given him this night – she needed change.

'We'll see what morning brings,' decided her husband, before dropping off to a troubled sleep. 'If she's still sweet and loving, and acts the same when we reach journey's end, then Deborah's a liar, and the sooner she's dismissed the better 'twill be for the pair of us.'

The morning brought fog, a clammy cold air drifting past the window when Linnet, the first to awaken, threw wide the sash. She dressed hurriedly, and was fastening her gown when her husband opened his eyes.

'What's the haste?' he murmured. 'We've the whole day before us, haven't we?' His wife, so clinging at midnight, did not deign to throw him a glance today. 'The sun's deserted us,' she said briefly. 'We'd best be off before the weather spoils my hat.'

Then he understood. This was the sort of weather when anyone in their senses stayed in town. He yawned and stretched. 'We'd be more comfortable here,' he remarked, his eye upon her. 'Another day's shopping and so home, giving the Indian Queen a miss.'

She paused, her hands now busy with her hair, and came to the bed.

'Shame on you, Mark Lewarne,' she said, pulling the sheets

from him, 'afraid of a bit of mist. Why, it will be bright enough on the high ground. Every one of your friends foregathering at the Indian Queen, and the landlord of Troy's Rose and Anchor dare not stir.'

If his spirits sank it was not because of the weather, but at sight of her cold eyes, her determined chin. The bait must be strong to lure her some nine miles in doubtful weather to a comfortless spot in the clay country. When they descended, dressed, and ready to mount the carriage, the White Hart landlord stared at them, astonished.

'You're never leaving in this fog?' he cried. 'Why, 'twill be thick as a blanket round St Denis. I decided against it myself as soon as I put back the shutters. I tell you, Lewarne, you'll find the dinner cancelled. No one will drive from Bodmin to Truro when they see how it is.'

Lewarne glanced at his wife to see how she took it. Linnet, unsmiling this morning, held out her hand to their host.

'Thanks for your advice,' she said, 'but we're not accepting it. It isn't often my husband and I take a holiday. If we lose ourselves we'll just draw in to the side of the road and sit tight. He'll not regret it.'

At this the landlord of the White Hart set up a roar of laughter, and slapped his friend on the shoulder. 'Why Lord, nor would I, in his place,' he said. 'There's one thing, ma'am, if the dinner does come off your husband will be the most envied man at the table.'

Could be, thought Mark Lewarne, could be. But only if the woman he'd held in his arms last night was his alone. And that, in this morning's light, was doubtful.

'Wosh! and away there,' called Tim Udy, who at the prospect of a couple of nights' free liquor consumed in freedom, safe from a scolding wife, would have driven the horses to perdition; a further few bleak miles, and another point of hospitality, would serve only to raise a double thirst. He reckoned, and so had Linnet, on improving conditions. But it was one thing to climb up to St Denis and the clay country on a fine morning, with all the landmarks clear; another to cover the same ground in growing fog, the road seeming to branch in all directions. Were they, in fact, on the St Denis road at all, or striking away from it to the bare downs? The horses plodded on, Tim Udy peering to right and left, cursing the scarcity of signposts, while within the carriage Mark Lewarne sat silent, aware of his wife's hands restless within her muff.

'He's missed the road,' she kept saying. 'I tell you the fool has missed the road.'

'If he has,' replied her husband, 'we can always turn back again.'

No answer to this, save an impatient tapping of her foot on the floor and a gesture of exasperation. Here was a different creature from the smiling, placating wife of yesterday; and his heart grew heavy within him.

It was nearing midday when, peering from the carriage window, Mark Lewarne discerned a river to the left of them. 'It must be the Fal,' he exclaimed, 'in which case we're miles off course and may as well give up.'

'Oh, God!' cried Linnet, 'and you sitting there like an idiot to allow it? Get out and make inquiries — there's a cottage yonder in those trees.'

It was indeed the Fal, her husband told her, on his return from knocking on the cottage door. They had left the St Denis road some miles back, thus making a detour, but that this road must bring them eventually to their destination.

'Eventually?' asked Linnet, 'and what's eventually?'

'Why, half past one to two,' replied Lewarne, 'depending on Tim's handling of the horses, and if the carriage can squeeze part the hedgerows. Time enough for us to rest and change before the dinner set for five.'

'The dinner!' Linnet flung herself back against the carriage cushions. 'May it choke you and the rest of them, for I'm not having any.'

So Deborah had been right. The gaiety of the preceding day had been a blind, or what was worse, anticipation – with the sweetness of the night a foul deception. He felt in his pocket for the phial Deborah had given him and held it tight.

It was close on two in the afternoon when the carriage turned from the side-road on to the highway, and drew up before the Indian Queen. The mist was as thick as ever, and a thin mizzle drifting with it. No other vehicle but their own was stationed by the inn; the door was closed, and the garish sign swung to and fro above the porch, the new paint running from the dark-haired beauty's eyes.

'It wanted only this,' said Linnet, not stirring from her seat; 'the place to be barred and bolted, and the folk gone elsewhere.'

A face showed itself at the window, and by the time Mark Lewarne had descended from the carriage, the door of the inn had opened, and the landlord, Bill Hext, stood before them, mouth open in astonishment.

'My gosh,' he exclaimed, 'if it isn't Mark Lewarne, and the only one to brave it to the present. Others may drop in by and by, and we'll have some fun yet. Come in, come in, and your good lady too.'

Linnet, once she had entered and looked about her, saw surroundings very different from her own spick-and-span hostelry at Troy. Here was nothing but a roadside inn, low-ceilinged, cramped, the rafters black with smoke, a long trestle table set for a dozen or more with plain glasses and cutlery, none too clean, the room already stinking of ale and tobacco; while her host in his shirt-sleeves, scratching his head and grinning, betrayed by his grubby linen he had no wife to care for him.

'You'll not want company, my dears,' he said, 'for though none may turn up from ten mile or more, we'll get some stragglers in, and the miners, and make a night of it. There's half a sheep been roasted for this caper, and I'm not wasting it.'

Already he was thrusting glasses into his guest's hands, and shooing the cat off the seat in the chimney-corner. 'Sit down, my dear, sit down,' he bade Linnet. 'Throw your shoes off if you've the mind – the cat won't scratch you.'

Mark Lewarne, uneasy, watched his disdainful wife. The slightest trouble now, and his own plan might miscarry. Or rather Deborah's plan.

'Half a tumbler of cider for the missus, please, Bill,' he asked. 'She don't touch spirits,' and in a slightly lower voice, as though to his host alone: 'To tell you the truth, she's a bit put out from the weather. She had it all planned to walk and see the country.'

Bill Hext lumbered to the bar, and stretched out his hand to the cider barrel. 'Walk?' he laughed. 'Well, she won't walk this day, unless she wants to lose herself on Goss Moor yonder. Give her this, and I'll tell your fellow where to put the horses. There's a room up over for you both, and the bedding's aired – I saw to it myself this morning.'

Mark Lewarne, his back to Linnet, who, scorning the offer of the chimney-seat, stood warming her hands at the fire, poured the drops of liquid from the phial he held secreted into the tumbler of cider. When Bill Hext had gone outside, shouting to Tim Udy, Lewarne carried the glass to Linnet. 'Drink it down,' he said, speaking with a rough, odd tenderness. 'I'm as vexed as you are that the day has gone amiss.'

She took it from him, and to his surprise and his relief, swallowed the draught instantly. 'That's better,' she said. 'Your friend keeps good cider if nothing else. I'll get my walk yet.'

Her husband said nothing, but watched her with curiosity.

A few moments later Bill Hext returned, slamming the door behind him.

'My gosh,' he said, 'we'll have to bring 'em in directly with a bugle – there's nothing else will do it, and reaching up to a nail above the bar, he brought down a battered brass horn and put it to his lips.

'Spare us for heaven's sake,' cried Linnet, dropping her muff and putting her hand to her ears. 'Blow it after dinner if you care to, but not now. Where's Castle-an-Dinas, Mr Hext, and how far from here?'

Their host, wiping the mouthpiece of the bugle on his sleeve, stared at his guest in some surprise. 'Some three miles if you go direct,' he answered, 'but if that's where you wanted to walk you'd never have found it. There's nothing to see there, not even in fine weather. Just a hill, with ditches around it.'

Linnet stood for a moment uncertainly, looking towards the door.

'Show me the road,' she said. 'I don't care how far it is. Show me the road.'

Now, though, her voice faltered, and moving a step towards the door she stumbled. 'I must go there,' she said. 'I have to go there.'

Her husband caught her as she fell, and gathering her in his arms, the expression on his face a strange mixture of awkwardness and shame, he stammered: 'She's not quite herself, that's the truth. You know how it is. May I carry her upstairs?'

His host, dumbfounded, nodded. 'Why certain sure,' he said, 'but to faint like that, so sudden. There's family on the way, I take it?'

Mark Lewarne did not answer. The question had never been put to him before, but it sounded bitter-sweet now it was said. Let Bill Hext think what he had a mind to think, and tell the company the same, if company came. He laid Linnet down on the bed in the small bare room over the bar, and covered her tenderly with the rough, grey coverlet.

Then he turned the key in the door and joined his host downstairs.

28

The Indian Queen

When Mary, glancing over her shoulder in St Columb church, saw that Amyot was no longer with them, she knew at once that something was wrong. She did not waste time looking about her in the church, but went straight to the door, and out, and across the church-yard, and saw his back disappearing up the narrow street to the right. Instinct made her wary; he must not know that she was following him, and indeed he strode ahead with confidence, never once thinking to look behind him. Instead of turning left to Tresaddern by the lane they had entered the town that morning, he continued on uphill, past the shops and houses, until soon St Columb itself lay behind and there was nothing before them but the open road. Now Mary paused, for the signpost had 'Truro' marked upon it, which she knew lay in the opposite direction from the farm, and was at least fifteen miles or more away. The weather was worsening, a fine rain falling, and already Amyot was striding away into the mist ahead of her, and would soon be lost to sight. It was useless any longer to play the spy, and she began to run, calling to him as she did so.

'Amyot!' she cried, 'Amyot, wait for me!'

She saw him turn and stare; and when she reached him he did not smile down at her, as was his usual way, but stood there watching her, in an odd grave fashion.

'Don't be angry,' she said, almost ready to cry. 'I saw you had left the church, and I had to follow you. There's something wrong. I knew it when we came to Tresaddern yesterday, and you had that letter.'

He did not answer her immediately, and when he did his voice sounded different from the Amyot she knew. It was harsh, the voice of a stranger.

'You'd best go back' he said. 'There's nothing you can do.'

He turned on his heel, and was walking ahead again, and she caught at his hand, running all the while beside him.

'Amyot,' she said, her tears now falling fast. 'you promised Father. You gave your word to Father. You are not free to do as you please.'

He tried to shake her off, his face pale, almost frightening in its unwonted gravity. 'I gave my word to another before I gave it to him,' he answered, 'and it isn't that it pleases me to do this, but because I must. It's something stronger than myself, and it can't be denied. Go back, Mary, before you make me angry.'

'No,' she sobbed. 'No, I won't. You're too dear to all of us, and I won't let you be destroyed.'

Then he stood once more, looking down at her, with St Columb now swallowed in mist, and the country all bare and bleak about them, and, pulling her to the side of the road, he said: 'You are dear to me too, Mary. You and Johnny and the rest, even poor Mr Tregentil with his kind ways, but you can't any of you stop me now.'

'It's Mrs Lewarne, isn't it?' said Mary. 'That's why you're running away. You're going to meet Mrs Lewarne. The letter was from her.'

'Call her that if you like,' said Amyot. 'I never have, or any name for that matter. She's dearer than life itself, that's all I know.'

Then Mary knew that nothing she could say would deter him, or prevent him going to her. He spoke almost as if he were already by her side, or in some dream, and that standing in the road there had no meaning for him, and no reality. It was real enough to the child. Every instinct told her she must be firm with him, and cunning too, or she would lose him.

'Yes, Amyot,' she said, 'I understand. You love her, and there's nothing else for you in the world but her. I'm not blaming you. Let me come with you till you find her, that's all I ask.'

It seemed to her she had grown suddenly old and wise, and he was a little child, younger than Johnny, in need of protection. He did not know he was in danger, and she must keep the knowledge from him.

'She'll never find her way there in this mist, that's what worried me,' he said, looking beyond them up the road. 'She'll step out bravely and lose herself and come to harm. That's why I've taken the Truro road, which should bring me to the Indian Queen before three miles.'

'The Indian Queen?'

'Yes, the name of the inn where they'll be lodging, to attend some dinner there by and by. She counted on being there before midday, and asked me to meet her at Castle-an-Dinas between one and two.'

The boldness of the request shocked Mary. How did Mrs Lewarne know Amyot was in the district anyway, and how could she have the effrontery to demand a meeting at the castle, with Mr Tregentil in charge of their party, and she herself in her own husband's company?

'If we hadn't gone to St Columb, and the morning had been fine, and all of us picnicking up at the castle as we did yesterday, how would you have explained her presence to Mr Tregentil?' she asked.

He shrugged his shoulders, strangely casual, as if such a dilemma had never occurred to him. 'I'd have gone on the road to meet her, just as I do now,' he said. 'It's no use, Mary, there can be no stopping us – I've told you that already. Come on, then, and walk beside me if you will. I daren't delay matters any longer.'

He strode off once more, and she was obliged to hasten her

steps to keep pace with him. Anyway, she thought, this mist must have hindered the travellers going to their dinner, and if Mr Lewarne himself was at the Indian Queen, and other folk too, Mrs Lewarne would be out of her senses if she tried to keep to her plan. Amyot would surely realize his folly as they drew nearer, and then, with further persuasion, agree to return with Mary to Tresaddern Farm.

A lane branched to the right of them, and another presently to the left, but still Amyot kept upon his way, despite her questioning, for this high road, he insisted, must bring them to a cross-roads eventually, and he would inquire for the Indian Queen once they approached a dwelling. Mary, who had already walked from Tresaddern to St Columb, was becoming footsore, and more than a little weary, with anxiety, too, adding to her distress; for what would Mr Tregentil think of them both? Would he search for them in St Columb, then call the police, and Amyot be seized and put in prison again?

The Indian Queen . . . the Indian Queen . . . She kept repeating the name to herself in a sort of jingle, keeping time with her steps, and it was not the name of an inn at all, but Mrs Lewarne herself, falsely smiling, beckoning them on, all decked about with jewellery round her throat and hair.

They came at last to a cluster of cottages, at the first of which Amyot asked his way, and when he returned to Mary she saw that for the first time that morning he was smiling, and looked once again like the companion she knew and loved. 'We're not far now,' he told her. 'The next turning to the left should bring us to the inn itself. The woman in the cottage thought I was bidden to the dinner, and I was not going to deny it.'

Now Mary's heart began to beat faster, for what in the world was his intention when they reached the Indian Queen? To go boldly in, and ask for Mrs Lewarne, with the landlord there himself, and other company?

They took the turning to the left, as directed, and soon emerged on to a great highway, with a dwelling standing on

244

its own, across the way, that could be none other than the Indian Queen itself. But what a fine and mighty name for so humble a place, and how unlike Mrs Lewarne the queen above the porch. As Amyot and Mary stood there, watching, for the inn looked deserted enough in all conscience, they heard the sound of wheels coming out of the mist to the right of them on the highway and voices, too, and swiftly Amyot drew Mary beside him into the ditch, and they crouched there waiting for the vehicle to pass. It hove into view, a wagonette, laden with a group of laughing, singing men, and drew up before the inn with enough noise and clatter to rouse anyone within.

'They've come for the dinner,' whispered Mary, 'though it isn't half past two yet, and we don't even know if Mrs Lewarne is there.'

Amyot put up his hand, warning her to silence, and they continued to watch as the men climbed down from the wagonette, shouting at the tops of their voices; then the door of the inn opened, a voice bade them enter, there was more laughter, more clatter, and some seven or eight men crowded their way inside. The driver of the wagonette turned his horses and drove back along the road whence he had come, perhaps to fetch more guests for the dinner. Slowly, the 'clop' of his horses died away in the distance, and all was still once more.

'What are you going to do now?' asked Mary.

Amyot looked down at her. His hair was damp with the mist and the fine rain, his face streaky, too, with mud from the ditch ditch that sheltered them, and now he looks a real vagrant, thought Mary, even a thief; if he knocks at the door yonder they won't admit him.

'Wait here,' he said. 'I'm going to see if there are stables behind the inn. If so the horses may be there, and their barouche.' And he was off in a moment and across the road, disappearing round the corner of the inn. How bleak and desolate it seemed, waiting there in the ditch for his return; no light yet in the windows of the inn, the only sign of life the smoke coming from the chimney, and the creaking of the Indian Queen herself as she swung to and fro upon the hinges.

Amyot, soon back, showed himself once more, beckoning her to cross the road, which she did, when he drew her under cover by a rough stable yard.

'The horses are there, and the barouche,' he said. 'The driver's inside. I saw him from that window, seated at a table – a kitchen I fancy. I have a plan, Mary, and I want you to trust me if you will.'

He was smiling again, and confident. She supposed it was because he believed now that Mrs Lewarne could not be far away, and they would be together soon.

'What is it, Amyot?'

'I want you to wait in the stables near the horses,' he told her. 'It's warm there on the straw, and you'll be safe enough. Wait until I return – I can't promise how long I shall be. But first, have I changed in appearance since a year ago?'

'How do you mean, changed?' Mary was puzzled. 'You're taller and broader if that's what you mean, and anyway, dressed the way you are, and wet too, it would take a friend to recognize you today.'

'That's what I thought.' Amyot seemed better pleased than ever. 'He only saw me once, and that when I flung myself before this same carriage, and he half mad with fright.'

Mary realized he was talking of Mr Lewarne. *She* would recognize him, of course, but not her husband. Anxiety was with her once again.

'Be careful,' she urged. 'Oh, Amyot, be careful.'

'I shall knock on the door,' he said, 'and ask if they want a musician for their dinner. I have no instrument, but I can sing for them. I'll say I'm a strolling player who's quarrelled with his company and lost his way. If I'd only not burnt my fiddle it would be true.'

He might have been Johnny, inventing some foolish game. He was not like a grown person at all. How was it he could

246

turn himself so swiftly to make-believe? It was dangerous what he proposed to do, but he did not care.

'I'll wait for you,' she said, 'but please, please Amyot, don't be long.'

Then he disappeared again to the front of the inn, and she crept into the dark stable, near the horses, and flung herself down amidst the straw. There was no sound now but the soft movement of the horses as they munched their hay and the ticking of her own watch, and all the while the feeling of apprehension growing within her for what might be happening inside the inn. She was hungry and tired and wet, but none of this mattered. Her fears were all for Amyot and the danger to him because of Mrs Lewarne. It was she who had brought all this trouble upon them, and but for her they would be safe and happy, sitting comfortably in the parlour at Tresaddern Farm.

An hour passed, and he did not come; and then, creeping to the yard, she could hear the sound of singing and laughter coming through the open window of the kitchen, and surely a bugle blowing – it must be a bugle – but harsh and out of tune. Greatly daring, she drew nearer to the window, and she saw that the kitchen itself was empty, but a door within wide open to what must be the bar, and a crowd of men were standing about there, drinking and laughing, while one of them, not Amyot, held a great brass trumpet to his mouth. Then she saw Amyot. His coat was off, and his sleeves were rolled up above his elbows, showing the strange armlet he always wore, picked up, so he had told Johnny, from a ditch; and above him, suspended from a lighted lamp, there was an apple on a string, and he wove this way and that, trying to bite the apple, while the men rocked with laughter and applauded. Then she remembered. It was Hallowe'en. These were the games they played at home, on Hallowe'en. But here at the Indian Queen it was somehow frightening and different, not like the merriment at home; and the crowd of men drinking and shouting, even Amyot himself, his hair falling over his eyes, looked savage, queer. There was no sign of Mrs Lewarne. There were no women there at all. Tim Udy, their driver, was there, very red in the face, propped up against the wall, and over at the far end of the room, the landlord of the Rose and Anchor himself, in his shirt sleeves, too, like Amyot, swaying on his feet, and drinking.

Suddenly Amyot ducked, seized the bobbing apple between his teeth and held it, and there was a great burst of cheering from the men, and another strident note from the bugle.

'He's won the queen,' someone yelled. 'Brave lad, he's won the queen,' and they swarmed about Amyot, clapping him on the shoulder, and Amyot himself, with shining eyes, crunched the apple in two, throwing one half over his shoulder. It hit the landlord of the Rose and Anchor between the eyes, who advanced, shaking his fist, half drunk for all the world to see, and another man in shirt-sleeves caught hold of him, laughing, and cried: ''Tis your turn now, Lewarne, for the four choices. If you choose aright, then you can up and join your sleeping lady.'

The four choices – yes, that was a custom, too, but one their mother never let them play, for it wasn't seemly. Four bowls must be placed in the four corners of a room: one bowl filled with pebbles, the second to be empty, the third filled with clean water and the fourth with dirty. The test was for someone to be blindfolded, and to creep upon all fours. He who found the pebbles found gold and would be wealthy; and he who found the empty bowl would end a pauper. The bowl with the clean water foretold a faithful marriage partner, but the bowl of dirty water signified adultery. This was why Mrs Bosanko forbade them to play the game.

Now they were blindfolding Mr Lewarne, and forcing him upon his knees, and all the men crowding to watch, laughing and jeering, too.

'Oh, let him choose the pebbles and be wealthy,' breathed Mary, half sick at the sight of the elderly man degraded; for there he was, crawling like a beast, not knowing which way to turn. There was a sudden hush as he made for the left-hand corner, and, coming upon the bowl, dabbled his hands amongst it.

A yell of laughter broke from the crowded company when the landlord of the Rose and Anchor, sitting back on his haunches, tore the bandage from his eyes. 'He's found the muck!' they all shouted. 'He's put his hands in the dirt!' Once more the bugle sounded.

As Mark Lewarne rose to his feet, dazed and shaking, his two hands black with mud, his eye fell straight upon Amyot, smiling, crunching his apple, and he lunged towards him, shouting: 'It's you that's done it – it's you that's played the trick!' and he bent and seized the bowl and flung it towards Amyot, but it shattered the lamp instead and plunged them into darkness.

The oaths and laughter and breaking glass that followed was like all of hell let loose, and Mary, terrified, hearing them crash towards the kitchen, ran out of the yard and into the road, and so out on to the highway, which way she neither knew nor cared, anywhere so that it might take her from the sound of the drunken men.

A horse and carriage came towards her out of the mist, and she ran towards it, crying at the top of her voice: 'Come quickly and stop them fighting. They're fighting down there at the inn.'

Then she recognized the horse, Captain, and Mr Dingle the coachman on the box, and the man who stepped out of the brougham and put his arm about her was none other than Doctor Carfax himself, come suddenly, and most wonderfully, to her aid.

29

'L'Amer alone doth trouble me'

I taste not wind, nor sea,
L'Amer alone doth trouble me.

Mr Tregentil, a hastily cut ham sandwich in his hand, did his best to answer the doctor's questions before they set forth together in the brougham up the steep hill from Tresaddern, *en route* for the Indian Queen. All, he insisted, had gone well with the excursion, until Amyot and Mary had disappeared from St Columb Church. The preceding day had been enjoyable in every respect, except perhaps for some unexpected boasting on the part of the Breton lad, who thought he knew his history when he most evidently did not; and because he chanced to locate the quickest entrance to the earthwork, and guessed where to find water, took it upon himself to play the leader, though luckily not for long. The evening had been uneventful. No, he knew nothing of any message from Mrs Lewarne, although now it seemed, from what Mrs Polwhele told them, Amyot had received a letter. He himself had been so preoccupied in preventing the ham from being put in the pot that he had small time for anything else. The whole party had been tired, and retired early to bed.

'And indeed, Carfax,' continued the irate patient, 'you are always determined to make me scapegoat for anything that happens to young Amyot. It is not the first time. As to Mrs

Lewarne, I am thankful to say I have not set eyes on her since the unfortunate time we encountered her at Woodget Pyll, and were obliged to walk her back through the grounds of Penquite.' Mr Tregentil snatched another bite at the ham sandwich, endeavouring at the same time to change his damp shoes.

'Never mind Woodget Pyll,' said the doctor; 'the damage has been done as far as that is concerned. But you might have had the perspicuity to inform me, when you returned my papers, that Bosanko's mother was a Hoel.'

'I did so in a footnote,' exclaimed the astonished Mr Tregentil, 'but what in the world has that to do with the present situation?'

'Nothing,' replied the doctor, 'or rather, everything. We are dealing with matters beyond our understanding, my friend, and because of it we cannot neglect coincidence. Do you mean to tell me the dog was fortuitous too?'

'The dog? What dog?'

'The dog that young Johnny gave to Amyot, and Amyot to Mrs Lewarne, and bears for its name, heaven spare us – Pettigrew!'

Mr Tregentil stared. 'I know nothing of any dog.'

'No, no, of course not.' Doctor Carfax swallowed a sandwich himself and turned irritably to the door. 'Nor did I until this morning. And if I had what could I have done? He played no part in the original tale, anyway, except to give his mistress a few years' pleasure. In this case, only weeks. We are seeing the past through the wrong end of the telescope, that's the trouble. Mrs Polwhele?'

Mona's sister came bustling though from the kitchen. 'Yes, doctor. What can I do for you, doctor?'

'Keep young Johnny here in the house until we return, and don't let him out of your sight. The weather's not fit for him without. Goodbye for the present. Mr Tregentil and I must away on business.'

Doctor and patient stepped into the brougham, and Mr Dingle, whose night's lodging in St Columb had not altered his opinion on the expedition's folly, coaxed Captain to step bravely through the mud that lay ahead.

'I really must tell you, Carfax,' began Mr Tregentil once more, 'you've been talking to me in riddles.'

'I know that,' snapped the doctor, 'but you must accept it. Tell me, there are two distinct versions of the death of Tristan, are there not?'

'Yes – yes, I think so, but I can't for the life of me see—'

'Then don't attempt it. One version, the later, is that he married King Hoel's daughter in Brittany, was wounded in some fight and, dying, sent for the queen to come to him – which she did, but arrived too late. The death was hastened, anyway, by the lie of Tristan's wife, who, through jealousy, poor soul, declared the barque bearing the queen carried black sails, instead of white, as a signal that the queen was not on board – confound this mist!'

Doctor Carfax rubbed the window of the brougham with his handkerchief. 'Yes, that is so,' agreed his bewildered patient, 'but of course my discovery would prove the event took place in Cornwall, and not Brittany at all. And Gottfried von Strassburg—'

'Never mind Gottfried von Strassburg,' interrupted the doctor impatiently. 'The second version, less popular, has the maid Brangwyn betray her mistress to King Mark, who, coming upon Tristan singing to the queen, wounds him with a poisoned spear, and locks Iseult in her chamber to prevent her following her lover. Tristan flies to his friend Dinas, and dies at his castle: the queen, as in the other version, arriving too late to bid him farewell. In both cases Tristan dies from a poisoned spear. The question is—' He broke off, for the brougham had drawn in against the hedge, and the coachman was descending from the box.

'What's the trouble now?' called the doctor, lowering the sash, and leaning from the window.

'Captain's gone lame, sir,' reported Dingle in a voice of studied gloom. 'It's only to be expected, seeing the state of the road by

253

the farm. There's no smithy handy, and I must remove the stone myself as best I can.'

Mr Tregentil fumbled surreptitiously for the remaining sandwich in his pocket. 'Extremely unfortunate,' he said, 'but this time not my fault. You were saying, doctor?'

Doctor Carfax, already out of the brougham and taking his own clasp-knife from his pocket, turned a furious face upon his patient.

'I was not saying anything,' he retorted, 'that would make the slightest sense to either of us today. Luckily spears, poisoned or otherwise, are hard to come by, but if we do find ourselves mixed up in a tragedy of some thirteen hundred years ago, who is to play the part of Dinas, you or I?'

Then he went forward to help the coachman, leaving his patient much perplexed. 'I have no desire,' Mr Tregentil muttered under his breath, 'to play the part of Dinas or anyone else. I sometimes wonder if Carfax is altogether right in the head.'

Although Captain obligingly stood still, the stone proved hard to extract, and when it was finally drawn, and they were on their way once more, time, which was all too precious, had been lost. Further consultation, as to the best road to take on reaching the top of the hill, wasted more minutes, and neither medical adviser nor his patient were on the best of terms when the brougham finally emerged, from a devious lane, on to the right road not a quarter of a mile from the Indian Queen, and so to the running figure of Mary Bosanko, waving her arms and crying.

It was only a matter of moments then before Doctor Carfax, after a few words of reassurance to the child, with strict injunctions not to stir from Mr Tregentil's side in the brougham, thundered with his stick on the door of the inn and burst inside.

The scene that met his eyes was one of complete confusion: a broken lamp, a table overturned, glasses and bottles strewn about the floor, and a bunch of hilarious men lying, sitting or straddling the bar, too helpless with drink and laughter to clear the mess. At the sight of the doctor there was a sudden hush, and one fellow, holding a bent bugle in his hand, advanced towards him brandishing the instrument above his head.

'And who may you be, Mister Hollower?' asked this individual. 'Another one come to dip his hands in the muddy water? If so go up and join the other pair – you're welcome.'

Shouts of delighted laughter greeted this sally, but the new arrival, walking to the centre of the room, kicking the recumbent form of Tim Udy as he did so, was not to be shouted down.

'My name is Carfax, and I'm a doctor in Troy,' he called loudly. 'A terrified child has just run out from here, seeking protection. What the devil do you think you're doing, behaving like a pack of beasts?'

His accusation was met with silence, save for a low murmur, and then the fellow with the bugle, looking about him said: 'There's no child here, nor has been at any time. We was only having a bit of fun. I'm landlord of this place. I know how to keep the peace.'

'It would seem so,' replied the doctor. 'Hearken to that!'

For in the room overhead there was tumbling and shouting, the crash of furniture, the splintering sound of breaking glass.

'By gosh, they're at it again!' exclaimed the landlord. ''Tis none of our doing, doctor, but two of the fellows here fell out, and they're at each other's throats up there, that's what it is. Come on then, we'd best stop them before more blood's spilt. Lewarne's a proper devil when he's roused.'

'Lewarne?' uttered the doctor, and in a flash he was at the stairway and up to it, with the landlord of the Indian Queen and a handful of others close at his heels. As they passed the stairhead Lewarne himself staggered from the broken-down door of a bedroom.

'This way!' he roared. 'This way! He's jumped for it. I hope to God he's broken his neck.'

Doctor Carfax strode into the room. There were two

windows, one facing the road, the other giving on to the stable yard. The second window was smashed to pieces, and there, below him, having leapt the distance, was the flying figure of Amyot, heading for the stables.

'Stop him, some of you,' cried the doctor. 'Seize him and hold him, but watch out for yourselves – he's not responsible . . .'

There was further clatter on the stairs as the three or four men tumbled over themselves to reach the bar, and so pass through the kitchen and to the yard; but the confusion below impeded them, and by the time they were clear, and stumbling through to the stables, Amyot, astride one of Lewarne's horses, was riding out into the yard, obliging his pursuers to scatter on all sides and let him pass.

'*Holà!*' called Amyot, '*en avant!*' And he was away and down the road, past the brougham, and out of sight, the carriage horse galloping like one possessed, while the half-drunken men and the landlord of the Indian Queen stared after him, dumbfounded.

'*Le saut Tristan,*' murmured Doctor Carfax, 'but like the rest of the puzzle pieces it fits too late.'

He turned back into the room, and looked down at the sleeping figure on the bed. It was Linnet, and her husband was kneeling beside her.

'She can sleep through all this racket?' said the doctor, and stooping, he felt her pulse, then turned her eyelids.

'Drugged,' he said, 'but with what? Can you answer me that?'

Mark Lewarne rose slowly to his feet. He was sober enough now, and grey with fear. ''Twas only a sleeping-draught to keep her quiet,' he answered. 'Deborah, the maid gave it me, in case of trouble.'

'What sort of sleeping-draught?'

The landlord of the Rose and Anchor drew a small phial from his pocket. 'There's none left,' he said. 'Deborah said to give her all of it. It acted more sudden than I thought.'

He handed the phial to the doctor, who removed the stopper and sniffed.

'Apple juice,' he declared, 'or near enough.' He put one finger within the phial and tasted it, and was instantly reminded of the evening a year ago, when he and Ledru had been given each a stirrup cup, and by Linnet herself. But this phial had contained a draught more pungent. 'Do you know where the maid found this?' he asked. 'Have you stuff like it in your cellar?'

The landlord shook his head. 'No doctor, not to my knowledge. She's going to be all right, isn't she?'

Doctor Carfax, seized with a strange misgiving, gazed down at the sleeping Linnet. 'I don't know,' he said slowly. 'The draught was potent, and without knowledge of the strength—' He looked across at the landlord. 'You remember how a spasm of the heart took Notary Ledru not twelve months since, and beneath your very roof?'

'Why, good God, doctor, you're not thinking—'

'I tell you, man, I don't know. But I'm deeply worried.'

His eye was caught by a bangle on Linnet's left wrist, and touching it he perceived it to be the same armlet that she had found amongst the earth that time the pair of them had sheltered from the storm at Castle Dor. 'Does she wear this always?' he asked.

Mark Lewarne stared. 'I've never seen it in my life before,' he answered. 'She didn't have it when I carried her here. It's that damned rascal who broke in the door – he's put it there. By God, I'll settle with him.'

Doctor Carfax laid his hand on the landlord's shoulder. 'Let him be,' he said quietly. 'I'll be responsible. He's not ridden far: only a few miles up the road if I judge correctly. Come now, help me wrap her in blankets and we'll carry her down. We must get her to hospital, and Bodmin must be all of thirteen miles.'

He leant out of the window, and hailed the coachman, who was standing by the brougham.

'You've a long drive ahead of you, Dingle,' he called, 'and a sick woman as passenger. Will you please request Mr Tregentil

257

and Miss Mary to step down, and give place to Mr and Mrs Lewarne?'

He turned once more to the landlord. 'With your permission, Lewarne,' he said, 'I'll harness the remaining horse to your barouche and drive it myself. No easy matter, but it can be done. I have two other patients in my care and must get them to their lodging. If your wife should wake on the way to Bodmin' – he paused and let his eyes dwell for a moment on the armlet encircling Linnet's wrist – 'it is very possible she may not recognize you, but will call upon young Trestane, using his surname, thus. If she does, bear with her, if you can, and ask no questions.'

Mark Lewarne, his face crumpling in grief, plucked at the doctor's sleeve. 'Don't leave me alone with her, doctor,' he begged. 'Let's go in company, or part of the way at least. You're not driving all the way to Troy this night, surely?'

'No,' said the doctor, and his voice was strangely quiet. 'My next call is barely two miles distant, and perhaps, as you suggest, we would do well to keep in company.'

Some ten minutes later two equipages drew away from the now silent Indian Queen. The brougham followed the barouche. Then instead of continuing straight long the road to Bodmin, Doctor Carfax, the leading driver, suddenly swung left, and took the lane across country that led to Castle-an-Dinas.

❧

30

'Then I must die for love of thee'

For if thou wilt not come to me
Then I must die for love of thee.

Instinct bade Doctor Carfax take the shortest route. If he judged rightly this narrow lane would bring them past the old tin mine he had noticed earlier that morning, and so to the foot of Castle-an-Dinas itself. This was the way that Amyot too would have chosen, riding like a madman some ten minutes since. What demon of the past possessed the lad scarce mattered now. He was no phantom figure, born of this moorland mist, but a living boy of flesh and blood who, after a drunken scrap, might come to misadventure. The road at least was firm to horse and vehicle, and the rain had ceased; only the drifting fog was with them still.

Doctor Carfax, glancing behind him over the top of the barouche, saw that the brougham was following some twenty yards in the rear. Lewarne must have given his orders to the coachman, preferring even the hazards of this detour, to continuing alone with his drugged wife to Bodmin. A mile or two out of the way, did Linnet's husband but realize it, might make all the difference between her life and death; yet Carfax had not the heart to draw rein and tell him so, and order the brougham back on to the Bodmin road. Reason and judgment had played little part in the happenings of this day, and it could well be that at some point on the drive to Bodmin Linnet would wake up from that deep sleep that held her, and, with a return to consciousness, struggle to be free, and so condemn herself. Somewhere in the mist ahead her lover rode. Once found and apprehended, he could perhaps with persuasion be sent back to Tresaddern in charge of Tregentil and young Mary, and Carfax himself would conduct Lewarne and his wife the whole thirteen miles to Bodmin.

This was the gamble. There seemed no other course. The only enemy was time; not the gathering dusk that would encompass them, nor the passing hours; but the freakish, ghostly time that had come upon them out of the buried past, holding them all in thrall.

The barouche had nearly covered the second mile, with the lane already sloping to high ground and Castle-an-Dinas beyond, when Merlin, the landlord's remaining horse drawing the vehicle, pricked his ears, paused in his stride and whinnied. An answering whinny came out of the mist ahead, and as Doctor Carfax drove the barouche to the side of the lane, raising his whip on high to warn Dingle on the brougham, Merlin's stable companion Merman came charging down the road towards them. He whinnied again on sighting his partner and pulled up short in his tracks. He was riderless, and trembling from head to foot. In a matter of moment the doctor descended from his seat, secured the runaway, and with the aid of the coachman who had drawn up the brougham alongside, coupled the frightened animal to the shaft of the barouche with his companion.

'He's thrown his rider,' observed Dingle, 'and small blame on him.'

'Or been set free,' returned the doctor, 'the rider having reached his journey's end.'

He stared at the country on either side of him, or rather what he could see of it through mist. Casting his mind back to the morning's walk he recollected that the lane they were now upon touched the road beneath Castle-an-Dinas within a hundred yards

260

or so of a tin mine. He himself had noticed the chimney and the sheds, built on a slope to the left of the road, and now peering through the murky dusk ahead it was that same chimney he could make out standing like a giant sentinel, but seen from the opposite side. When seated in the parlour at Tresaddern, waiting for the St Columb party to return, he had glanced at Tregentil's map lying upon the table, and had seen the name of the tin mine, Royalton. This, of course, was modern English for Tre-kyning, or 'ruler's town', and the manor of the present-day Trekenning was a couple of miles or so westward of this position. But royal in Cornish was also *ryal*, and through the centuries it well might be that a tin mine, constructed on the site of the ruler's house beneath the fortress, would carry the ancient name of its former splendour, and so be Royalton. Thus, if his surmise was correct, and a ruler's house had stood once beneath the fortified Castle-an-Dinas, would not a friend and brother-in-arms of that same ruler, Dinas, when seeking sanctuary after a private encounter, look for his friend in his house, and not his fortress?

Blot out the centuries, accept the fact, or the fantasy, that time – at any rate for Amyot and Linnet – was then, not now, and it would not be uphill and beyond to the castle where Amyot would descend and dismiss his horse, but here, fifty yards or so ahead, at Royalton mine.

Mary, obedient to the doctor's order, had not stirred from the barouche, but now, as he looked down at her and Mr Tregentil, having coupled up Merman to his companion, she could tell from his grave expression that he feared, even as she did herself, that mishap might have come to Amyot.

'Mary,' he said, his voice concerned, 'when you picnicked at the castle yesterday, do you remember if Amyot perceived this mine that lies beyond us now?'

Mary leant from the barouche, and she too could see the outline of the chimney just beyond them in the mist.

'I don't think so,' she answered. 'If he did he made no mention of it to me. His talk was all of the old days long ago.'

'Of which, very naturally, he knew next to nothing,' interrupted Mr Tregentil hastily, 'but the lad has an eye for country, that I grant him. I noticed the mine of course, but did not discuss it. Mining was not the object of the expedition.'

'No, indeed,' said the doctor; 'the object of the expedition was to reconstruct the past, which in the light of all that has happened was successfully achieved. A man living thirteen centuries ago sees what stood then, and not what stands today. Amyot perceived Royalton, very probably, but not Royalton mine.'

He left the barouche, and went behind it to the brougham. Linnet was still lying as he had seen her last, wrapped in the blankets, sleeping, her head on her husband's knees. Mark Lewarne, white-faced and drawn, held her close.

'She hasn't stirred, doctor,' he said. 'Is she any worse?'

Doctor Carfax felt his patient's pulse, and kneeling within the brougham put his ear to her heart.

'No change,' he said. 'Keep her warm, as you do now, and within a short while we shall be, all three of us I trust, upon our way to Bodmin.'

'You're not going to delay things by searching for that rogue?' asked the landlord. 'Let him break his neck, or do what he wills, I'll bear him no further grudge if we can but get Linnet to hospital.'

'Have patience, man,' replied the doctor. 'If I see no sign of him within five minutes we'll drive on, and leave the search to Tregentil and his coachman.'

Leaving the two vehicles and the horses in charge of Dingle, Doctor Carfax walked slowly upon the lane, his eye on the ground for hoof marks, and here they were, just as he had surmised, leading off the road and through a gap in the hedgerow, and so on to the broken ground that formed the back premises of the mine itself. The chimneystack, black and threatening, loomed before him, and the low slated roofs of the sheds.

262

All was still. The mine, even if in working use, would have been deserted since morning. Saturday night and All Hallows' E'en had bereft the spot of even a solitary watchman. Perhaps the men who worked here were amongst those who had been drinking this past hour or more at the Indian Queen: but the rider who had leapt from his horse and plunged forward here amidst the piled up earth and all the debris, what had he sought – or worse, what had he found?

Dinas, friend to Iseult and Tristan, seneschal to his overlord King Mark, paced up and down this piece of territory once, his dwelling-house perhaps where the sheds stood now, or even beneath the engine-house itself, topped by the chimney yonder. Miners drained the lode, deep in the earth, besides which, centuries since, the servants toiled, and the disused shaft amidst the furze a few yards or so ahead ringed about with rotten fencing, might have seemed – to a traveller in time who knew his way – the entrance to a stairway.

The hoof prints ceased, the muddied ground was trampled, as if the horse had taken fright and fled, and straight to the shaft through the furze lay the new-beaten track. Nor was the fencing rotted. The posts leant sideways because they had been smashed.

'Amyot!' called Doctor Carfax, 'Amyot!'

The echo mocked him, flung back from the empty sheds, and in the mist and darkness the chimney stack loomed larger than before. It seemed to the doctor, standing there by the black pit which perhaps less than a dozen years or so ago had served as a mine shaft and been discontinued, that he hovered now in strange and sickening fashion on the threshold of another world. Whatever he said or did in the present time would only be repetition of a day gone by, and anyone who listened to his voice calling in the darkness would hear it as the voice of another, dead these thirteen hundred years.

'Trestane!' he called. 'Trestane!' and the sound of the changed name was not foolish in his ears, but strangely ominous, for the echo came back to him without the sharpness of his first cry. Now with a melancholy haunting note, the widely flung 'Trestane' sounded and died, and the echo was a whisper scarcely louder than a sigh.

Then, gripping his stick firmly in his hands, yet holding his breath with wonder, Doctor Carfax watched a figure rise slowly from the pit beyond him, climbing hand over hand from the depths, now slipping, now secure, and there was black mud about his head and shoulders, and blood upon his face, and the eyes were wild and staring, the eyes of Amyot.

'Who calls?'

The voice, half strangled in a sob, was faint and breathless, and the doctor, knowing that a sudden move and one false step would send the climber back to the unknown depths from which he struggled, remained motionless, knee-deep in the furze beside the broken barricade.

'It is I, Dinas,' he said softly, 'Dinas, your friend.'

The boy stared back at him without recognition, and clinging with one hand to the more solid earth above him, thrust back with his free hand the matted hair that fell about his eyes.

'You've played me false,' said Amyot, 'you or some other. The stairway's gone. They've dug a pit to trap me and I'm held.'

The doctor, leaning forward, saw that the lad's left foot was enmeshed in wire, and if he bent to clear it he would fall.

'Steady,' he said. 'Hold fast with both your hands. I'll come and free you,' and was moving towards the brink, when Amyot shouted: 'Keep back, for I'll not trust you. The fox is abroad tonight and all his men. Dinas serves his king before he serves his friend.'

Suddenly, with a supreme effort, he kicked his foot clear from the tangling wire, and, grasping the edge of the pit, dragged himself to safety.

'Good lad,' cried the doctor. 'Here, seize my stick,' but his leap forward into time proved his undoing, for Amyot, taking both words and gesture as hostile to himself, and the stick a weapon, sprang sideways, and in a second had flung his whole weight upon his unsuspecting ally. Together they wrestled in the furze, each fighting for supremacy, not three yards from the open shaft, and Carfax, no longer held by the past, knew that, unless he overcame his assailant, death would take him in the present.

Already Amyot, in his blind rage and fear of what he thought betrayal, had seized the clasp-knife from the doctor's pocket; already it lay open in his hand and pointing at the doctor's throat, when the older man, forcing back the wrist that threatened him, threw his opponent on his side, so driving the knife into his shoulder by mischance. The blood spurted, and as Amyot cried out in pain the cry released his anger and his fear. He ceased struggling, and was still. Then, drawing the knife from the swift-bleeding wound, he stared back at his late enemy in wonder.

'Doctor Carfax,' he said, 'what have you done to me?'

The doctor did not answer, but flinging off overcoat and jacket proceeded to divest himself of his own cambric shirt, and tear it into strips to staunch the wound.

'There, lad,' he said. 'Keep still, I'll bind you, somewhat rough and ready, but it must suffice' – his voice calm and steady that scarce three minutes since had been nigh choked out of him as he struggled for existence; but even as he spoke, with practised hands applied the only possible dressing of clean handkerchief, with strapping of cambric shirt, the dark stain spread down the forearm, and Amyot fainted.

As Doctor Carfax knelt there in the furze at Royalton, beside the disused mine-shaft, and hallooed with all the strength in his lungs for Dingle the coachman, or Tregentil his patient, to come to his aid and so help bear young Amyot to the barouche, (for there would be two to carry to hospital in Bodmin instead of one), he gave no thought to the death he had himself so narrowly escaped. He stared down at the lad who now lay white and senseless in his arms, bleeding from the wound inadvertently given; and it was not the depth of the wound that bothered him, nor the loss of blood that must inevitably follow before the proper dressings could be applied, but the fact that it was his own clasp-knife, used barely an hour ago to take stones from a horse's hoof, and grimy still with mud and grit, that had pierced the tender flesh of Amyot Trestane, thus playing, fatefully and ironically, the role of a long-vanished poisoned spear.

The mist had lifted. The countryside, shrouded and murky for so long, was now clear, save for its own natural cloak of darkness. A light wind, coming from the north, would scatter the last clouds and clean the sky. The track to Castle-an-Dinas wound away in the distance above the road, and Mr Tregentil, before descending the lane to Tresaddern to keep Johnny company, foretold a fine tomorrow.

When he had gone Doctor Carfax knelt once more on the floor of the brougham and felt for Linnet's pulse. The armlet dangled from her wrist.

'She hasn't stirred?' he asked.

'No, doctor. Once I thought she made a movement with her lips, but no more than that. It was when you were away there, by the mine.'

Mark Lewarne, his wife gathered to him, searched the doctor's eyes. 'They'll be able to waken her, won't they, when we get her to hospital? They'll have medicines and that to do it, won't they, doctor?'

Carfax gently replaced the blanket round the sleeping Linnet, and with a queer twist of the heart remembered that day, some twenty years ago, when he had slapped life into a little child, so producing her first cry. She had been reluctant, in those few moments, to greet the world: but later, with what fervour and delight had she seized upon life, daring, in thoughtless mood, even to risk marriage with this man old enough to be her father. If she would but cry now, and draw breath in bewilderment and pain, as she had that first birthday morning at Castle Dor, so proving the will to live . . .

'Everything that medical skill can do will be done for her in hospital,' he told her husband. 'I cannot promise more. Did I know what the draught contained I could speak with more authority.'

'As to that,' said Lewarne slowly, 'unless she wakes to tell us, we shall never know. Deborah filled the phial from some bottle, which she then smashed, saying she had drained it to the last drop.'

'And you permitted it?'

'What was I to do?' cried the agonized landlord. 'She swore it was from some old recipe that could do no harm.'

No harm – yet the same draught had taken an old man in his sleep. Carfax signalled to the coachman to mount the box, and went himself to the barouche. Amyot, recovered from his faint, but deathly pale, smiled at him from the corner.

'The strapping holds,' he said. 'Mary says you want to take me to hospital, but there's no need of it.'

'Let me be the judge of that,' answered the doctor. 'Mary here shall keep you company, and we'll be in Bodmin within two hours.'

'What I don't understand,' said Amyot frowning, 'is how we came to be on the moorland there, and both of us fighting. I never touch strong liquor, but I fear I must have done.'

'No matter if you did, it's done with now.' The doctor glanced at Mary, who, like a young nurse, nodded imperceptibly, guessing his meaning. If Amyot had forgotten the events of the past few hours it was better so. Doctor Carfax climbed once more to his seat and took the reins. Amyot had not as much as asked what he was doing in Mark Lewarne's barouche. Mercifully then the immediate past was blotted from his memory. The lad was no longer a wanderer in time, caught up in a past that was not of his own seeking, but a simple Breton sailor, wounded through misadventure. He, Carfax, would take all blame for what had happened. There had been no fighting, and no quarrel. Amyot would not have to face the long process of the law again. His last enemy would not be Mark Lewarne, nor any other living soul. The battle must be fought, just as Tristan's had been fought and lost, against an unseeing foe, hitherto unconquerable, that even now, multiplying a thousandfold, coursed through his bloodstream, militant, unchecked.

Mary, stealthily tucking the carriage rug about her charge, for fear he should take cold, saw that he had once more closed his eyes. Presently, his voice coming as it were from a distance, he said: 'We made a pact once, long ago, she and I. If I ever needed her she swore she'd come to me.'

Mary did not answer. Amyot must not know that Mrs Lewarne, taken ill at the Indian Queen, was in point of fact on her way to hospital too.

'I left my armlet with her as she lay sleeping,' continued Amyot. 'When she wakes she'll recognize it, and no matter who tries to prevent it she'll follow me.'

So memory was breaking through, and might do some damage, unless she took great care. 'You're dreaming, Amyot,' she said. 'Mrs Lewarne is sleeping safe and sound in her bed, and doesn't know of your accident.'

He opened his eyes. 'I swear I heard her call to me just now.'

Mary patted his knee and smiled indulgently. 'It's just your fancy,' she told him. 'Don't fret yourself, but take your ease and rest.'

It seemed to her that he was now listening intently, straining to catch some sound upon the road.

'We're not the only travellers,' he said. 'There are other wheels behind us – I can hear them. Whose are they, Mary?'

Fearing he would lean too far forward, and in his fever do further damage to his wound, Mary took his hand gently and settled him against the cushion. 'Strangers,' she answered, 'a carriageful of folk from Truro bound for Bodmin, same as we. They lost their way in the fog, I suppose.'

'Are you sure, Mary?'

'Certain sure. They have a brougham something like Mr Tregentil's, but painted black.'

She went on holding his hand, believing, in her young heart, that because it gave her comfort it brought him strength, and she did not know that the hope that had been his for a brief moment, on hearing the sound of carriage wheels behind them, was now ebbing, like the life within him. The lie, spoken on impulse to spare him distress, had failed in its purpose.

When presently he whispered a few words in French she guessed him to be wandering, in fancy, back in Brittany, watching the white seas break on the steep shore. '*Dieu vous garde*,' he whispered. '*Je ne vous verrai plus.*'

Epilogue

A local poet – a native of Troy who died young – left an imperfect poem in manuscript. It opens bravely:

Westward, between the Dodman and the Rame,
There lies a Haven: on this side a Cross,
On that a Fortalice. There, twice a day,
The tide, and ever with the tide my heart—
Yea, with such urgence as the tide's my heart—
Homes to be land-locked by a little town
Grey, ancient, with bitten garden walls
Coped by the rose valerian; brimming yet,
To surge by wharves, black jetties, anchored ships,
To open on a land all strange to trade,
To flood its wildfowl-haunted river flats,
And break in seven channels, mazily
Lost between heronries and hanging woods,
O'er glades thro' which the upland harvesters
Pause in the swathe, shading their eyes to watch
Slow barge or schooner stealing up from sea;
Themselves in sunset, she a twilight ghost
Parting the twilight wilds.
    Ah, loving God!

271

Grant, in the end, this world may slip away
With whispers of that water by the bows
Of such a barge, bearing me home – thy stars
Breaking the gloom like kingfishers, thy heights
Golden with wheat, thy waiting angels there
Wearing the dear rough faces of my kin!

On such a quiet surge of the tide did Doctor Carfax, now some eighty-odd years of age, and some while since retired from medical practice, pull over in his gig the Gilly flower to the piece of land he rented as a garden, known as The Farm – although no farm upon it – and where, most afternoons between two and four, he chose to take the exercise that suited him best, which was sawing up a score of logs or so for his library fire.

Here, separated by a stretch of water from the more prosaic pleasures of book and slippers, or the delights of the table – for his was no jaded palate despite his age – or yet again the constant stream of visitors, most of them ex-patients, who winter and summer still knocked at the surgery door from some force of habit and were bade welcome, Doctor Carfax gave himself up to that blessed solitude and peace, which seemed now more than ever to be the very source of life itself.

He had two companions: a robin, who watched his labours with bright eye and pecked the sawdust, and a tortoise, who ignored him, preferring to trundle in a cabbage patch near by in quest of food.

The pleasing rasp of the saw, the rhythmic movement, induced a sense of well-being to Doctor Carfax, pervading his whole nervous system, and this, he told himself, was surely how Man was meant to live from the beginning; making use of the fruits of the earth, the timber, all that sprang from the soil, and the sea beside it; the very seasons, rainy, warm and chill, bringing nourishment to all living creatures, from the greatest genius down to the merest maggot.

Tommy Tortoise himself was no mean philosopher, withdrawing, when winter came, to the good earth, until one day in spring, long after the first daffodils were in bloom on the hillside, he would peek out from his snug lair to view with a grave air his hardier friend the robin, who bursting his small heart in joy, gave thanks for the sun's renewal.

It was fretting that turned Man sour and lost him Paradise: not tasting forbidden fruit, like Eve and Adam, nor stealing fire from heaven, as Prometheus, but striving to seem important before his fellows; buying, selling, building, destroying, laying waste a countryside in name of progress, inventing machines which by their very nature must end in mechanizing their inventors too. What changes in the last years! More ships, more jetties, the mineral railway cut along the river's bank from Lostwithiel past St Sampson's, and on top of it all a slump, so that Cornishmen everywhere were packing up and seeking their fortune overseas.

Trade would return of course. The slump was passing. And one day, when he himself was gone. Troy would become a thriving hive of industry, houses and terraces built way up past the Rope Walk to the castle hill. Progress – perhaps. To one thing only he granted full respect. The advance in medicine. Today the young fellow he had trained, and who was about to take up practice in Troy itself, knew more about microbes and how to combat them that he, Carfax, had ever dreamt would be discovered. What made a good physician? Understanding of human nature, yes; the ability to make a quick decision, yes; and furthermore, imagination in full measure. Young Johnny Bosanko had all three qualities, the last especially. The kings and queens of legend had not played him false. The dreams of childhood, quickening perception, had brought great depth to his maturer years. Young Johnny would go far; healing the sick in body, and in mind as well. And Mary, too, caught up in the same desire to lessen pain, had led the way as elder sister by turning nurse at seventeen, and now, sister in one of the big London hospitals, would one of these days, if she did not marry meantime, become matron.

Curious how both those children had dedicated themselves

to the same cause: to save life, and prolong it, much to the grat-
ification of their proud parents, though Gabriel Bosanko was
left without a farmer son to succeed him. And sometimes, when
taking a glass of wine with his ex-patient Tregentil, who had
built himself a fine house overlooking St Austell Bay, finding
the northern aspect of Penquite finally unsuited to his liver,
doctor and patient would discuss the careers of their *protégés*,
dating this same dedication of two children to the moment
when they were first shocked by death.

Old men forget. Mr Tregentil, babbling of his new craze,
astronomy, and how a star's source of light lies many million miles
away, had little interest now in legends or etymology, or even his
own ancestors, still sleeping undiscovered beneath Pyder hills; but
Doctor Carfax, whether smoking an after-dinner pipe, browsing
over books and papers, or sawing logs in great tranquillity on his
hillside overlooking Troy harbour, would feel at times nearer than
he had ever done to solving the mystery of man and maid, and
how love caught them unawares and made them one.

From the minstrels down, poet after poet had attempted to
explain the genesis of love and had failed; still it loomed larger
through their failures, asserting itself through them to be greater
than any man's telling.

Nurtured on this soil, his young eyes having fed on this very
landscape, he had not been able to stay a senseless repetition of
one of the saddest love stories in the world. His own roots
made him participant. Senseless perhaps, yet not entirely so. The
pleasure and pain of love, once breathed upon the air, rose but
to fall again, like blossom or like rain, infecting all things living
with pain and ecstasy.

Because of this a boy now healed the sick. Because of this
a girl brought consolation to the suffering. And he himself, an
old man near his time, uttered eternal thanks for that redemp-
tion that had swept him like a tide some years before, when
the hapless Amyot laughed at the wound that killed him, and
the dying Linnet stirred in her sleep and smiled.

Now you can order superb titles directly from Virago

❏ The Birds and Other Stories	Daphne du Maurier	£6.99
❏ The Du Mauriers	Daphne du Maurier	£7.99
❏ Frenchman's Creek	Daphne du Maurier	£6.99
❏ Gerald: A Portrait	Daphne du Maurier	£7.99
❏ The Glass-Blowers	Daphne du Maurier	£7.99
❏ The House on the Strand	Daphne du Maurier	£6.99
❏ Julius	Daphne du Maurier	£7.99
❏ The Loving Spirit	Daphne du Maurier	£7.99
❏ Mary Anne	Daphne du Maurier	£6.99
❏ My Cousin Rachel	Daphne du Maurier	£6.99
❏ Myself When Young	Daphne du Maurier	£7.99
❏ Rule Britannia	Daphne du Maurier	£7.99
❏ The Scapegoat	Daphne du Maurier	£7.99

Please allow for postage and packing: **Free UK delivery**.
Europe; add 25% of retail price; Rest of World; 45% of retail price.

To order any of the above or any other Virago titles, please call our credit card orderline or fill in this coupon and send/fax it to:

Virago, P.O. Box 121, Kettering, Northants NN14 4ZQ
Tel: 01832 737526 Fax: 01832 733076. Email: aspenhouse@FSBDial.co.uk

❏ I enclose a UK bank cheque made payable to Virago for £.............
❏ Please charge £............. to my Access, Visa, Delta, Switch Card No.

❏❏❏❏❏❏❏❏❏❏❏❏❏❏❏❏❏❏❏❏❏❏

Expiry Date ❏❏❏❏ Switch Issue No. ❏❏

NAME (Block Letters please) _____

ADDRESS _____

_____

Postcode:_____Telephone: _____

Signature:_____

Please allow 28 days for delivery within the UK. Offer subject to price and availability.

Please do not send any further mailings from companies carefully selected by Virago ❏

Delphine du hamien

Daphne du maurier

maurier

Daphne du mau

Daphne du maurier

maurier

Daphne du mau

Daphne du maurier

maurier

Daphne du mau